Pink Punch

Pink Punch

Laura Kinch

Moof Books

To my sister.
Who has likely not even read the draft copy I sent to her yet. Kara, if you point out any errors after this is published, I will shoot you.

K ris scrunched down in the police vehicle, arms folded, her peaked cap pulled down to hide her flushed cheeks. She'd been caught. How was she going to talk her way out of this?

"Kris, what am I supposed to do with you?" Her father, John, sat in the driver's seat beside her, his attention on the road and his jaw set.

"What's the problem? I wasn't drinking or anything." Luckily, her father had caught only her out at the local skate park. Which wasn't abnormal; her parents knew it was a frequent hangout of hers. What they did not know, at least, not until tonight, was that she also frequented it after 12 a.m.

"The problem? The problem is you're a teenager. And as long as you live in my house, you need to follow my rules. Curfew is 10 p.m. And no, I'm not just being difficult. I've told you it's dangerous out at night. That's when the worst of the vigilantes are out."

Kris pointedly stared out the window. Mostly to hide the roll of her eyes she found impossible to suppress.

John sighed. "I get it, all right? I was a teenager too. And I know you're upset because your best friend is away. But that doesn't mean you can play up."

Kris bristled. "Away? More like locked up. And don't blame

Penny. What about you and Mum? Don't you think the way you two have been acting might be just a little upsetting for your kids?"

John shifted in the driver's seat. The VCU issue Commodore was a standard sized sedan but, with his broad shoulders and bulky biceps that pressed out on his short-sleeved work shirt, John managed to make it look cramped. "Your Mum and I are working things through. It's just that, you know... shit!" John slammed on the Commodore's brakes.

A dark brown body, thick like a tree trunk and scaled like a crocodile, slithered out across the street. The police vehicle slewed across the road, momentum dwindling. They had almost stopped by the time they reached the beast. The bonnet of the car made a dull thud as it tapped the creature's side.

The snake whipped around and hissed. A human torso swayed atop the body. Red eyes and dripping fangs gleamed beneath his hood; a hood made of polyester. Snake seemed to think he was quite the gangster. A tacky gold chain adorned his neck.

"It's Snake," Kris said. More than a simple description, it was the name the mutant had chosen to describe himself. Not very imaginative. But probably more terrifying than 'Brett.'

John threw the Commodore into reverse and floored it. "How do you know its name?"

"Don't you have your Tech-taser? Isn't that supposed to take guys like that down if you set it up high?"

"I'm not going to attempt to arrest that with you here." John's glare cost his concentration. They climbed the curbing and hit a lamp post with a clang. John cursed. The gearbox grated as he forced it into first.

Snake slithered toward them, fangs dripping. Then the lamp post flew over their car and caught Snake across his middle. Their car dented in the center of the roof, and the whir of motors sounded above them. A humanoid shape leaped down in a blur of pink to stand in front of them.

"It's Pink Punch."

John's panic subsided. But at the mention of the super's name, he fixed his daughter with an ice-cold glare.

Kris squinted back at him. "What? Yes, I know who she is. Everybody does. That suit's kind of hard to forget." Pink Punch was a recent addition to the scene. She'd only appeared on the news within the last few months, though she had never stopped to talk to the cameras.

The suit she wore was body armour, and appeared to enhance her strength and speed as well as provide protection. It covered every inch of her body, save for her jawline. And every inch of that suit was coloured in shades of bright, hot pink. Not Kris' favorite colour. But she could not fault the woman for making such a bold statement.

Snake hurled the lamp post aside and reared up.

Pink drew back a fist. A layer of pink, like liquid metal, issued from the cuff that circled her right wrist. It crawled up her fist and solidified to form a bulky gauntlet. She struck Snake across the jaw. The mutant swayed, then dropped to the pavement, forked tongue hanging from his lips.

In addition, she could make weapons from the same material as the protective suit. As well as Pink's trademark gauntlet, Kris had seen her produce a sword, a shield, and a club. All on television, of course. This was the first time Kris had seen her up close. Dad was going to have a fit.

Pink Punch lowered her fist. The extra bulk of the gauntlet lost solidity, turned gray, and then dissolved to dust to blow away on the night air. She looked over her shoulder at them, and a small smile played at the corner of her lips.

John tugged at his collar. "Wonderful, now she's saved my life. I am never going to live this down."

Kris mirrored her father's hand on the door handle, until he fixed her with a glare.

"No. You stay in the car."

"Dad! I'm nearly sixteen."

"Exactly."

Kris settled back in her seat, arms folded across her chest, and huffed. Once her father was out, she rolled down her window and leaned out.

John strode past Pink, pointedly not looking at her, and knelt beside Snake. He pushed two fingers into Snake's neck and felt for a pulse. "What the hell do you think you're doing? I hope you haven't killed him."

Pink put a hand on her hip. "You're welcome. You all right, sweetheart?" Her voice held a slight, warped buzz. The suit had a voice modulator built into it; Kris guessed to disguise her voice. Or maybe just make her sound cooler.

John stood and shook slimy goop from his hand. "My daughter's in the car. So, keep the sweethearts to yourself."

Pink frowned. Despite her lower jaw and mouth being the only part of her body visible, she seemed quite apt at using these to communicate her judgment. "You brought your daughter out on patrol?"

John flushed. "Of course not. She sneaked out." He jabbed a finger at Snake. "So, this what you're doing now? Beating up other vigilantes?"

"I was concerned he was about to go anaconda on your car with you, and apparently your daughter, inside. Besides, he's a villain. I don't know whether he's working for TechCorp. But the way things are going I'm sure he'll be on their payroll soon. I get the impression he likes nice things."

"Oh god," John rolled his eyes. "Not this again."

"TechCorp wants the cops to wear those suits, John. And it isn't going to end well."

John threw his arms in the air. "Yes, I know. They're the big bad villains. They're paying all the vigilantes to commit crimes, never mind that committing crimes is what you lot have been doing for years."

"Not all of us, John."

"Villains, supers, they're all the same. You're not a superhero. You're a vigilante. Same as slime-boy over there. Same as the rest of them."

"You really need to check that attitude."

John shrugged. "Yeah, well, you know the whole 'Vigilante Crimes Unit' thing? It's kind of in the job description."

"Don't hide behind that 'I'm a cop' crap."

"Says the lady in a supersuit."

Pink held up her hands. "All right. I'm not arguing with you. I just wanted to help. At least you can arrest this guy now." She poked Snake with a hefty pink boot. "Ask him if he knows anything about TechCorp. You never know."

John was already dialing a number on his phone. Kris groaned. She wasn't going to get to hang around; Dad would get the rest of the VCU to deal with Snake. The excitement was over but hanging around for the arrest might prolong the time until punishment, or perhaps even get her father to forget about grounding her. John finished making the call. The faint sound of sirens filled the air.

A smile tugged at Pink's lips. "I hope those are for Snake."

"You know I can't arrest you."

Pink waved at John. Like they were two old friends who'd met in the shopping center. Kris smirked. Pink had her father seriously flustered and it was monumentally fun to watch.

"Oh, and make sure you keep that daughter of yours in at night.

It's dangerous out here." With that, Pink leapt clean onto the second story roof of the nearest building and disappeared.

Kris scrunched down in her seat and rolled her eyes. Great. Pink Punch was controlling too. Superpowers made no difference. Adults were adults.

John waited for the police vehicles to arrive for Snake before returning to the car.

"I didn't realise you two got on so well," Kris commented.

"She won't hurt me. At least I can turn my back on some of them."

"I mean, Mum's barely been out of the house for three months and you're already flirting. With a vigilante." Kris made air quotes around her father's favourite term. "You know, I really don't think you should be throwing stones at your daughter for getting out for a bit of fresh air, even if it is at odd hours."

John ran a hand through his hair. "Not now, Kris."

2

"I heard she grew horns. So un-ladylike. No wonder her father sent her to the clinic."

Kris whirled around to face Amanda where she stood beside the Northberg High school gates. It would be so easy to deck the girl and put an end to her incessant prattle. Too bad she'd been taught not to start fights, despite the fact she could probably finish them. Kris lowered her clenched fists to her side. "You seriously need to stop talking about my best friend like that."

Amanda tossed her long blond hair over one shoulder. "Sensitive much? You don't even know who I'm talking about. Seriously though, Penny a vigilante. That must've been a shock. Did your dad arrest her himself?"

"She's not a vigilante. She didn't do anything wrong. And she didn't get arrested." Kris gritted her teeth, if only to stop herself talking. If Penny were here, she would have pulled Kris away. Or come up with a quick and witty retort to turn Amanda's cheeks red. Then walked away with Kris, laughing. That had ticked Amanda off so much. Of course, she was taking the opportunity to make fun of her when Penny wasn't around to defend herself.

Before Amanda could reply, a male voice broke in. "Of course, she didn't get arrested. Not legally anyway. Probably the only thing she did was manifest powers. And how is that un-ladylike?"

"A and B conversation," said Amanda. "C you later."

Kris mentally fumbled for the boy's name. Calvin. He'd only been at the school for a few weeks. He'd tried to talk to her once or twice before, but she had to admit she'd been a little short with him. With Penny's absence, and the positively weird home environment her parent's separation had caused, she had not been in the mood. This time, despite the fact he was clearly butting in, Kris found she didn't mind. He'd certainly been around long enough to notice Amanda's grating personality. Kris would take any backup she could get. "This B doesn't mind the interruption."

Calvin grinned at her. His short blonde hair was clogged up with product, not exactly abnormal for a boy his age. It was the outfit Kris still hadn't figured out. The school was mostly air conditioned, but here outside the school gates, long sleeves had to be uncomfortable. As well as the long-sleeved shirt under his mandatory school shirt, Calvin wore jeans. Northberg's almost constant heat didn't seem to bother him in the slightest. "We're talking about powers, right?"

"I," said Amanda, "was the one talking, before I was so rudely interrupted. And as I was saying, what's her supername now? The Freak?"

"People with powers aren't freaks," said Calvin. "They're just different. It's not a good enough reason to not be friends with someone who has them. Or with someone who's friends with someone who does."

"Well maybe not freaks. But they are entitled. They think they can do whatever they want."

Calvin snorted. "Entitled? Seriously?"

Kris rolled her eyes. "Amanda, please stop talking."

"Or what?"

Kris was just about to tell her what when a shadow fell across them.

"Ladies." Butch was big for his age, over six foot tall already, and broad across the shoulders. His dark hair was slicked back.

Amanda squared her shoulders. "What, you here to argue too?"

"Maybe I'll just eat you."

The girls wilted under Butch's toothy grin. Amanda regained her composure. "You like hanging out with boys better anyway, Kris, so I'll leave you to it. I mean, you practically are one. Later."

Kris rolled her eyes. "Thanks, Butch. But I don't really need your help to deal with Amanda and her minions."

"Why, because you have this guy's?" Butch poked Calvin in the shoulder.

Calvin took a step back to regain his balance. "Hey, watch it."

Oh no, this was all she needed. Butch was one of the only friends who'd stuck by Kris since Penny had left, even though previously they only spoke because they hung out at the same skate park. But he could be a little overprotective. "This kid? He's nothing. You can leave him alone."

"I'm just here because they were insulting supers," said Calvin. He looked Butch up and down, then settled on the big boy's toothy grin. "I'm guessing you wouldn't like that either."

"My change is coming. I can feel it. I'm not going to have to worry about the prattling opinions of a bunch of little girls. Or little boys."

Kris stepped between them. "All right, calm down."

Butch glared at her.

Kris gulped. She had to salvage the situation, and quickly. She would have actually liked to talk to Calvin more. Even just about vigilantes. Her father may have had a lot of information on them, but every conversation inevitably became a one-sided rant. But it was obvious Butch was about to get upset. "I didn't need your help, Calvin. They're just a bunch of bitchy girls. And now they're gone. So, I don't want to talk anymore, okay?"

Calvin stuffed his hands in his pocket and hunched his shoulders. "I was only trying to be friendly. Fine, I'm going."

Kris watched his retreating back, then glanced cautiously up at Butch. "I need to go home anyway, Butch. I'm grounded… I think." Dad had told her to come home after school, but Kris wasn't sure if it was his usual 'it's dangerous out there rant,' or he was mad about last night. It had been late, and he'd seemed more tired than usual.

Butch eyes narrowed, then he shrugged. "Whatever. If you still want to hang out with someone strong, I'll be at the skate park. You know, unless you're into pretty boys now."

* * *

Kris rolled toward home, listening to the clack of her skateboard wheels over the rough concrete edges. Skating along the sidewalk was boring. She wanted to go to the skate park and patch things up with Butch. But it wasn't worth getting Dad mad, especially after last night. Besides, he'd been so busy with work that if she didn't give him the chance to wonder where she was outside of school hours, he'd probably simply forget she should be grounded.

A blast of orange shot past overhead, and a wave of heat crackled through the air. This wasn't going to be a boring afternoon after all. Kris kicked off the concrete hard and followed the orange blur. Her father would kill her if he knew she was deliberately following a vigilante. But she wasn't about to miss a super-powered battle. This was one of the originals - Pyromaniac!

Kris rounded the corner and flipped her board up deftly into one hand. A small crowd had gathered at the side of the street and Kris pushed her way through. "Who's Pyro fighting?" she asked a woman beside her. If she were a few centimeters taller, she might be able to see.

A screech rent the air, and everyone clapped their hands over their ears. Kris used the opportunity to squeeze herself closer to the action. The screech was followed by a low bass note that vibrated every bone in her body.

Axe Man stood in the middle of the street atop a large loudspeaker, completely topless. Ripped jeans and a spiky green hairdo completed his villainous outfit. Whether you could call him a villain was debatable. Dad certainly thought disturbing the peace with 120 decibel guitar riffs was an indictable offense. And, technically, Axe Man did fall under the vigilante category. His superpower was his unbreakable guitar, and he could render his assailants unable to move under an onslaught of sound. He also played a pretty mean guitar solo.

"Bow to the gods of bass!" Axe said, then screamed as he strummed down on his guitar. The note blared out like an invisible wave. Car alarms went off. Windows in nearby houses shattered.

Kris clapped her hands over her ears again. Okay, mean guitar solos aside, Axe Man did make a hell of a mess.

But today he would be foiled. Because Pyro stood before him in his orange-clad glory, legs spread apart, hands on his hips. His tight spandex suit clung to every curved muscle of his body. Kris tried not to look too hard. The guy must have been close to sixty.

Not a lot of superheroes wore spandex nowadays. It had been used by the original supers when they had first declared their existence, back in the '90s. A few of the supers who'd acquired their powers in the subsequent Fallout had tried it. Most had declared it 'too itchy,' and now, Pyro was the only one. He was also the only original super still alive - the poster boy for the superpowers which had swept the area now known as the Northberg Triangle.

Pyro activated a ball of flame, then flung it at the loudspeaker, which burst into flames. Axe Man clutched his guitar and rolled to the ground. His guitar may have been unbreakable, but the rest of his sound equipment was not.

"Your gods of bass are on fire," said Pyro.

Kris snorted.

"What have you done?" Axe screeched.

"You can't go around assaulting the general population with your, ah, music, Axe," said Pyro. "There's a time and place for that kind of thing."

Axe flung his arms wide. "Dude, I can't even get any good gigs!"

Understandable. Any four-walled establishment stupid enough to let Axe and his unbreakable guitar inside would have to repair some serious structural damage.

"It's not fair!" Axe smashed his guitar on the asphalt, repeatedly. The road surface cracked under the onslaught.

The wail of sirens cut the air. A police vehicle slewed around the corner. VCU issue. Dad's Commodore. John and his partner, Detective Johansson, stepped out.

Kris ducked down behind the crowd.

John slammed the driver's side door far too heavily. "What the hell is going on here?"

Axe Man stopped his assault on the pavement, yelled, and flung his guitar at the two detectives.

Pyro hurled a ball of flame. It intercepted the guitar and flipped it up over John's head, where it crashed down onto the roof of the car and bounced off. But not before leaving a reasonably sized dent.

Detective Johansson drew in a sharp breath. "Ouch. Told you we should have waited a few weeks before getting that last prang fixed."

John's hands balled into fists. "Hey! That's police property you just damaged. You're under arrest. Both of you!"

Kris rolled her eyes. The VCU vehicles always seemed to cop a battering, but Dad always complained about it. The small crowd seemed to agree. Someone booed.

"Now hang on," said Pyro, holding up a hand toward the onlookers. "They're just doing their jobs. Or, you know, the part I haven't already done for them."

The crowd snickered.

John tensed, but Johansson stepped past him and put a hand on his arm. Johansson was a small, dark-haired woman. She was wiry, and deceptively unimpressive looking. Kris didn't know her first name. Dad said she hated it, though he and the other detectives occasionally called her 'Jo.' She'd taught Kris Taekwondo when Kris was younger. Kris had since given up martial arts for skateboarding.

"Now come on, Pyro," she said. "All you've done is make a great big mess."

Pyro smiled coyly. "I'd suggest, Detective, you concentrate on this fellow here. He was, after all, the one disturbing the peace."

Axe Man panted but drew himself up a little straighter. "And just how do you expect to arrest me?"

"Same as we do every other..." Johansson began.

Pyro flung a ball of flame. It smacked Axe in the face and the villain fell to the ground, his face covered in soot, unconscious.

Johansson closed her eyes briefly.

"You can't do that!" John barked.

"He's all yours, detectives."

John jabbed a finger. "And so are you, Pyro!"

"John, there's no point," Johansson pointed out.

Before they could argue further, a grey news van careened around the corner. It was followed closely by a white BMW. Kris could actually see the colour drain from her father's face. A news crew stepped out of the van. The BMW deposited a well-dressed, blonde-haired man of about thirty onto the sidewalk.

The cameraman set up in a blur. The reporter leapt out in front of the camera, a grin plastered to her face. "And it looks like we've just caught Pyro rescuing some cops. Tell me, Pyro, what are your thoughts on the role of vigilantes in the safety of Northberg?"

"Sorry, guys, not today," said Pyro. He gave them a sloppy salute and took to the air in a blur of orange.

That didn't stop the news crew. The reporter turned to the man who'd stepped from the BMW and quickly introduced him. The man didn't need one. Rick Richardson was loaded, but still seemed to find the time to have his say on vigilante rights. Rick slipped in front of the camera with practiced ease. "Don't worry about Pyro. He's just camera shy."

The colour had returned to her father's face. In fact, it had passed normal and was now almost red.

"Don't engage him," said Johansson with a tug on John's arm.

John pulled away. His partner shook her head and went over to put Axe Man in a bulky pair of handcuffs.

"… Of course, noise complaints are a legitimate cause for residents to feel upset," Rick was saying. "But if this was a normal Joe, would he be arrested for this crime?"

John stomped over. "He's being arrested for causing property damage. Something a normal Joe wouldn't be capable of doing."

Rick raised an eyebrow. "You feel he should be arrested for that capability?

"Feeling? It's the law!"

"A law that discriminates against anyone with superpowers. Or as you love to call them, vigilantes. You even have a whole crime unit dedicated to it…"

"… which is needed…"

"A crime unit that refuses to employ anyone with superpowers."

"Is it true you had one of your detectives tested at the TechCorp clinic just because you thought she may have been hiding powers?" asked the reporter.

"That wasn't…" John bit down on his response, held up his hands, and stomped away from the camera. He went to help Johansson load Axe Man into the police van which had pulled up, along with a few officers.

The crowd began to disperse, although Rick still prattled on in front of the camera. A superfight was fun. But no one was going to hang around to listen to Rick. If they had any interest, they'd see him on the new tonight.

"Kris, what are you doing here?" John had finished loading up Axe Man. He looked down at her, arms folded.

Kris shrugged as innocently as she could manage. "I was heading home, Dad. Like you told me to."

John ran his hand through his mussed-up hair. "Yeah, okay. Tell you what, why don't I give you a lift?"

"Aren't you working?"

"My shift is technically finished. I should have time to eat dinner with you kids tonight. I know I haven't been spending as much time with you as I should be."

Kris worked her jaw. Perhaps her father just wanted to make sure she really was going home. But since Mum and Dad had separated, they'd both seemed distant. Kris had only seen her mother a couple of times since she'd moved out. Heck, she didn't even know where she lived now! Dad had thrown himself into his work and seemed to be constantly grumpy. Not that he'd been a ray of sunshine to start with.

Time with her father, without him yelling at her, might be okay. "Yeah, Dad. You can drive me home."

John smiled faintly. "Great. Besides, I need to get away from Rick." His shoulders tensed as he said the man's name. "Jo, have you got this handled?"

"Yes, go," said Johansson. "Before you say something stupid."

* * *

For a drive that was supposed to give them time to catch up, it was awkwardly quiet.

"So, how's school going?" from her father, hadn't gotten much of a response. Kris knew she probably should have said more than 'good.' But the truth was, it wasn't good. So, what was the point making up a nice lie to fill the time?

They pulled into their street, away from the traffic. John slowed and squeezed his daughter's arm. "Come on, Kris, talk to me. I know you've been struggling. I know you wouldn't usually be sneaking out at night if everything was okay between me and Rachael."

"What do you want me to say, Dad? You're barely home. You haven't even seen how much Tommy's been on his computer playing his video games."

"We're not talking about Tommy; we're talking about you." John smiled encouragingly. He wasn't having a go at her for her escapades. Maybe, he might actually be interested.

Kris shifted in her seat. "Well, I mean, I miss Mum…"

John's attention snapped outside the windshield. "Please, not now."

An old, battered blue Mustang was parked up on the curb. Kris straightened up. As they pulled into the driveway, Kris spotted her mother at the front door. Tommy, Kris' younger brother, balanced a laptop on one hand and excitedly showed her his new game.

John's jaw was tense. He gripped the steering wheel tight. And his attention was very clearly no longer on his daughter.

"Well, obviously you don't miss her." Kris threw open the door and bailed out. She didn't wait for her father's response. If he wanted to ignore her, she could ignore him too.

Kris slowed as she reached her mother. Her heart hammered in her chest. How many times in the past few months had she been home? Maybe it wasn't just Dad. Maybe she didn't want to see her kids either. But Mum broke into a grin as she saw her daughter and threw her arms wide. Mum wasn't usually so huggable, so excitable. Kris ran into those open arms. "Mum, what are you doing here?"

Rachael released her. "Can't I come and see my kids? Have you grown?"

"I don't know. Are you staying?" She had to be staying, just for a little bit.

"Rachael," said John tersely.

"John."

"I thought you were busy with your new job. Are they paying you yet?"

"Is that all you care about? Money? You know, leaving TechCorp the way I did might make it a little difficult to get what you'd consider a real job."

Kris tugged on her arm. "What work are you doing, Mum?"

Rachael pushed a strand of blond hair back into her ponytail. Her hair had grown longer, though she usually kept it long. Easier to maintain, she didn't constantly have to be at the hairdresser's. "I've been developing some equipment for some clients. Freelancing. I'm afraid I can't be too specific - it's kind of private."

John snorted. "Freelancing. So that's what they call it."

"Your father's just cranky because he wouldn't approve of some of my clients," she lowered her voice, like she was imparting some great secret. "Some of them have superpowers, you know."

John bristled. "Do you really think it's appropriate to talk about this in front of the kids?"

"It's just her work, Dad," said Kris.

"But they're not even paying you. You were the Chief Engineer at TechCorp. Don't you think you could be doing something better with your life?"

"You mean something you approve of? Relax, I'm sure you can still afford all the bills."

"You know that's not the issue."

Rachael's voice rose, and she stabbed a finger at her husband's chest. "You had your chance, John."

Kris blinked and released her mother's arm. Mum didn't usually get mad. She wasn't unemotional; in fact, she usually seemed calmly happy. Like the world could do what it will with her, and she'd take it in her stride. But not since the separation, not since losing her job.

"I told you everything…" Rachael drew in a breath, her shoulders leveled, and when she spoke again, her voice was steady. "I told you what TechCorp was doing, John. I asked for your help. You're a cop; it's your job."

"I'm on the VCU. My jurisdiction is vigilante crimes. Not whatever corporate garbage you imagined your boss was up to."

"You get on well enough with Chief Thompson. You could have spoken with him; arranged something. You didn't. So don't complain now."

"And the way you've responded is completely inappropriate."

"Enough, all right? Like you said - we can't do this in front of the kids. I just came to get one of my hard drives. I'll grab it and be gone."

The front screen door slammed as Tommy ran inside.

Rachael frowned. "Is he okay?"

"Maybe he just realised he over-wrote your hard drive with one of his games," John snorted.

Kris' hands balled at her sides. "What's wrong with him? What's wrong with you? All you wanted was a stupid piece of hardware. Don't pretend you came here to see us."

Rachael put a hand on Kris' shoulder. "Kris, sweetheart, I've been busy."

Kris slapped her hand away. "You were always busy. It never stopped you spending time with us before. Now? I don't even know where you live! Why don't you let us come see you?"

Rachael shifted her weight. "My place isn't really in a good neighborhood."

"See, Rachael? This is messing with the kids. Why can't you just…"

Kris whirled to face her father. "And all you care about is that Mum lost her job. Who kicks out someone just because they're not bringing in a tonne of money anymore?"

"Kris," said Rachael. "Your father didn't kick me out. It's just easier like this, for now. We'll work it out. Things are just complicated."

"Just get your stupid hard drive." Kris ran inside and pegged her skateboard under the stairs. She'd probably scratched it, and it had left a sizable dent in the wall. She rushed upstairs and slammed the door to her bedroom, sat down on the bed, and put her head in her hands.

A few moments later there was a light tap at the door.

"Go away!" said Kris. Her voice cracked and she put a hand over her mouth.

"Kris," said Rachael. "Are you all right?" After a pause, she continued. "I know things are confusing right now. But it'll make sense soon, I promise. I just need to finish this project first. Then we'll talk, properly." Another pause. "I did come for some equipment, but I can talk for a bit now, if you want."

"I don't want," Kris growled under her breath. Mum probably hadn't heard, so Kris picked up a pillow and pegged it at the door. It didn't make as loud a bang as she'd hoped, but she probably shouldn't put more than one dent in the walls today.

Rachael said nothing more, but Kris heard her move down the hall into the next room, which had been her study. She could hear her clattering through the equipment she'd left there. The study was a mess. Dad hadn't tidied what Mum had left, and when he found things around the house that belonged to her, he'd just peg them into the study. She could be searching for ages. Kris put her pillow over her head and tried to block out the sound.

3

Kris fell asleep after her mother left and missed dinner. Her phone woke her; the jolting burp she'd chosen as her message tone indicating she had a text. It was Butch. He was at the skate park with a few of his friends.

Dad wasn't in his bedroom, so Kris assumed he'd gone back out to work. Tommy's door was closed, the faint sound of simulated gunfire leaking through. No one would notice she was gone. And so, Kris quietly retrieved her skateboard from under the stairs and headed out for the skate park. It wasn't like she was doing anything wrong. After 12 a.m., the air was a lot cooler, if still a little heavy. It was a far better time for physical exercise.

Kris scraped her board to a halt on the concrete as she reached the halfpipe. The park was silent save for the rustle of air through the nearby trees. She couldn't hear any skateboards. "Butch?" Her voice echoed all too loud in the night air, and she winced.

A heavy footfall sounded behind her, and Kris spun around.

A shape loomed above her. It was nearly seven foot tall, and broad. The torso rippled with muscle and a white singlet was stretched far too tight across the leathery skin. The creature had no neck, but the torso tapered into a thick head, the mouth lined with rows and rows of teeth.

Kris jumped back, automatically falling into a guarding block. "Back off!"

"You idiot," a familiar voice growled. "It's me."

The voice was thicker and deeper, but Kris hazarded a guess. "Butch?"

"Hmm," Butch mused. "I'm not sure about that. I still haven't figured out if I have any powers beyond this sweet body. But I definitely need to come up with a better name."

Kris looked him up and down. "You're a freaking shark."

"Half-shark." Butch held his hands out in front of him and turned them over, studying them. They were grey and leathery, and twice as large as they had been before. "Happened this afternoon. Kind of like a growth spurt, I guess. Except now I have teeth. Hmm... teeth..."

Kris reached up and brushed one of the oversized hands. The skin was rough. "I'm not sure how you're planning to skateboard. You'll probably break yours."

"Might have to get a bigger one," Butch shrugged. "But that's not why I texted you. I was hoping you'd come. And that you wouldn't freak out. I think it's time you met some of my other friends. They've also got superpowers."

"You mean like shooting fire, or..." Pyro was still on her mind from earlier.

Butch shook his head. At least, that's what Kris thought he was doing. His upper body kind of twisted from side to side. "Nothing so tame. I suppose it might have been nice to have inherited a power that doesn't turn me into a freak. Not that I'm upset." Butch held his hands up again and flexed his big palms into fists. "My friends have some of the more... exotic powers... like mine. You know, mutants. One of them is a werewolf."

Kris felt sweat start to prick her skin, despite the muggy air. "Werewolves?"

"Well, they're not true werewolves. But that's what everyone calls them. Pup's just a kid. But she seems pretty cool."

"And you want me to meet them? But I don't even have powers."

The corner of Butch's mouth turned up into a grin, making him even toothier. "Aw, don't worry about that. You made friends with me at school, even though you knew I was probably going to develop powers. And you didn't disown Penny. Even with your dad being a cop and all. I guess it's going to be a hard for me to sneak around now, same as it is for them. So here seemed appropriate."

"Yeah, I guess," Kris agreed. She hated to admit it. But whatever Butch was doing, even just hanging around at the skate park like a normal teenager, if he looked like this, her father would immediately pull over and want to know he was behaving himself. Even if he didn't actually arrest him, having powers didn't mean Butch should endure that kind of harassment.

"So, what do you say? You going to let me and my friends know what daddy and the rest of the cops are doing so we can keep out of trouble?"

"Wait, what? You want me to spy on my dad? I thought you wanted me to meet your friends?"

"Yeah, so you could help us avoid the cops," Butch said, a growl creeping into his voice. "I thought that was obvious."

Kris took a step back. Being friends with mutants was one thing. But passing information to someone her father might have to try and arrest? Butch's friends were probably okay, but she knew some mutants had to be downright dangerous. "Butch, I don't know, I need to think about this."

Butch grabbed her wrist in an iron grip. "Come on, I thought we were friends. Or do you like that pretty blonde-haired loser now?"

"Let me go!" Kris tugged backwards, trying to break Butch's grip. The self-defense she'd learned was too long ago, her mind had blanked, but she knew she was doing it wrong. "What the heck are you talking about?"

"What's-his-name, Calvin," Butch growled. He loosened his grip, but Kris still had no chance of breaking free. His skin against hers was like sandpaper.

"I talked to him like once!"

Headlights flooded the skate park. Butch released her and held up a hand to shield his eyes. "Jeeze, watch it."

Kris backed up toward the vehicle. It hadn't been parked there before. If it was her father, she was just going to die.

The door popped open. The driver's body was just a silhouette as she stepped in front of the headlights, armour cutting hard, dark, but unmistakable edges through the glare. Pink Punch.

Kris eyes adjusted to the lights. The vehicle was as brightly coloured as the woman's suit. A Mustang. Big and curvy and shiny pink, its paintwork polished to perfection.

"It's time for you to leave," Pink Punch said to Butch.

Butch growled and his hands bunched up into fists.

In response, the Mustang revved and jerked forward, throwing its light up into Butch's face. It was like a dog on the heels of its master. Pink simply stood there, hand on one hip, waiting for Butch to follow her order.

"I'm not even doing anything. You're as bad as the cops!" Butch stepped back, out of the headlights, and slunk into the bushes.

Pink Punch was right here. And, this time, her father wasn't around to stop her getting a nice close look at an awesome superhero. Maybe she'd give her an autograph.

"It's after midnight. What are you doing out this late?"

Kris' shoulders slumped. "Seriously? Look, thanks for your help. But I don't think Butch was going to hurt me. I know he looks scary, but he's just a friend from school. I think he just figured out he has superpowers. Must be kind of confusing."

"Looked like he was hurting you to me. You shouldn't put up with that. Whether from a shark or a so-called friend."

Kris rubbed her wrist. Butch could be a little aggressive sometimes, like he'd become with Calvin earlier today. But not with her. Not until now. And why would he want to hang out with her properly if he could hang out with people like him? Mutants. Maybe information on the cops was all he'd been friends with her for in the first place. "I suppose. But why are you helping some stupid girl who's out when she shouldn't be?"

"You're not stupid, Kris. I thought you might sneak out again. So, I followed you."

"Why are you following me? And how do you know my name?"

"Your father," Pink said eventually, "that night you were out. He said you were sneaking out. I keep messing things up for him, so I figured I'd help him out a bit tonight. It seems like he's rather busy."

Kris groaned.

Pink nodded to the idling Mustang. "Come on. I'll take you home,"

Kris nearly said no. Who did this woman think she was, telling her what to do? Superpowers or not, she had no right. "Wait, you mean take me home in the Mustang?"

"You'd rather I scoop you up in my arms and fly you there? Believe me, I would love to figure out how to make this suit do that."

Kris broke into a grin and climbed into the passenger side. Inside the seats were pink leather, accentuated with black. Everything was lit with a faint pink glow.

Pink slipped into the driver's seat. "I have to make a stop first. I'm meeting someone, and I can't be late. I hope that won't be a problem."

"No, of course not." Kris bit down on her lip to stop herself grinning even harder. She was riding shotgun with Pink Punch.

* * *

The Mustang's console was lit up like a Christmas tree. The newer Mustang interiors had a bunch of fancy switches and an entertainment display, but this had certainly been modified. The toggle switches looked more industrial and the display more complicated than the stock standard. Right now, it displayed a map. But there were blips and extra information and the map itself was cleaner looking than a simple navigation system. Kris poked one of the blips, and it let out a chirp.

Pink's eyes remained on the road. "Don't touch him. He's working."

"Him?"

Pink drove at a blistering speed, tearing around corners and slamming over speed bumps. Even if she had wanted to keep interfering with the dash, it would have given Kris nausea. Her heart was pounding, and she couldn't wipe the grin off her face. Within minutes they pulled up at a deserted alleyway. Kris wasn't sure of their exact location, although they must have been somewhere downtown.

"Stan, are you picking up any activity in the area?"

"One heat signature, down the alleyway." The tinny voice came from the console and held a slight twang. It seemed Pink had chosen the American, male voice for her vehicle's systems. It sounded bored. "No reports of villain activity on police scanners, and I am detecting nothing to indicate otherwise."

"Stan?" Kris mouthed. But Pink ignored her, so Kris poked the console again, eliciting a high-pitched chirp.

"All right, cut it out!" said the automated voice. "You keep fondling my dash, you have your feet up all over my leather. Could you just keep still?"

Kris slowly pulled her legs out from under her and settled them on the floor. "Your car talks, and it's called Stan?"

"Of course, I'm not an object."

Pink put a hand to her forehead. "Stan, please concentrate."

A pause. "Sorry."

"Wait for me here. I'll let you know if I need an assist." Pink opened her door and stepped out. "Oh no," she said, as Kris got out the other side. "Back in the car."

"Come on!" Kris threw her arms wide. "I'm too old to sit in the car."

"Not for this you're not."

"You're as bad as my dad!"

"Look, Stan has a feed direct to my visor." Pink leaned down and stuck her head back inside the car. "Make sure Kris doesn't miss a second of this, okay? And make sure she doesn't get out of you either."

"Yes, ma'am. Babysitting is an excellent use of capabilities."

Kris glared at Pink. Not that she could tell if it was having any effect. Pink's visor blocked her eyes, and most of her expression. "Fine." Kris climbed back into Stan, and gave the center console a poke. "How do you turn on your..."

"Quit it. I'll do it."

The screen flickered over to show an image, the feed from Pink Punch's visor. She sauntered down the alleyway. The view from the visor panned up, down, and around, readings Kris didn't understand flashing at its side. Pink Punch was looking for her contact. Or danger. Kris momentarily hoped she'd run into trouble. She had the best view of a super fight she ever would, even stuck inside this vehicle.

Kris tapped at the screen. "Hello?"

"She can't hear you."

"So let her."

"No."

"You're a car; quit telling me what to do."

Stan let out a disgruntled blip. "Typical. Well, this car has a mind of its own, missy. And if you want me to cooperate, you'll have to show a bit of respect."

Kris mashed the screen again, but it got her nowhere. "Okay, I'm sorry. Is that better?"

"Sorry only works if you mean it. Look, I don't like being stuck with you anymore than you do. But I can't be distracted. I need to protect Pink. She's already annoyed at me because of my programming quirks. Software is not her strong point, I'm afraid."

"What quirks? You mean because you can talk?"

"I'm supposed to talk. That's how she communicates with me. But just to feed her information. Not get frustrated at little girls putting their shoes up all over my leather. Now let me concentrate."

"Come out, come out, wherever you are," Pink said, her voice relayed over Stan's speakers.

Stan's screen showed only a deserted alleyway. The alley contained few discarded bricks and a large, overflowing rubbish skip leaning against one wall. Pink's gaze settled on the bin. "I can see you."

Kris couldn't. She squinted. And then she saw movement. From beside the bin a shapeless shadow emerged. It unfolded itself and solidified into a tall, broad-shouldered man in a leather coat.

Pink Punch took a step back. "Where's Steve? Is this a trap?"

The big man shook his head. "No trap." His voice was deep, though not quite as deep as Kris had expected. It had a hint of boyishness to it. Though this was clearly a man, and a very large one, he had only just grown into his beefy build. "I've been thinking. And speaking with Steve. He couldn't come but he is safe. His communications with you were compromised. So, he sent me instead."

"You, Greg? Why the change of heart? I'm not sure I believe you'd go behind the Boss' back like this."

"My name's Thunderclap, Pink, remember that." The man raised a black leather clad fist and pounded it into his open palm. Each wrist was bound in a metal manacle, and as his fist hit his palm a crackle of electricity crawled out of the metal. "You wouldn't want me going around using your real name, now, would you?"

"Point taken." Pink's gaze lowered to Thunderclap's fists, where tendrils of electricity still crackled around them. "But you've still got those wrist cannons. They're TechCorp property, and that makes me suspicious."

"Hey, at least I didn't steal my equipment," Thunderclap shrugged. "But I am honestly here to give you information. I've decided I don't like the Boss' plans for this city either, or the way she treats me."

"Like a lab rat? I'm glad you've come around, Greg... Thunderclap. She has no right to treat you like that."

Thunderclap shifted his weight. "Steve tells me this should be enough to convince your cop friends." He reached into his leather jacket and pulled out an A4 envelope. "Here."

Something on Stan's console flashed red. "Don't touch him, he's..."

Pink reached for the envelope. Thunderclap's fingers crackled with electricity as they contacted, and Stan's feed was enveloped in a burst of static.

"What happened?" Kris prodded the screen. She was rewarded with a marginally clearer picture. Instead of flat static, she could tell there was an image there, though it was impossible to make out.

"I knew she'd get herself in trouble." Stan floored it into the alleyway. He got as far as the rubbish skip, but the space was too narrow for him to squeeze past.

Several meters away, Thunderclap, electricity crackling over his fists, stood over Pink Punch. She was crumpled on the ground.

Thunderclap threw a punch straight down. It left a dinner plate sized crater in the concrete as Pink rolled away, back to her feet.

Thunderclap shook his hand and winced. "Steve also told me if I gave that device enough of a direct jolt, it might stop you building your little toys."

Pink rolled her shoulders. "Hurt a bit that close, yeah. And you're right; probably screwed up a few systems." A pink broad sword materialised in her hands, building itself like Kris had seen those gauntlets build the night before. "But not enough. Come on, you think I would've built this suit that easy to destroy?"

Thunderclap charged up his cannons and sent a shower of lightning toward Pink. The air cracked and fizzled. Pink's sword flashed through the air. Each bolt ricocheted off its shiny surface, lighting up the alley in a crackling display of blue tendrils.

"Right, she's got this. And I'm supposed to keep you safe." Stan backed up a few meters.

Enough that Kris couldn't see the action. She glanced at his screen, but it still showed static. "Sorry, Stan." Kris kicked opened her door, scraping it on the alley wall, and jumped out.

"Hey, watch the paintwork!"

Kris slipped past the front of Stan's bumper and closer to the skip.

Pink Punch slashed her sword at Thunderclap's arms. Sparks and clangs rang out in the night air as the man deflected each blow with his wrist cannons. Pink forced him back. Despite the obvious difference in build, Pink's slight frame, Thunderclap's hulking muscles, Pink Punch was stronger.

Thunderclap grunted, lost his footing, and slammed back into the alley wall. The tip of Pink's sword rested against his throat.

"Sorry, Greg. I'm afraid you'll have to go back and tell the Boss I'm not so easy to take down."

Kris cupped her hands to her mouth. "All right, go, Pink!"

Pink jerked her head over her shoulder. "Kris! Get back in the bloody car!" Her sword lowered from Thunderclap's throat.

Thunderclap grabbed at the only exposed part of Pink's flesh - her lower jaw - and sent a massive jolt of electricity right through her. Pink clutched at her throat and collapsed to her knees. The sword turned to grey dust and vanished.

Thunderclap grinned. "So, Steve lied to me. Whatever. Your suit might be pretty good at withstanding my attacks. But you're not. Under that suit you're just as weak as anyone else."

Pink Punch pushed herself shakily to her feet. "And what about you, Greg? All that tech grafted to your body. You don't have super-powers either."

Thunderclap's lips twisted into a scowl. Electricity built around his fist, and he slammed it into Pink's stomach. He grabbed her by the throat and hoisted her up against the alley wall. He breathed heavily. "I'm stronger than you. I'm stronger than everybody! But I won't let you distract me; I've got a job to do." He reached up and tore off her helmet. The armour went brittle along the tear, turning to powder. Thunderclap closed his fist on the remainder of the helmet and that too exploded into dust. He leered into the face of the woman revealed beneath. "Hi, Rachael. I knew it was you. But the Boss wanted me to check for sure. Before she takes back what's hers."

Kris jaw dropped. "Mum?"

Thunderclap looked between the two of them. "Wait, so this is a mummy-daughter date? Interesting. Maybe we'll have to get rid of your little brat too."

"Kris," Rachael said, her voice strained. She grabbed at Thunderclap's wrist, but she didn't have the strength to pull him off. "I got this. Get in the car."

The wail of police sirens came to them on the night air, growing in the distance. Maybe it was Dad; maybe if he got here everything would be okay. Stan's passenger door clicked open. Kris swallowed, moved back, and slipped inside, but she didn't pull the door shut completely. How could her mother be Pink Punch?!

"Yeah, that's a good plan. Better get rid of the kid too so she doesn't tell anyone what happened here." Thunderclap's wrist crackled with electricity. But instead of shooting out the bolt, the wrist cannon began to whine, the tone steadily increasing in pitch. Thunderclap took a step back and fumbled at the device with his big fingers. "Wait... what... what's it doing?"

Rachael dropped to one knee as Thunderclap let her go, but she didn't drop her gaze from his panicked face. "Something wrong with your wrist cannon? Did I touch something I wasn't supposed to?"

Thunderclap tugged and swore as he dragged at the cannon. It looked like he was trying to rip off his own hand. He became increasingly flustered, sweat pouring off his face. He whimpered when it became clear the device wouldn't budge.

"She hasn't... oh bloody hell..." Stan slammed the door on Kris so quick he nearly took off her fingers. He threw himself into reverse, careened back down the alley and scraped his side as he spun out into the street.

Kris grabbed the door handle. "Stan! Wait, it's my Mum."

A boom rocked the alley. Bricks and mortar, dust and rubbish spewed out after them. A crackle of electricity played over everything, lighting up the settling dust.

Kris fought with her door, then she kicked it. "Mum! Damn it! Let me out!"

"Don't. I'm still..." Stan screeched to halt.

Kris kicked the door again, and it popped open as Stan released it. She stumbled out and held a hand to her mouth so she wouldn't choke on the settling dust. "Mum!"

The alley was trashed. Parts of the walls were blown out, bricks strewn everywhere. Kris froze. Tears pricked the back of her eyes.

She wiped her hand across her face. A flash of pink caught her eye amongst the rubble. The suit crackled with electricity, parts of it had lost the bright pink colour and were now closer to grey, like Pink's weapons before she let them crumble to powder. Kris rushed over and threw off the bricks that had settled across her mother.

Rachael coughed, and a small trickle of blood ran from the corner of her mouth. "Kris, are you okay?"

Kris grabbed her hand. The armour was bulky, like lifting a chunk of metal. "I'm fine, Mum. But you… you're Pink Punch."

Rachael smiled faintly. "I hoped you wouldn't find out. She's made things complicated enough already."

"Just hang on. You're wearing armour. It must've protected you."

"Not so much when Thunderclap's wrist cannons self-destruct," Rachael said, then she smirked. "I told them not to make that function so easy to activate."

There was movement at the other end of the alleyway, and dislodged bricks clattered. Something moved across the rubble.

Rachael grabbed Kris' arm. "Thunderclap. He said he'd hurt you…" The pink suit dissolved in a wave, crawling from Rachael's feet and up her body, then down her right arm. The wave ended at a cuff on Rachael's wrist, no bigger than an oversized chunky bracelet. Then the cuff snaked off Rachael and wrapped around Kris' forearm.

Kris drew in a sharp breath and held her arm away from her. "Mum, what's it doing?" The cuff locked in place, and then the pink wave rolled up Kris' arm. It made her skin prickle with pins and needles, and then the suit solidified. Kris wore Pink Punch's suit, complete with a newly formed helmet.

"Don't fight him." Rachael said weakly. "The suit will protect you. Just get back to Stan." She slumped into the rubble and her head lolled to the side.

Kris choked over a sob. "Mum?"

"Hey!"

Kris eyes watered as she shot to her feet. Her hands balled into fists and her body tensed. Thunderclap. She'd beat him to a pulp for what he'd done. But it wasn't Thunderclap. The man who stood atop the mound of rubble was Kris' father.

"For crying out loud. Who is it this time? Do I get to arrest them, or did you blow them up completely?" John picked his way down the rubble. His focus was on his footing, and he grumbled to himself the whole way down.

Kris' jaw worked, but no words came out.

"You realise I'm going to have to clean up your mess again..." John's gaze fell on his wife's crumpled body, and he stiffened. "Rachael?"

"She was... I didn't mean..." Kris' voice sounded strange to her, warped by the voice modulator in Pink's helmet.

"Who the hell are you!" John arm shook as he raised his Tech-taser. His eyes filled with tears, then the tip of the weapon sagged down. His voice caught over a sob. "Get out of here! Go!" John dropped the taser to the pavement and sank down at Rachael's side.

Kris bolted back to Stan and slammed the door behind her. She collapsed into the seat and hugged herself, tears streaming down her face.

"Hang on, sweetheart. I'll get us out of here." Stan backed out of the alleyway. All Kris saw before her vision blurred completely was her mother's crumpled body and her father crying over her as he pulled her into his arms.

4

The next morning Kris woke late. She sat up and swung her legs over the side of her bed, then stared at an indeterminate point on her bedroom wall. Last night, Stan had taken her home, deactivated Pink's suit, then driven away. Pink Punch's cuff still encircled her wrist. Kris spun it around a few times, and the wires and circuitry beneath its smooth, translucent pink surface caught the morning light. She couldn't see how to remove it. One thing was sure: the cuff was real; not a dream. Just like the events of the night before.

Kris eventually worked up the motivation to stand and, moving automatically, she dressed and slouched downstairs. Her father sat at the dining room table. He wore his clothes from the night before, but his collar was undone and his tie loose. He stared listlessly at the steaming cup of coffee he clutched in his hands.

"Dad, are you all right?"

John flinched at her voice. "Hey sweetheart. Is your brother up yet?"

Kris shook her head.

"Okay. Come over here. I need to talk to you."

Kris slipped into one of the dining chairs, her jaw tense. She already knew what had happened but what was she supposed to say? Saving him the pain of explaining would only reveal Mum had

34

been Pink Punch. She couldn't betray her. And finding out his wife had been a vigilante would hurt Dad even more.

John fumbled with his coffee cup. "It's your mother. She was out last night doing… I'm not sure what. I don't want you to get upset. She's fine. But she's in hospital, on life support. She's in a coma."

Kris shoulders slumped as tears pricked her eyes. She blinked them back. "Wait, what do you mean a coma?"

"Aw, Kris." John reached out and squeezed her arm. "It'll be okay. She just needs to be in one to recover."

Mum was alive. Kris forced a smile. "I'm okay. As long as Mum is. But what about you, Dad? I mean, was it you who found her?" That look on his face when he'd seen Mum lying there had burned into Kris's brain. She couldn't remember the last time she'd seen her father cry.

John's hands tightened on his cup. "Pink Punch was there. She… the woman in the suit. She did something to Rachael."

Kris stiffened. "You think Pink Punch hurt her? But she seemed so nice that night we saw her."

"Nice? She's… so stubborn…" John waved away his words. "Forget it. What happened to your Mum is nothing you need to worry about. It's police business and I'm going to take care of it."

* * *

Kris sat on the edge of the halfpipe and rolled her skateboard back and forth beside her. She couldn't be mad at Dad for blaming Pink Punch. He'd found her standing over Mum's unconscious body. If Mum hadn't been Pink Punch, this wouldn't have happened. And if Dad knew the truth he and Mum might never get back together. But it wasn't really Mum's fault. She'd been a vigilante for months, and she'd been fine. She'd been handling Thunderclap too. She'd had him cornered. Right up until Kris had called out to her, distracted her. And then the battle had turned.

Calvin wandered over the grass toward her with an air of nonchalance, skateboard under one arm. He was wearing his long sleeves and jeans again, and his short blonde hair was spiked up at random angles. It hadn't been that spiky yesterday. He slowed as he reached Kris, then cleared his throat and sat down beside her. "Not skating today?"

"Aren't you hot?"

Calvin grinned. "Why thank you."

"That is not what I meant."

"I don't really feel the heat." Calvin frowned. "Are you okay? You look a bit down."

"My mum's in hospital. In a coma."

"Oh. Kris, I'm sorry."

He sounded so genuine. Kris blinked, then shook her head. "Why do you care?"

"You mean I shouldn't?"

"I was mean to you yesterday. With Butch." All because she didn't want to scare off the one friend she thought she had. Butch had only wanted to use her for her connection to the cops. Pink Punch, Mum, had been right. If only Mum had hung around, instead of going off to be Pink Punch, maybe she would have told her something like that sooner. Kris wasn't sure she would have listened.

"I thought you might still need a friend. Besides Butch."

"Yeah, well, he turned into a shark."

"Shark? I would've called him something like a…"

"No! Literally."

"That's the power he was talking about getting?"

"Yup. All teeth and scales and everything. And legs."

"Wow. That's going to make it hard for him. Not the legs, he needs those. I mean, some supers just shoot fire balls or something. But they can hide it; look normal. The cops will be all over Butch.

But like I was saying, he seems like a bit of a jerk. I'm glad you're not friends anymore. So, what do you say?"

"Huh?"

Calvin pulled at a piece of grass growing in a crack in the concrete. "Needing a friend. Don't get me wrong, I'm not just doing this for you. I'd like a friend too. I haven't been able to make too many since starting school."

Kris stared at the clump of glass Calvin was mutilating. Perhaps she shouldn't have dismissed him so quickly. She could hardly complain about people ignoring her when she was doing the same thing to someone in the same position as her. "All right, Calvin. I guess I can give you a chance." She jumped on her skateboard and rolled across to the other side of the halfpipe.

Calvin stood where she'd left him. He stared at the halfpipe and chewed his lip, but other than that, did not move a muscle.

Kris rolled her eyes, then skated back over to him. "Do you even know how to use that skateboard?"

Calvin squared his shoulders. "Of course I do. I'm just better on flat surfaces."

"Well, I suppose I can teach you. I don't want to hang around here anyway."

They dropped their skateboards on the sidewalk and rolled off. At least Calvin could skate in a straight line, so that was a start. He wobbled a bit, and Kris had to slow down so he could keep up. "So, are you new here? You've only been at school for a couple of weeks."

Calvin shook his head. "Up until recently I was home-schooled. My father..." He concentrated on his footing for a moment. "Look, I get how you feel about your mother, because my father passed away recently. I live with a foster family now."

Kris jerked to a halt. "Oh. I..."

"It's okay," said Calvin with a faint smile. "It was a few months ago. We weren't particularly close, and he liked me to stay at home. I've got more freedom now. So, I thought I'd learn to skate."

Kris swallowed. Great. Calvin's skateboarding was so lousy, she'd thought he'd only brought the skateboard as an excuse to talk to her. "I'm sorry."

"Don't worry about it. And your mother's going to be fine."

They hadn't made it far from the park when a crash sounded and an alarm started to blare. Both kids jumped off their boards, and without any consultation searched for the source of the commotion.

"There." Calvin pointed to a nearby pet store. A fluffy tortoise-shell cat pelted out of the store and ran across the road. It flicked its tail about and let out a low growl.

"Oh no."

"That's one of Catlady's, isn't it? She's harmless. I mean, she's robbing a pet store. That's all she does. She's got enough cats; she's got to feed them somehow."

"Yeah, Catlady's harmless. But her cats aren't. Just ask my dad."

The tortoiseshell decided they weren't a threat and turned around and yowled. Four more cats spilled out of the pet store, followed by an older woman. The woman was wrinkled with grey, curly hair, and wore a tight black outfit.

Calvin winced. "Yeah, definitely Catlady."

Catlady threw her arms wide. "Be free, my pretties!"

A half dozen nervous kittens slunk out of the store, the freed captives of the confines of domesticity, and sniffed the air. The four adult cats stood guard, tails flicking aggressively.

"She doesn't have a lot with her today," said Kris.

Another dozen cats spilled out behind Catlady. They tugged along bags of food and toys.

"Nope, I was wrong."

The tortoiseshell growled, and her tail flicked harder. Seconds later, the wail of sirens filled the air and a police vehicle skidded around the corner.

Two men jumped out of their car. They were a couple of officers Kris didn't know, not dedicated to the VCU. They shouldn't get hurt, but they wouldn't have the equipment to deal with Catlady. She put a hand on Calvin's shoulder and led him back from the edge of the footpath so their backs were against the storefronts behind them. "Careful," she said, "this is about to get ugly."

Calvin snorted. "Seriously? It's just Catlady."

"What's going on here?" said one of the officers.

The cats all stopped dragging their catch and turned toward the cops as one. The big tortoiseshell hissed.

"Get them!" Catlady picked up the nearest cat and hurled it.

A dozen felines launched themselves at the unfortunate officers. They ducked back inside the car. Cats bounced off the windshield, the door. One skidded across the roof with a clatter of claws. The vehicle revved and jerked forward; cats were thrown in all directions.

"I know she's just got cats," said Kris. "But would you really want a dozen angry cats attacking you? Yeah, she's harmless, but the cops hate her."

"Amanda said your dad was a cop on the VCU. But you were still friends with Butch. Are you really happy for these guys to arrest harmless people like Catlady?"

"She's robbing a shop," Kris pointed out. But as much as her father complained about how dangerous vigilantes were, he certainly didn't mean Catlady. The cops should be concentrating on the dangerous ones. Not the one trying to feed her animals, and certainly not teenagers who just happened to be developing super-powers. Kris' hands tensed at her sides. "You want to know why I was hanging out with Butch? Because of Penny. That's what Amanda was prattling on about yesterday. My best friend developed superpowers. And the Police Chief wasn't having a bar of that, so he just threw her in the clinic."

Calvin's jaw dropped. "Wait, hang on. The cops can put teenagers in the clinic?"

"Not exactly. The Chief's her father."

A few cats hung around; an orange tabby even sat quite contentedly on the bonnet of the police car. The pet shop owner came out of the nearby alley with a hose. The big tortoiseshell, the last to leave, waited right until the man shot a spray of water at it, then darted deftly to the side, hissed, and bolted.

"They're not helping. They're just harassing people. Supers would be much better suited to handle supers," said Calvin. "And they wouldn't automatically treat them like criminals."

Kris scuffed a shoe over the pavement. She honestly didn't know what to say to Calvin in response. Then her phone chirped, and the interruption was not unwelcome. Kris skimmed the text message. It was her father. They could go visit Mum.

* * *

The hospital was cold, and the corridors a stark white. Kris rubbed at her arms. Tommy was silent as he walked beside her. Their footsteps echoed. Mum had her own room, and as they reached it Dad stopped with a hand on the door.

"She just looks like she's sleeping. But you guys have nothing to worry about; she's going to be fine." John opened the door, and let the kids step in ahead of him.

Rachael lay on a bed with a dozen different apparatus strapped to her. Her chest rose and fell, but that false breath of life was provided by a machine. She looked pale and haggard; far worse than if she were just sleeping. Kris fiddled with the pink cuff on her wrist. Mum had been caught in an explosion. This could have been far worse.

"Mum?" Tommy's breath caught in his throat. He choked down a sob, then sat at his mother's bedside and took her hand.

John squeezed Kris' shoulder. "She's going to be okay," he said softly. Kris wasn't sure if he said it for her benefit, or for his.

If only she hadn't distracted her mum. She'd caused this. And she had to make up for it.

Her mother had felt something to do with TechCorp was important enough that she'd become a vigilante and had chosen to leave home to figure it out. She'd gone to see Thunderclap, had fought him, for a reason. Something important, perhaps dangerous, was going on, and for all Kris knew the only person who could stop it was out of commission. She had to figure out what Pink Punch was onto.

5

Whenever Tommy arrived home, he would inevitably rush up the stairs, to his bedroom, to play his video games. When she'd been younger Kris had made a game of trying to beat him up there. But she hadn't bothered racing him in years. She was too old for that now. Besides, the last time they'd both fallen, and Tommy had started screaming, Kris was certain to demonstrate his sister was the one who had caused all the trouble and he was just the poor victim.

Today she pushed past him at the front door, much to his shock, and charged for the stairs.

"Hey!" said Tommy. Kris felt a wad of her shirt grabbed, but she was bigger and stronger, and her brother's grip did nothing to slow her down.

John shouted after them both. "Get back down here. You've got to eat dinner!"

Kris fixed a glare on her little brother. He held the wad of material for a second longer in spite, then released it.

Kris rolled her eyes, pushed past him, and slouched into the kitchen. "Dad, you don't have to cook something now." Not that he wasn't capable. He and Mum had shared the task when she lived with them.

John ripped open a frozen pizza box and tossed the solid disk in the oven. "I'd like to make you something a bit healthier, but I don't have time. I need to get to work."

"Dad, it's fine."

John slammed the oven door and set the thermostat. Then he turned and took his daughter by the shoulders. "Kris, I really need your help right now. I know I've been busy lately, and you've already been looking after Tommy when I'm not here. But you've also been sneaking off at night. I'm not mad. But with your Mum in hospital, I'm probably going to be even busier. Can you just promise me... just make sure the pizza doesn't burn, and your brother eats some?"

Kris jaw worked. "I..."

"That's my girl." John ruffled her hair, then dashed upstairs to change.

Kris waited until her father left, and the pizza was cooked. Then she dumped half of it beside Tommy at his computer and locked herself in her room. She stood in front of her mirror, a pizza slice hanging from her mouth, and held out her wrist so she could see the pink cuff. There was circuity beneath the translucent surface. But no obvious buckles or buttons.

Kris scoffed down the pizza, then flung out her arm. "Activate!" Nothing. She spun the cuff around so it sat differently. "Turn on, um, engage... go, go, gadget supersuit!" Still nothing. Kris groaned and flung herself onto her bed, staring up at the ceiling. "Stupid superheroes. Why do they have to make everything so complicated?" Tommy might be able to figure out how the gadget worked. But there was no way she was asking. Her little brother couldn't get involved. He'd get in the way, or worse, tell Dad. She could have asked Stan. But Kris had no idea where the talking car had got to, or how to contact him. With a growl, Kris rose to her feet. "Pink's a stupid colour anyway. What were you thinking, Mum?" But it didn't matter. She didn't need a super suit to discover what her mother had been investigating.

Kris flung open her cupboard door and dug into the pile of clothing crammed inside. She tossed shorts, shirts, and jeans over her shoulder, as well as a single dress which had long ago slipped off its designated hanger and become buried. Eventually, she located a pair of black jeans and one of her few long-sleeved shirts, also black. She stood in front of her mirror and turned her body every which way. That would do. In the darkness, she wouldn't be seen. Except for her face.

Kris dragged open her second dresser drawer to reveal a far more ordered collection of baseball caps. She selected a plain black one from the back, one that didn't have any writing or brand names on it. She crammed it on her head and pulled the peak low.

Kris opened her bedroom door and listened. Tommy's door was closed, the chatter of simulated gunfire coming from within, louder tonight. She raced downstairs and collected her skateboard. An old cricket bat sat beside it in the under stairs cupboard. She snatched that up too.

Suitably outfitted, Kris slipped out into the night and dropped her board to the street. The only indication of her presence was the clack of skateboard wheels on the sidewalk as she headed into town.

*** *** ***

Kris dismounted her board and held out her arms. "Aw, man." Her clothing was soaked with sweat. It may have been well after dark, but it was still hot and muggy. She hadn't been certain where the alleyway was, and it had taken her almost an hour, once she'd got into town, to locate it.

Kris slipped under the police tape. No sign of any cops. She rested her board against one wall, changed her sweaty grip on the cricket bat, and began to pick her way over the rubble. Half-way down the cluttered alley, she stopped. What was she looking for? Mum had been here for information, something to do with

TechCorp. But other than that, Kris had no idea what Pink Punch had been doing. All she could see were mounds of broken brick, and the mangled rubbish skip. If there had been anything here that might have helped her the cops would have already taken it. She kicked at a loose brick and swore. "Ow."

"This is why I wear steel caps."

Kris whirled around and brandished her cricket bat.

A teenage boy stood on the top of the overturned rubbish skip. He wore tattered jeans and a sleeveless, hooded top. The hood was up, obscuring his face. His bare arms were bound in a whirling band of bright blue tattoos that glowed faintly in the dark.

"Who are you?"

The boy looked to the sky and groaned. "Typical. If I could do something interesting, I might actually get on the news. The name's Zero K. Zero, if you prefer." Zero jumped off the skip and kicked a loose brick into one of the walls. He spun back around, arms raised. "See? Didn't hurt a bit."

Kris lowered her bat ever so slightly.

"And you are?" Zero prompted.

"None of your business!" Kris flushed under her cap. She had no intention of revealing who she was. She should have come up with some dumb vigilante sounding name before coming out here.

Zero's voice took on an edge. "It is my business. Because you're poking around a crime scene I'm supposed to be investigating. Seriously, what can I call you?"

"Your name's not that great either. What does the K stand for? Zero clue?"

Zero's mouth dropped open. "That's... that's not even the right letter." He cleared his throat and squared his shoulders. "Okay. So, your uniform sucks, but you seem to have a handle on the insults." A grin crept onto his face. "Zero K as in..." He flung out his arms.

His tattoos glowed brighter, built and swirled, and almost seemed to lift off his skin. He flung a sparkling blue comet at her.

Kris jumped clear. The comet struck the pavement and left a crackling mass of icicles where she'd stood. "Hey!"

"… as in absolute Zero. Now tell me what you're doing here. Or I'll hit you for real this time." Zero's arms still glowed brightly, but he held them at his sides.

Kris gripped the bat tighter. This guy was powerful, and she didn't have any powers. Her muscles shook; she wanted to run. "I'm here to find out what happened to Pink Punch. Do you know something?"

Zero K frowned. "I want to find out what happened to her too. Come on, are you a hero or a villain? We can't help each other unless I know."

Kris swallowed. Surely Mum had been a hero. But she was unsure about this guy. "I'm a vigilante just like you," she eventually said. "They're all the same, right?"

Zero laughed. "Good one. You sure you're not a cop? No, that's silly. They'd never have you."

The wail of sirens filled the air.

Zero tensed. "Wait, you're not a cop, right?"

"They're not with me!"

"We'd better get out of here." Zero fired a blast of ice at the ground. It propelled him upward and he landed on the edge of the roof, gained his balance, then looked down. "Go on. Get out of here. You want to be arrested?"

Kris backed up the way she'd come, but the glow of blue and red was already lighting the alley walls. Great. She hadn't even started, and the cops were going to catch her. And then Dad would find out.

Zero stared at her. "Do you even have superpowers? Oh shoot, you're just some dumb kid who wanted to play superhero."

"I'm not a dumb kid!"

A vehicle nosed into the alleyway, sirens blaring. Kris held up a hand to shield her eyes from the glare.

The door opened and a silhouette stepped forward, framed in the headlights. "What the hell are you doing here?"

Kris drew in a sharp breath. Dad. His voice was strained, and the TechCorp branded taser he held out before him shook. Kris raised her hands above her head. The VCU tasers were built for people with superpowers. She didn't know what her father usually had his set on, but she most certainly did not want to find out.

A bolt of blue shot from the roof and knocked the taser from John's grasp. He cursed and clutched his hand.

Zero K dropped to the rubble between them. "Steady there, officer. She's not a threat."

John snatched his badge from his belt and held it up like it could actually protect him. "I'm Detective John Mahrone," he said, emphasizing his rank, "and I'll be the judge of that. What are you both doing here?"

"Just a little investigative work, officer," said Zero with a casual shrug. "Same as you blokes."

"You're not a bloke, kid," said John. He turned to Kris. "And what about you? We don't need any more of you lot around here."

Zero snorted. "Typical. You think we're all the same. Anyone with powers - we're all vigilantes to you, no matter what we've done."

"One of you bloody vigilantes put my wife in hospital. And you're here now. So, I think it's a fair assumption you might know what happened, and you can damn well tell me about it."

Detective Johansson stepped out of the passenger side. "Take it easy, John."

John drew in a breath and clipped his badge back to his belt. "You should be careful where you poke your nose, kid. I honestly couldn't care less what powers you have. But start using them to hurt people, well, looks like you're young enough to keep out of jail. But I bet the clinic would take you."

Kris' arms tensed at her sides. "Is that what your boss taught you? Send any kid whose powers scare you to the clinic?" She pushed past Zero K. "Zero's not a threat. He's just snooping, and now he's leaving."

"And I should believe you because?"

Kris pulled off her baseball cap.

John stared at his daughter, jaw working. He swallowed hard. "Kris?"

Zero blinked. "Kris? Oh, so that's your name. Better than the black bandit, I suppose."

"Great." Johansson turned to Zero. "If what you say is true, and you're not a threat to us, not a villain, if you prefer I put it that way, then get out of here, son. I think we've got other things we need to deal with here."

Zero K took a step back and nodded. Then he ice blasted himself onto the roof and disappeared.

John stood frozen, as surely as if Zero K had caught him in an ice blast. He blinked himself out of it, but when he spoke his voice was strained. "Kris... I... what are you..."

"I'm trying to help! You said Mum got hurt here, so I wanted to see if I could find out anything, and..."

"It's the middle of the night. I left you at home. I told you to look after your brother."

"Dad..."

"Don't Dad me! Get in the car!" John pointed a finger at the Commodore. His arm shook.

Kris ducked around Johansson, picked up her skateboard, and slammed the door behind her. John spoke with Johansson for a moment, then joined Kris in the car. Kris pressed herself further into the passenger seat. John wouldn't look at her. He fumbled with the ignition, then backed out the alley and started driving home.

It took him a few minutes to speak. "What were you thinking, Kris? I trusted you."

"Dad, I'm fine. I was just trying to help."

John threw the car into third gear. The gearbox grated. "What if you weren't? Your mother was out here last night. She got hurt. Then I find you in some bloody outfit and with some kid with superpowers. Do you think you're some kind of vigilante?"

"No!" She tugged at her shirt. "This was just so no one would see me."

"Well, that worked out swell. What if that ice guy had hurt you?"

"He wasn't going to."

"How would you know?

"And how would you know he's dangerous? You wanted to shove him in the clinic just like they did Penny."

"Kris, you know we don't just send kids with powers there. I got angry. I was trying to scare him into behaving himself. You know, so I don't actually have to arrest some stupid kid who thinks having powers means he can do whatever he wants."

Kris folded her arms and glared out the window.

John pulled up at the side of the road. "Listen, Dave sent his daughter to the clinic because he thought it was the best thing for her. He thought it would keep her safe. And that's all I'm trying to do now; make sure you're safe. I don't want you to get hurt like Rachael did." He paused, and when he spoke again his voice was strained. "If I'd just listened to her maybe this wouldn't have happened."

Kris waited, but her father remained quiet. Eventually, she snuck a look at him. He stared out the windshield, hands gripping the steering wheel tightly. She reached across the car and squeezed his arm hard. "Dad, if you're still worried about Mum, that means you still love her, right?"

John blinked. "Of course I do."

"So, why'd you break up?"

John shifted in his seat and looked away. "Doesn't matter now, does it? We've got to be there for her when she wakes up." He turned back to Kris and put his hand over hers. "And you need to stop trying to figure out what happened, okay? That's my job. Promise me you won't go out like this again? I've got enough on my plate."

Kris couldn't hold her father's gaze; he stared into her eyes like he could see her answer there before she spoke. She pulled away, and her fingers went to the pink cuff under her black shirt sleeve. "Okay, Dad. I promise I won't go out like this again."

6

"Kris, wait." Calvin jogged up beside Kris at the school gates. He stopped for a few seconds, hands on his knees, panting, then drew himself upright. "I wanted to check you were okay. You ran off pretty quick on Saturday to see your mum at the hospital."

Kris picked up her skateboard from the sidewalk. If Calvin had been a few seconds later, he'd have had no chance of catching up with her. "I'm fine. Did you want to hang out again?" She cleared her throat. "I mean, only if you want to."

"Actually, I want to show you something. It'll be really cool, I promise." Calvin shifted his weight from foot to foot. "It'll, um, it'll mean you won't have to worry about what might have happened to Pink Punch."

Kris stiffened. "What about Pink Punch? I mean, she's that pink superhero, right?"

The corner of Calvin's lips quirked upwards. "Come on, Kris. Don't pretend you don't know about Pink Punch. I know you were out looking for her Saturday night."

Kris grabbed Calvin by the shirt sleeve and dragged him off the sidewalk, away from the dwindling stream of children leaving school. "How do you know about that? Are you spying on me?"

Calvin's cheeks flushed. "I'm not spying! I thought I was pretty direct about it." He glanced over Kris' shoulder. The kids walking past were engaged in conversation with each other, but Calvin positioned himself between Kris and any potential onlookers. "I was only worried about your safety. That's why I tried to protect you from those cops."

"Well, seeing as one was my dad that hardly..." Kris eyes widened, and she took a step back. "Wait, what?"

Calvin tugged up the edge of his shirt sleeve just enough to reveal the network of blue tattoos wrapped around his forearm. "I'm Zero K."

Kris stared, mouth open. She yanked Calvin's sleeve back down. "Why are you even showing me that?"

"Rick says we shouldn't need to hide who we are. And since I saw you out there last night, I thought you might like to know a competent superhero was on the case. I don't need to know who Pink Punch is to you. But at least now you know the situation is under control, so there's no need to do anything stupid like go out at night without superpowers."

Kris still had his sleeve, and her grip tightened on his wrist as it hit her. "Wait, Calvin, you can help me. We can go out and figure out what happened to Pink, and..."

Calvin held up his hands. "Hey, I told you so you knew it was under control. I want to protect you, not put you in more danger."

"I can look out for myself. And why should I believe you just want to protect me? We've only been speaking to each other for the last couple of days. Why would you tell me something like this? Seriously, my dad's a cop."

Calvin paled. "No, you can't tell him! I thought because you were saying all that stuff about Butch, and you disagreed with your dad about the clinic..." He grabbed his upper arms and hugged himself tight. "No, I'm going to be in so much trouble."

"Calm down. I won't tell him." Kris mind churned. She had to get Calvin to help. She put a hand to Pink's cuff. If only she could prove she'd be safe, but she couldn't even figure out how to turn on the damned suit. And even if she could, it did not seem a great idea to reveal a secret identity to someone she'd just met.

Which was something that only now seemed to be dawning on Calvin. He began to pace. "I shouldn't have told you. Please don't tell me you feel the same way about supers as your dad? I mean, you can't, you were out at night, you were basically being a vigilante..."

"Calvin! My dad is a cop. It's his job to distrust vigilantes. But it's not mine." She shrugged. "It's complicated, I guess. I don't agree with him on a lot of things. Look, all you need to know is I am not going to tell on you."

A grin played at the edges of Calvin's lips. "Yeah? Okay, okay... So, you want to hang out?"

"Well, now I don't know. That depends on whether you're going to help me find out about Pink Punch."

"It's dangerous!"

Kris rolled her eyes. "Yeah, you know what, forget it. I didn't ask for your help in that alleyway. And I'm pretty sure I did a better job at protecting you than you did me."

"Kris, come back, I'm not being a jerk. It's just because I've got superpowers."

"You want to hang out? Help me find out what happened to Pink Punch."

Calvin glanced around nervously at the mention of the super-hero's name. Like talking about superheroes was more suspicious than showing off your superpowered tattoos.

Kris jumped on her board and rolled off, fast.

"Kris, wait."

Kris didn't turn around, or slow down. A moment later a crash sounded behind her, and Calvin cussed.

Once she was sure Calvin had no hope of keeping up with her, Kris slowed. She didn't want to get home too quickly. She cut across the carpark of the abandoned supermarket a short distance from her house. It would have been convenient, had it been open. Now, most of the supermarkets operated from Northberg's two competing malls, overcrowded, but certainly getting enough customers to justify their existence.

She rolled past the only vehicle in the cracked parking lot; an old, pale blue Mustang. It sat silently in a corner not visible from the main road, dripping oil. It looked exactly like the one Mum had kept in the back yard and taken when she'd left.

Kris scraped to a halt, turned around, and frowned. "Stan?"

The Mustang was silent, save for a faint plink as a drop of oil fell to the puddle under its hood.

Kris kicked a tyre. Then she shook her head at herself. "Man, I am really getting desperate."

The Mustang rumbled. "Go away."

"Wait, Stan? Stan, it is you." Kris leaned hard against his side, until his body started to rock back and forth. "Stan, talk to me, please, I need your help!"

"I'm sorry about your mom. I failed her. I was supposed to be her backup." Another plink of oil.

"Are you crying?"

"Don't be silly. Cars can't cry."

"Um, you know she's not dead, right?"

"What?" Stan's engine roared to life. His body lifted on its suspension and a wave of pink crackled across him. His bodywork solidified to solid pink and his edges smoothed down to his modern Mustang body. "Why didn't you tell me right away? Is she okay?"

Kris rested a hand on his hood. "Settle down! I didn't even know where you were. You're parked in the middle of nowhere. You don't even look like you."

"Camouflage."

"Was Mum living around here? I thought she said it was someplace shady."

"It is. And no, it's nowhere near here. After I dropped you off, I parked myself here. I didn't know what else to do. Rachael created me, gave me life, even though I don't think she fully intended it. What was I supposed to do when I failed at the one thing I was created for?"

"You didn't fail. Mum's in hospital, she's in a coma. But Dad says she's going to be okay."

"Thank Ford," said Stan. "At least I didn't stuff up this whole thing for her."

"This whole thing is kind of what I wanted to talk to you about. Mum was investigating something in that alleyway. I think it had to do with her old job, and it might be important. I need to find out, and to do that you're going to have to show me how to activate this suit." She held out her wrist and pointed at the cuff.

Stan rolled back with a jerk. "What? No! Your mother told me to protect you. Not put you in further danger."

He was as bad as Calvin. Kris put her hands on her hips and glared at the vehicle, the way she'd seen Mum do whenever she told her and Tommy off. "If she stays in that coma, what's going to happen, Stan?"

"This city could be in a lot of trouble. TechCorp, the company your mother used to work for, has been trying to sell suits, very similar to the one you're wearing now, to the VCU. It's supposed to help them combat the rising vigilante crime rate."

Kris' guts tightened. "Dad."

"Yes, so you see, Rachael has a vested interest in stopping TechCorp. Honestly, it would have made it a lot easier if your father had just listened to her when she told him what they were up to in the first place."

"Dad's job is dangerous enough already. Wouldn't something like Pink's suit protect him?"

"The suit itself? Probably. Your mother did design them. But she believed TechCorp was also paying villains to commit crimes, to raise the crime rate. The cops didn't want to take the suits to start with. But now with rising vigilante crime? It all seems rather suspicious. TechCorp already seems to be controlling many of the villains by giving them money, and tech, and getting them to commit more crimes. That bit is easy. The VCU, not so much. But once the cops take them up on the offer, Rachael believed TechCorp would have control of them too."

Kris let out a pent-up breath and leaned against Stan's bonnet.

"Please don't lean on me like that."

"Sorry." Kris straightened up. "Don't you see? Mum needs my help, and yours. She can't do anything from hospital. If I wear this suit, I'll look exactly like Pink Punch."

Stan rocked back and forth on his tyres for a moment, then settled. "All right. But if we're going to do this, first you need to learn how to be Pink Punch."

* * *

Kris crossed and uncrossed her arms and then slumped back in Stan's seat with a groan. They had waited until nightfall, and then Kris had sneaked back to the abandoned parking lot. Stan said he wanted to see how she handled the suit. And for that, he'd decided they needed to locate some villains. Now they were trundling through backstreets at a ridiculously slow pace. "Is it always this hard to find bad guys? Can't I just try punching a tree or something?"

"They're villains. Not koalas," said Stan.

"Can I at least get out for a bit?"

"I'm scanning the police frequencies. As soon as we find something that looks like villain activity, we'll head there."

"I thought you said villain activity was increasing?" Kris threw her arms wide. "I see zero activity."

"Increasing means there's more of it. It doesn't mean we're going to find them on every street corner. No villain is stupid enough to randomly attack people or make themselves unreasonably visible."

"Yeah, but… cat!" Kris pointed out the windshield.

A dark shape stood in the street. It glared at them, and its tail flicked side to side. Stan braked. The cat waited until he stopped to jolt to life and finish its mad rush across the street. Then, at least two dozen felines spilled across behind it. The rattle of dragged packages and the clatter of tins, interspersed with the yowls of the cats, filled the air.

"Well," said Stan. "There're some villains for you."

"You want me to fight cats? I can do better than that! I did take Taekwondo, you know. I can throw a punch."

"But not in a superpowered suit. Go on. Practice time."

Kris rolled her eyes and stepped out into the street. This was stupid, but if she wanted Stan's help, she had no choice but to play his games. Besides, they were cats. What could go wrong?

"Right, first you need to activate the suit. All you need to do is think of activating it. You have to do it very consciously and deliberately though."

"Seriously? I already tried that."

"I locked the suit down when I dropped you home that night," Stan admitted. "Your mother gave it to you to protect you. Not as some toy."

Kris grumbled and held out her wrist, focusing on the cuff. "This is dumb."

"Once you do it once, it's a piece of cake."

Kris focused. She told herself that she needed the armour, that she needed to fight. "Go-go gadget supersuit."

Stan groaned. "Oh, for the love of Ford. Please don't do that every time."

Kris didn't plan to. But it was enough to help her focus on what she wanted. The suit built itself over her in a wave, and her skin tingled. Kris couldn't be sure it was the contact against her skin or just knowing she was suddenly ten times as strong that made her feel so giddy.

"Now, you'll need to make a weapon," said Stan.

"Like a gun?"

"No! Why would you want to shoot cats?"

"I don't! I'm just saying…"

"Projectile weapons won't work," Stan grumbled. "The suit is programmed with swords and shields, bats, and clubs."

"And the gauntlet?"

"Yes. Pink's weapons need to be in contact with the suit to stay solid. They're built out of the same nanites as the suit. But they won't know what to do if they're not in contact with you."

"So, if I imagine something like a ball…" A cricket ball sized sphere built itself in her hand. Kris broke into a grin. "Holy crap! I just thought of it!"

"Yes, but that's still technically a projectile."

"How long do you think it'll last though?" Kris drew back her arm, and hurled the ball at the river of cats. The ball flew from her hand like a rocket, and Kris' guts caught as she realised that would easily take out one poor little cat. The ball exploded into dust, right in front of the huge tortoiseshell.

"A few seconds; at least until any significant impact. So I guess that works. Not that I'd try hurling things at anything larger than a cat. You'd only make a full-sized villain angry. Besides, it's inefficient."

The tortoiseshell turned around and hissed. Her fur stood on end and grew into jagged spikes. They shot from her body and stabbed into the asphalt. A couple impaled themselves in Stan's bonnet, and Kris held up an arm to shield her face. A plink, plink, plink sounded from her armour, and the spikes that hit her fell to the ground, but she didn't feel anything. "It's got freaking spikes? Why has a cat got superpowers?"

"Don't you listen at school? The Fallout didn't just affect humans. But I suppose animals don't usually go around using those powers to take people's stuff." Stan's bonnet rippled, and the orange and black spikes which had struck him fell to the ground. "Unless some human is nice and feeds them in exchange. Catlady doesn't have powers, but I guess her cats do. May I suggest a shield?"

"Shield?" said Kris. As soon as she pictured it, it materialised in her hand. The next round of spikes smacked into it and fell harmlessly to the ground. Then twelve kilos of cat flung itself onto the shield with a clatter of claws. Kris spun herself around and threw it off. She didn't put too much effort into it. She didn't want to splatter the cat across the concrete like the ball. The cat flew through the air, yowling all the way, and landed smack in the middle of the cat pack.

"I'm really not sure I should be picking on cats. I'm pretty sure all they've got is cat food."

Thunder cracked overhead, and it started to rain. It rarely rained in Northberg, and there certainly hadn't been any indication tonight was going to be one of those rare times.

The cats cried and grumbled, picked up their haul, and then bolted into the nearest alleyway. The tortoiseshell yowled, shook her fur, and brought up the rear, disappearing into the darkness.

"Well, it's nice to know you're all right," said a voice from above. "Though I can't imagine why you're fighting a bunch of cats. Are they in on this whole TechCorp conspiracy too?" A woman floated above Kris, seemingly suspended on the clouds that surrounded her. She wore a white dress that billowed around her, and her red hair lashed about her face. The rain let up, and the woman's hair settled as the wind died down.

"Who…"

"Pink Punch knows her," said Stan. "That's Nimbus."

Nimbus. Kris hadn't seen her on television, but she knew she was Rick's wife. Dad often included her in his rants. Something about causing trouble behind the scenes whilst her husband plied vigilante rights in the spotlight. Kris couldn't remember her showing up on the news having dealt out some vigilante justice, as Pyromaniac often did, but her father had mentioned he suspected her of being involved every time there was odd weather. Which sounded paranoid, but in a place like Northberg, where there was basically one type of weather, maybe not so much.

Nimbus touched down on light, bare feet. "So, any particular reason you're harassing cats?"

Kris shrugged. "We didn't want to run them over. But what are you doing here?"

Nimbus raised an eyebrow. "I'm putting out spot fires, as you've called it in the past. Well, actually, I spotted your car, and then you. No one has seen you for days. After that explosion, we've all been worried."

Stan snorted. "She's worried because Rachael promised to make them a bit of tech. They're hardly being helpful otherwise."

"What tech?" Kris asked.

Nimbus frowned. "Pardon?"

"Kris, I have a direct feed to Pink's helmet. Nimbus can't hear a word I'm saying."

Kris' cheeks flushed under her helmet. "Nothing."

"I know we've got you working for us in, I guess you'd call it in a contractor capacity. But your skills could be far more useful to us than just making us a few toys in your spare time. Whatever our differences, we should help one another."

Kris' heart leapt. Forget Zero K. She could get help direct from supers who she'd actually heard something about. "Oh great! Because there's this whole thing with TechCorp going on and…"

Nimbus held up a hand. "Yes, so you've told us. And we told you if you would give us a hand with the tech we needed and help us put a damper on some of these spot fires, we'd see if there was anything to your theory. Don't get me wrong, TechCorp isn't any vigilante's favorite company. But we're not interested in vengeance. There are plenty of villains committing crimes we can stop now, if you're willing to help us."

"Rachael told them TechCorp was paying villains to commit those crimes," Stan grumbled in her ear, "and they still won't listen."

Kris chewed her lip. She still wasn't entirely sure what was going on. But all Stan had her doing so far was fighting cats. She needed to ramp this up if she was going to have any hope of helping Mum. "Hey, I'll help you with anything, so long as you return the favour."

Nimbus smiled. "I was hoping you'd say that."

"Maybe that explosion knocked some sense into me."

"Well then, you can help me right now. Zero K was supposed to be tracking some werewolves. We'd heard they'd planned to cause trouble down at the night markets. Zero insisted it had something to do with your TechCorp theory. He really does look up to you, you know. But he hasn't reported in yet. He's young; and I'm starting to worry he might take on more than he can handle."

"Yeah, Zero seems kind of into showing off," said Kris.

"So, will you help us check this out?"

"Definitely."

"I'm glad, Pink. We're on the same side, so it certainly helps to pool our resources. Thank you. Follow me." Nimbus lifted into the air and floated down the street like a red-haired apparition.

Kris climbed back into Stan. He started up with a rumble and trundled after Nimbus. "You need to listen to me. And how do you know this Zero K?"

"He goes to my school. He told me who he was." That was the simplest explanation. Stan wouldn't want to hear about her sneaking out without even Pink's suit for protection. He'd been cautious enough about letting her use the suit as it was.

"Kids these days. I hope you don't go telling people you're Pink Punch too. It's dangerous. And how do you think you're ready for this? You need to practice first. And just talking to Nimbus like that... you need to be in character! You're supposed to still be Rachael."

"I'm wearing a mask. How would she know? All I need to do is act like an adult. And if you're here to fill me in on what Pink Punch should know, and how she acts, I'll be fine."

Stan rumbled around a corner. "I suppose. I will admit you seem to have got Nimbus on side far quicker than your mother did. She just argued with her. Maybe helping them is the way to go, but I'm still not sure you're ready. Just promise me if you get in a fight, you'll listen to me?"

"Deal."

7

Zero K surveyed the alleyway from his vantage point on the rooftop. He was a silhouette against the night sky; a tall lithe shape watching over the city against the backdrop of the full moon. At which point he remembered the whole point of surveillance was to not be seen, and crouched back down, cursing softly. Not only did the full moon render him starkly visible, but rumour had it that it made the mutants he tailed more powerful. Whether this were true, or simply folklore surrounding the creatures the mutants closely resembled, Zero wasn't sure, but he shouldn't take any chances. He'd kept downwind of them, as he'd been told, and so far, he'd followed without incident. Zero had no intention of stuffing this mission up.

A growl came from the alley below, followed by a sharp yap. A bin clattered over.

"Gran, would you keep an eye on Pup?"

"I'm not your babysitter," grumbled a deep voice. "I did my dash raising you, didn't I?"

"It's Barry I'm worried about… Barry! Stop sniffing that!"

Another yap. It sounded like someone had earned themselves a cuff.

Calvin moved along the roof line, keeping far enough back

that he wouldn't be seen. He winced as another bin crashed to the ground.

His targets were illuminated as they passed through a beam of bright moonlight shining down between the buildings. Five big furry shapes moving through the streets below. They were man sized, but at least twice as broad, and completely covered in shaggy fur. Like big dogs, but humanoid. Werewolves.

The two shapes at the front of the small pack huddled together as they loped along. "As long as the Boss comes through, I'm happy to stir things up a bit," the bigger shape growled. "We need the money."

"I know, Spike, but I'm still not sure Pup is big enough for this sort of thing."

Spike's furry face split, and teeth glinted in the moonlight. "Our daughter's tough, Fang. She'll be fine. You saw how she ripped into that mangy mutt that was sniffing around her."

Fang snorted. "I suppose. But aren't you suspicious that someone would pay us simply to cause havoc down at the night markets? Should we have asked why?"

Spike shrugged his shaggy shoulders. "I'm not bothered. Everyone will have a good feed. And we'll get some money out of it. It'll do those humans good to know they've still got something to fear from 'the likes of us.'"

"Just don't bite off more than you can chew."

"Never, my dear."

Another crash sounded behind them.

"Pup!" Fang barked.

"It wasn't me, Mum."

"Goddamn it, Barry, stop sniffing the bloody trash cans!"

Calvin waited until the wolves were out of sight, then made an ice bridge and crossed the gap to the next building. He held out his arms and gritted his teeth as he struggled to keep his balance. At least this was a little easier than skateboarding, and he wasn't worried he would fall, but he still needed to get his body in better shape. He was pretty sure his balance had improved since Nim had started letting him help with missions, but if he was going to become a fully-fledged superhero, he still had work to do.

Calvin grinned faintly. He had managed to keep his movements well-honed when he'd met Kris, out searching for Pink Punch, the other night. At least one person thought Zero K was cool.

Once he was safely on the other side, he allowed himself to ponder the wolves' words. Pink Punch had said the Boss was associated TechCorp; the same name Spike had just mentioned. Calvin was certain Pink was onto something. He wouldn't be here, not working with Rick and Nim, if it hadn't been for Pink Punch. As far as Calvin was concerned, he'd believe anything she told him. But his foster parents had yet to be convinced. And so, they'd given him this mission. He'd have liked to think it was because they trusted him, but he was still suspicious they only gave him a crappy job to occupy his time. Maybe they didn't think he was capable of anything. Just like his father had.

Calvin swallowed. That wasn't fair. Rick and Nim had been kind enough to let him into their home. If anything, they simply thought he was still learning, not ready yet. At least they were giving him the chance to try. And they didn't treat his failures like a capital offense. A part of him still wondered: if he did something stupid enough, would he lose their trust? But he'd show them. As soon as he found out what was going on here, and he could prove Pink Punch was right, they'd see he was useful.

He hoped Pink Punch was okay. Nim had told him the cops had found one woman on the scene, who was now in a coma, but there was nothing to indicate she was Pink Punch. No flamboyant pink suit. She was probably just some poor innocent, and Pink Punch was still around, lying low. She'd show up eventually, and he could fulfill his promise to Kris, and let her know her friend was okay.

Zero K crept to the roof edge and spotted the pack again, still making as much noise as, well, a pack of wild dogs crashing through alleyways. He should call Nim now to let her know the wolves were about to stage an attack. But instead, he let them continue on their way. To prove himself to his foster parents, and to pay Pink Punch back for what she'd done for him, he'd need more than one of the wolves simply mentioning this Boss. "It won't hurt to let them actually get to the markets. Then I'll stop them." Calvin grinned. "Besides, it's about time people saw my powers too."

* * *

Nimbus led Kris and Stan down to Northberg's foreshore. The markets were held here a couple of times a month, along the strip of concrete path that wound its way between the landscaped grassed areas the council had installed on the otherwise desolate beachfront. For some of the supers with more artistic powers, it was a perfect place to sell their wares, along with those people with more traditional artistic talent. For whatever reason, those who had not manifested powers didn't seem to mind those benign, artistic powers so much, especially when they resulted in a particularly interesting gift for a loved one.

Nimbus stood on the footpath, her dress billowing around her in the ocean breeze. She would fit in with most of the night markets patrons, as long as she didn't levitate. Stan's flamboyant paint job, and growling engine, stood out far more. Perhaps that was the reason they had stopped some few hundred meters from the bright lights of stalls and floodlamps, on a quieter stretch of the foreshore.

"I'll be in contact," said Stan. "I'll be able to see and hear everything you do, and talk to you, from here. Just listen to me, please?"

"I promise I'll be careful. Relax." Kris joined Nimbus on the footpath. "So, where are these villains? I hope you don't want to wander around and buy jewelry. This suit is going to draw attention."

Nimbus smiled faintly. "You do make quite an entrance when you're ready." She slipped a mobile phone from her pocket. Her dress had pockets. A frown touched her lips as she checked the screen. "Zero still hasn't been in contact. I told Rick he's too young for this sort of thing, but he's too trusting. You're probably right about him. Not that it's abnormal for a teenager; but I think he just wants to show off."

Kris swallowed. Calvin was no older than her. Nimbus would certainly not want Pink's help if she knew who she really was. "I'm sure he's doing fine. Just because he's a kid, doesn't mean he can't be a hero, right?"

A scream sounded from the direction of the markets, and Nimbus' head jerked up, green eyes alert. A howl rent the night air. Then a flash of blue shot into the sky. One of the floodlights tilted and crashed down, throwing a bright beam high into the sky until it was snuffed on impact.

A wind gust whipped past Kris as Nimbus lifted into the air. "Damn it, Zero. They're werewolves, Pink. Likely more than one. I'm still not sure how best to work with you. But if you see Zero just make sure he doesn't get himself hurt." Nimbus shot up into the sky, completely enveloped in a growing cloud.

"Werewolves?" Kris' shoulders tensed.

"Oh boy," said Stan. "Okay, so this is not what I had in mind for a practice run; I much preferred the cats. Just…"

"Be careful, I know." Kris gritted her teeth and ran toward the flashes of blue and howls.

People ran past her from the other direction, fleeing the markets. "Hey, it's Pink Punch. Help us!"

"What do you think I'm doing?" Kris kept running. She flew along, barely expending any energy. She was fit from skateboarding, she could run, but she still got puffed. This was amazing. "Hey, Stan? Think I could make a skateboard?"

"Well, most of the swords and clubs were previously programmed into the suit by your mother, so she could build them with just a thought. However, it's a bit difficult to make something from a thought from scratch. What you're actually doing is referencing a library of the 3D models Rachael previously programmed. Basic shapes like your ball, however…"

"Stan! Yes or no?"

"Unless she already programmed… well, look at that."

A skateboard materialised in Kris' hand. Kris grinned, tossed it onto the concrete, and jumped aboard. A single kick propelled her along faster than she had ever gone before. Kris entered the market, past stalls set up displaying various wares, and was nearly on the flashes of blue when a bunch of screaming people exploded from the stalls to her left. "Help!"

Kris slowed and jumped off the board. Her big metal boots cracked the concrete as she landed. The skateboard skittered off under its own momentum and exploded in a shower of pink against a palm tree.

The terrified market goers were followed by a furry beast, black and streaked with grey. Seven foot tall, broad shouldered, and full of teeth, the werewolf pointed its nose to the sky and howled. It turned its attention to an unattended food stall and began snuffling down burgers.

"Hey!" said Kris, "I hope you're planning to pay for those."

"Go away, I'm eating." The beast turned back to its meal.

Kris imagined a ball, and a pink one quickly built in her hand. She hurled it at the wolf's head. "Hey, wolf-man, fetch."

"I told you to go easy on the projectiles!" Stan grumbled in her ear. "You're wasting nanites."

The ball exploded on the wolf's head. It turned and bared its teeth. "That's wolf lady to you, you disrespectful whelp!" She snarled and leapt on Pink Punch.

"My bad..." Kris slammed into the ground as teeth snapped inches from her face. Even with the body armour she felt the impact. Something in Pink's suit whirred and she held the wolf back. Her heart hammered in her chest. "What do I..."

"Knife," said Stan.

"Knife?" Kris already had her hand on the wolf's shoulder and the knife shot straight into flesh. The wolf jerked and yelped. Kris called up a gauntlet. As they were Pink's most used weapon, they had to be effective. She smashed it into the wolf's face, and she swayed and backed off.

"Easy, stay with the gauntlet for now," said Stan. "If you ask the nanite generator to make too many weapons too quickly it won't work. It needs time to recharge."

"Got it," Kris said, even though all this talk of nanites and 3D modeling was going over her head. But 'hold onto your weapons and don't make too many too quickly' she understood.

The werewolf circled then launched herself, teeth bared. Kris threw a punch into the wolf's jaw. She sailed clean over the burger stall and crashed onto something behind it in a splinter of wood.

"Whoa." Kris stared at her fist as the gauntlet fizzled out. She knew how to throw a punch, but she'd never sent someone sailing like that.

A howl sounded, followed by a blast of blue shooting into the air. Zero K's ice. Kris ran down the path to the source. In the middle of the open oval at the centre of the markets, Zero K was circled by a werewolf. It was slightly larger than the one Kris had fought, but all black, and its movements were quicker and less lumbering. It wore a spiky dog collar around its broad neck.

"Enough with the banter, boy," the wolf growled. "You can't hit me, and I'm going to eat you up."

Zero K flung a flurry of icicles, and the wolf leapt aside. "But you can't get any closer," he taunted, his voice taking on a singsong note. He circled the wolf a good ten meters away, tense, ready to bolt at the next attack, but not moving any closer. But his attention was on the big wolf. Not the smaller, lither, werewolf that silently padded up behind him.

"Look out!"

The second werewolf pounced. A bolt of lightning shot out of the crackling clouds above and the wolf spun away with a yelp.

Zero K stiffened and whirled around. "What the..."

"Mama!" With a snarl a flash of fur sprinted from between the stalls and tackled Zero. "You hurt my mama I'm gonna bite off your face!"

Zero crashed to the ground and scrabbled at the ball of fur that assaulted him. "Get off me!"

This wolf wasn't much bigger than a large dog, but she fought ferociously. Zero K pushed and pulled, he shot ice off in all directions, but still the wolf stayed, arms wrapped around his head, trying to bite him.

The big werewolf loped over to the fallen one. "Fang, are you okay?"

Fang hauled herself up and shook the smoke from her fur. "I'm fine. Get Pup, Spike. I'll round up the others. This is too dangerous."

Spike turned his attention to Zero K. He snarled and charged toward him, gaining speed.

Kris ran in front of Spike. "Hey, big bad... oh crap..."

Spike ran smack bang into her. They rolled over on the grass, and when they came up Kris straddled the chest of the startled beast. Spike looked at her cross eyed and broke into a grin. "Pink Punch, huh? How hard is your punch, really?"

"I'll show you."

Spike flung up a paw and blocked her. His muscles shook, but he stopped her, and held her fist captive in his big paw. He grinned. "Decent, now try mine." Spike landed a punch that made Kris' head spin. In fact, it sent her whole body reeling through the air.

Somehow, Kris found herself back on her feet. Her head still spun, but she was upright.

"Are you okay?" said Stan. "Your suit will help compensate your balance. It should complement any muscle movement, actually. That's why you can hit so much harder."

"Keep it simple, Stan. Also, can I please have a sword!" Kris raised her voice as Spike barreled toward her.

A broadsword was in her hands. Spike huffed and puffed in her face. His claws scrabbled at the sword.

"Okay, good, now how do I use it?"

"Why'd you want a sword if you don't know how to use it?" said Stan. "You want simple? Pointy end goes in the wolf."

"Because claws." She slashed at Spike, and metal rang against claws as he blocked each blow.

"Stop talking to yourself," Spike growled. "Seriously, you had really good banter when I saw you on TV. Now I'm getting bored. Or do you just save that for those cops you like picking on?"

Kris slashed Spike's paw and he took a step back to steady himself.

Zero K yelled. Kris whirled around. She'd nearly forgotten him! A ball of glowing blue snowflakes built around Zero and the smallest werewolf. Like a blizzard in a two-meter diameter ball.

"Damn it, Fang will kill me." Spike shoved Pink out of the way and lunged for Zero. He reached into the snow and hauled the white-flecked werewolf out by her scruff. Then he slapped a paw into the snowstorm.

Zero K collapsed to the ground and the snow exploded around him in a poof of white.

Spike pointed his nose to the sky and howled. Three mournful wails answered him. Spike picked up the smaller, shivering werewolf in his jaws at the back of her neck. And then he bolted.

Zero sat up, rubbed at his head, and groaned. "Wait, Pink Punch?" His eyes widened. He shot to his feet and dusted himself off.

Kris lowered her sword as it dissolved. "Yeah. Glad to see you're okay." Not only because she cared if Calvin got hurt, but Nimbus had specifically told her to look out for him. Kris doubted failing her first order from one of the supers would have gone down well.

"I was tracking those werewolves for you." Zero scuffed a foot through the grass. "They said something about, you know, the Boss. So, I figured I, ahem…" He straightened himself up, hands on hips, and got control of his voice, "could use my considerable skill to bring them down and find out what they were on about for you."

"Well, thanks, but you seemed to be in a bit of trouble there. You basically fell flat on your face. Maybe you need a bit more of that skill." Compared to Zero, Pink's voice sounded strong and measured. A great deal of that was the voice modulator in the helmet. It made her voice deeper, more adult. It certainly helped her confidence level.

Zero's grin faltered. "But I…"

"No, I just mean… there were like five of them. How'd you expect to fight them all?" This was not the self-assured young man who'd attempted to rescue her the night before. "What's happening?" Kris said, voice low.

"Not that Rachael told me a great deal of what transpired. But from what I've seen, he's a bit of a Pink Punch fanboy," said Stan.

"She's right, Zero." Nimbus floated in from above, dress swirling as she landed. "You were supposed to follow the werewolves, find out what they were up to, and then contact us. Before they caused trouble."

Zero folded his arms. "I was handling it."

"Does this look handled?" Nimbus swept an arm behind her to

indicate the upturned stalls. Food and merchandise were strewn everywhere.

Kris couldn't recall when she had last seen such havoc caused by vigilantes. Not in a public area. Dad had mentioned banks or warehouses being attacked and damaged. But those happened in the dead of night. Things were stolen; those attacks had made sense. These werewolves had just caused a great big mess. Worse: there had been tonnes of people around.

"I didn't do that, the werewolves did!" Zero protested.

"True. You're lucky Pink and I came in time to send those werewolves running. People could have been hurt. You could've been hurt."

Zero looked at his feet. "You keep giving me garbage missions..."

"We do trust you, and this mission wasn't garbage."

"Exactly," said Zero, his mood rallying. "This mission wasn't garbage, and I haven't stuffed it up. I heard the werewolves talking. They said they'd been paid by the Boss to trash the markets." He turned to Kris. "She's TechCorp, right; that's what you're always saying?"

TechCorp paying villains to commit crimes. Like Stan and Mum had said. This was the first Kris had heard of 'The Boss' though. No, wait. In the alleyway. Mum had said something to Thunderclap about someone called the Boss. "Yeah, that's right. So, you believe me now? You'll help me?"

Nimbus stared at Zero, arms folded. "I know you want to trust her, Zero. But we still don't know her that well."

"Nim! Pink Punch was right, something is going on with TechCorp. They nearly blew her up, now this, we have to trust her. I'm glad you're okay too, by the way."

"Um, thanks." Kris still couldn't quite understand what was going on. Zero was certainly keen to help Pink, despite barely knowing her. Kris barely knew him, but she did know Calvin. Maybe if she hung out with him more, he'd tell her more.

"All right, Pink, I guess you've got our attention," said Nimbus. "You did help us tonight, without argument, and that's more than you've done in the past. I tell you what, finish up those bits of equipment you were working on for us, and bring them around. I think that with your actions here tonight that's enough to put you on the team."

"Relax, the equipment she's talking about is in your Mum's workshop," said Stan. "About time. At least having some more supers around means I won't have to worry so much about you getting yourself hurt."

She'd done plenty okay tonight without anyone else' help. Wearing the suit, she was indestructible. But she did need these guys to help her finish Mum's mission and she would not be foolish enough to turn that away. "All right. I'm in."

Nimbus nodded. "We'll be in contact. Now, I suggest we all get out of here before…"

The wail of sirens filled the air.

"Right on cue. Zero, let's go. Pink, I assume you can take care of yourself." She smiled faintly. "Unless you want to hang around and tease your boyfriend. We'll speak soon." With that she took to the air.

Zero flung out a chute of ice, then made himself a platform no bigger than a skateboard. He shot off on top of the trail that glittered and started to melt only seconds after he'd passed over it.

Kris frowned. "What did she mean boyfriend? She didn't mean Zero."

"She means your father," said Stan. "Pink Punch did have a habit of flirting with him whenever they met. Or arguing. I never could figure out which."

Kris cringed. "Please tell me you don't want me to stay in character and flirt with him."

"No, I think you would be best to avoid him entirely. Speaking of which, you do realise the cops and possibly the man himself are only moments away?"

Kris' eyes widened. "Oh, shoot." She looked left and right in a panic, orienting herself back to the direction Stan had parked.

A police vehicle slewed over the top of the hill and vibrated as it navigated the grassed area. Detective Johansson stepped out and surveyed the damaged stalls and scattered merchandise. She froze as her gaze fell on Pink Punch. Hard to miss in the bright pink suit. "John…"

John stepped out beside her, and his fists tensed at his sides. "Hey! I want to talk to you."

Kris turned and bolted, her boots stamping deep footprints in the grass. She ran back along the footpath, past the trashed stalls, back to Stan. "Stan, come get me."

"It's just your father. Pink Punch will outrun him easily."

"Pink, wait!" John ran behind her, breath chugging. "I just… want to talk…" Her father was fit, but he struggled to keep up.

Dad had always seemed to get along with Pink, as far as vigilantes went. Understandable, as, even though she couldn't tell him who she was, Mum would have known how not to upset him. Kris slowed. But imagine how he'd felt finding Mum lying there, hurt. Of course he wanted to talk; he needed to know what had happened. She couldn't tell him everything, but maybe she could put his mind at ease.

John jogged to a halt with some ten meters between them. He didn't seem keen to close the distance. Fair enough, Kris didn't know if he'd notice the height difference, or anything else that might give her away as a different person to her predecessor.

"Okay, I've stopped. What did you want to ask?"

John drew in a few more breaths, until his voice was steady. "That doesn't belong to you."

"What?"

"The damned suit!" John burst out. "You took it from my wife. I want to know who you are, and why you took her suit!"

Kris' jaw dropped. "Wait, you knew Pink's identity?"

"What's wrong? Does that put a spanner in whatever your little plan is? Of course I knew! She's my wife. At least I can trust her not to do things behind my back. Nope, she just says it straight to my face and goes and does it anyway."

"So, I'm giving you one chance. Maybe you were there to help her. I can't ask her who you are because she's in a coma. But there's also a chance you were the one who hurt her, and you stole her suit. So, you'd better tell me a damn good story about why she got hurt and how you had nothing to do with it. Because if this was your fault..."

A lump rose in Kris' throat. Back in the alleyway, Mum had turned at her voice. If she hadn't been there, Thunderclap wouldn't have hurt her. "I'm sorry Da... Detective Mahrone."

"Sorry? Sorry for what? What did you do?"

Stopping was a mistake. Kris turned tail and ran.

"Come back!"

Kris pelted back to where Stan was. Or should have been. "Stan, where are..." She ran smack bang into something that sounded metal and bounced back onto the road.

Stan grunted. "You'd better hope I can repair that." Thin air cracked open and revealed Stan's interior. Kris rolled inside and slammed the door, just as John pelted off the foreshore and onto the road. He slowed to a halt, looked left and right, and then put his hands to the back of his head. His chest heaved as he caught his breath.

"Can we go?" said Kris. She fought to keep the tremor from her voice.

"No, he'll hear my engine."

"You're invisible."

"Not entirely. This may be my best camouflage, but it still looks odd in the middle of nowhere if I move."

John looked around again, then yelled into the night air. "All right, I gave you your chance. I will find you, and I will make you tell me what happened to Rachael. You can't hide behind that bloody pink suit forever!"

"He's upset about Rachael," said Stan, "he'll calm down once she wakes up."

"Why didn't you tell me he knew? I could've been ready to talk to him, I could've... explained..." Explained what? Kris hugged herself tight.

Johansson jogged up from the foreshore footpath. She caught her breath and put a hand on John's shoulder. "Hey, we'll get her. She's always been relatively cooperative. We'll get her to talk."

"You know what, Jo? Those TechCorp suits are starting to sound pretty damned good about now."

8

It all made sense now. Mum and Dad's separation, the arguments. Quitting her job at TechCorp may have preempted it, but it was not the reason her parents had decided Mum needed to move out. Mum had discovered that TechCorp planned to, somehow, control the police force through the suits she had been designing. Dad had told her he couldn't help. His jurisdiction was vigilantes. This was either true, or he simply thought she was overreacting.

So, Mum had taken matters into her own hands. She had stolen a suit from her ex-employer and become Pink Punch. But she hadn't been doing it behind her husband's back. She'd told him. And then she'd moved out. A vigilante and a cop whose sworn duty it was to arrest vigilantes could hardly live under the same roof.

Kris just wished they had told her and Tommy. The last few months had been confusing as hell. She'd thought her Mum didn't care about her family, and all her father had cared about was the money his wife made. Tommy she could understand, but they could at least have told her something. She was old enough to know; she would have kept it secret. And that knowledge might have helped her in her mission now.

Kris was mulling over this outside the school gates when Calvin appeared at her shoulder. "Hey, Kris."

"Where'd you come from? Please don't tell me one of your powers is sneaking up on people."

"Afraid not. Look, I just wanted to let you know, Pink Punch, your friend, or whatever. I saw her last night. She's okay. So, you don't have to worry about her. You might have heard about those werewolves at the markets. I helped her chase them away. I don't think she could've done it without my help."

Kris raised an eyebrow. "Wow, your powers must be really awesome," she said, making an effort to keep any hint of sarcasm from her voice. She had no reason to be mad at Zero K, although perhaps Pink Punch should be as he was trying to steal some of her credit. But he'd made the effort to seek her out to let her know Pink was all right. Maybe she had found a legitimate friend. "Thanks for letting me know she's okay."

Calvin bounced on his heels. "So, you free to hang out?"

"I've... I've got to go to the hospital to see my mum."

"Oh, of course."

Kris scuffed the toe of her shoe on the concrete. "You know, you could come, if you want."

Calvin grinned. "Yeah? If I'm not intruding."

"She's unconscious. You can hardly intrude."

* * *

Mum lay in her hospital bed, hooked up to the apparatus that breathed for her. Kris gritted her teeth. She hated seeing her like this. She almost regretting bringing Calvin. She wanted to tell her mother what she was doing for her, that Pink Punch had everything under control. But she wouldn't have had that opportunity anyway. Dad was already there at his wife's bedside, absently stroking her hair.

Kris swallowed. She hadn't seen him yet today. Not after the events of last night, when he had shouted at Pink Punch. "Dad, what are you doing here? You should be asleep. You were on night shift."

John lifted his head and smiled at her faintly. He had dark circles under his eyes. "I've slept enough for today, sweetheart. Who's your friend?"

Calvin stood frozen in the doorway. Even though John wore plain clothes, his police badge was clearly visible on his hip. Calvin stared at it like it would jump off and bite him.

"This is Calvin. He's new at school."

Calvin tugged one of his long shirt sleeves down a little lower on his wrist but forced a smile. "I've seen you on TV, Detective Mahrone."

"Just call me John, son." He rose to his feet, but his eyes lingered on Rachael, and he swallowed hard. "Your mum's still out of it, Kris. The doctor says he doesn't know when she'll wake up. I'm sorry."

"That's okay, Dad." It looked like she'd have to be Pink Punch for a while yet.

"I was going to go straight to work after coming here, but your mum can't hear me anyway. Besides, Johansson will quiz me about whether I've eaten properly. Why don't we go home, and I make you kids a proper dinner? Calvin, you're more than welcome to join us, if you'd like."

Calvin still looked like he wanted to run as far away from the policeman as he could. Perhaps understandable, but he had already known her father was a cop. "Um, yeah," he finally said. "I'd love to."

"Good," said John. He glanced one last time at Rachael, then shook himself and turned away. "It'll be a good distraction."

* * *

"I know it's not much, but it's the best I could throw together from what's left in the fridge. I need to get to the supermarket."

Kris stared at the bowl of fried rice and raised an eyebrow. Dad had found half a kilo of bacon in the back of the fridge, as well as a hodgepodge of half-eaten vegetables, and thrown this together. It looked like they'd have enough for the next three days. "You could've just bought takeaway."

"Yeah, takeaway tastes good when you're not the one paying for it. We've been eating far too much as it is."

Tommy started hoeing into the rice like he hadn't eaten all day, which was quite possible. Kris had often seen him engrossed in his computer at lunch time at school, instead of eating his lunch. He was thin as a twig.

"So, Calvin," said John. "Did you just move here?"

"No, I was home-schooled, but now I'm not," Calvin forced a smile. "But that's kinda boring. Actually, I wanted to ask you about some cop stuff."

John lips twisted into a cheeky smirk. "No, I can't give you a pair of handcuffs. Especially if you've just made friends with my daughter."

"Dad!"

Calvin prodded his rice around with his fork. He hadn't eaten any of it yet. "Actually, it's about all the vigilante stuff."

Calvin didn't know what he had started. John dropped his cutlery to the table with a clatter, so his hands could be more appropriately used for the gestures necessary to support the practiced rant. "You'd best not believe everything you hear on TV, son. Crime is getting worse, and most of it is because of those vigilantes. They think they can do whatever they want, just because they won the Fallout lottery and ended up with abilities that make them stronger than the rest of us. I hope you're not thinking of sneaking out at night to get a look at them." He glanced briefly at Kris. "I think we can all agree that's kind of dumb."

"By vigilantes you mean villains, right?"

"There isn't a difference."

"Well, superheroes try to help you, right? Whereas villains are the problem."

"I thought you said you saw me on TV? So, you know what I think."

"Yeah, I did. And I disagree with you," said Calvin, meeting the older man's gaze. "Superheroes and villains are different. And what about people who just have powers but aren't out on the streets causing trouble? Are they criminals just because they have powers? Just because you can't tell the difference doesn't mean there isn't one."

"Hey, I'm out there on the street at night. Not you. And I know what goes on..."

"You work for the VCU. You're biased."

John slammed a closed fist on the table. "I wasn't biased when I found my wife unconscious and I thought she was dead! And who was there? A self-proclaimed 'superhero'. So don't you dare try to tell me there's a difference!"

Tommy flinched. Calvin's reaction was even more pronounced. He pressed back in his chair with such a jerk it squeaked back on the tiled floor.

John stared at his fist as if it were some unattached animal misbehaving. He winced and uncurled his fist. "Er... sorry."

"Dad, are you okay?"

Calvin blinked himself back from whatever had held him rigid in his dining chair. "Is he okay? What about me?"

Kris chewed her lip. With Butch, she'd constantly felt like she needed to stop him getting upset. Calvin wasn't nearly as emotional as he had been. But she wasn't going to start that again. She shrugged. "Well, you kind of started it."

Calvin threw his cutlery onto his plate with a clang. "Forget it, I'm leaving."

John would have told her or Tommy off if they'd treated the

dishes like that. But he wouldn't even look at Calvin as he stomped out of the house.

Kris caught up to Calvin in the middle of their driveway and stepped in front of him to block his path. "All right, stop. What happened in there?"

"Your dad obviously has some pretty strong opinions about vigilantes. Which is fine. But if he can't handle someone disagreeing with him without getting violent…" Calvin shoved his hands in his pockets and stared at his feet. "I don't have to sit around anywhere I don't want to and get abused."

"Violent? He got cranky, that's all. I'm sure the table will survive. Look I'm sorry, I didn't know he'd react like that. But it's not his fault, he's just upset about Mum."

"Whose fault is it then? Mine for making him angry? Rick says that's not a thing. I'm not responsible for anyone else's emotions, or what they choose to do because of them."

"What the heck is so great about Rick? I get you have powers, but all he does is rock up at crime scenes and talk to the press. He doesn't even use his superpowers. You know there's a conspiracy theory he doesn't actually have any…"

"Rick is my foster dad. He's a heck of a lot better than my real one was." Calvin jabbed a thumb over his shoulder. "And from what I saw in there it looks like he's a better one than yours too."

His foster parents were Rick and Nimbus. Zero K was working with the supers because he was their kid. The piece of information clicked into the mental puzzle Kris had been constructing. But it sure as hell wasn't what she was going to focus on right now. She jabbed a finger into Calvin's chest. "Don't talk like that about my dad!"

"He was being a jerk."

"Mum's in hospital. You should be smart enough to know he doesn't need you harassing him right now."

"I thought you agreed with me. They put your friend in the clinic, for goodness sakes."

"His boss did that. Dad's just... it's his job..."

"Well, at least you think supers count as people."

Kris rolled her eyes. "Calvin..."

"You don't get it; you don't have superpowers."

"What, because I can't shoot ice out of my hands?" Kris waved hers in the air.

Calvin glanced back at the front door. "Keep your voice down."

"My dad won't hurt you."

"He's a cop. Worse, VCU. And I'm a vigilante." Calvin pushed past her and headed down the driveway.

Kris' hands tensed at her sides. "I bet your powers aren't really that great. I haven't even seen you on TV yet. I bet all your super friends just give your lousy jobs and have to help you all the time."

Calvin faltered and glanced back over his shoulder. Then he just huffed and continued on his way.

Kris stomped back inside and slammed the screen door.

John met her in the front hall. "Hey, calm down. Is Calvin okay? I didn't mean to shout like that. He's just a kid."

Kris shrugged. "I guess so. But what about you?"

"I'm just stressed out. Your mum..." He swallowed hard and looked away. Then he smiled, but it was thin, and just made him look immensely tired. "But she's going to be okay. You don't need to worry about me flipping out on your friends. That won't happen again."

"I'm not sure Calvin's going to want to come around again." Kris threw her arms around her father's middle and pulled him in tight. "Mum's going to be okay." She wished she could tell him Pink would take care of everything else; that he didn't need to worry about the super's new identity. A hug would have to do.

John held onto her a little longer than he usually would, then pulled back and ruffled his hair. "Nah, he'd be lucky to have you as a friend. I'm sure Calvin will be back. He did seem pretty fired up about vigilantes though. He doesn't have powers, does he?"

Annoyed as she was at Calvin, Kris had made a promise. And something inside her still knotted up at the question. Something that doubted her father only wanted to know that information because the boy had shown interest in his daughter. "No, Dad. Calvin's just a fanboy."

9

The Boss strode through the corridors of TechCorp's bottommost labs, her heels clicking on the pristine white floors. She pushed open the big white double doors that led to the operating theater where her latest creation was being reassembled. Thunderclap was a colossal idiot, but he'd be grateful for the upgrades. He craved power, and that certainly made things a lot easier.

The Boss donned a white lab coat over her crisp, blue business suit. "How are things progressing, Steve?" she asked her Chief Engineer.

A balding man in glasses, also wearing a lab coat, though his was stained from the process he was implementing, turned to face her. "Fine, it's going fine. Well, it is now. We almost lost him a few times."

The Boss turned steely grey eyes onto him. "Nearly lost him? Steve, Greg is family. I would take it quite personally if he died on your watch."

Steve swallowed. "He'll survive."

"Good. Besides, I've invested too much technology in him. I don't like losing an expensive asset."

Thunderclap was spread out on the table, his exposed torso cut open from neck to belly. Machines were wired to his body. Tubes fed fluids to keep his flesh alive. Electrodes were connected to the pulsing hunk of metal grafted directly into his open chest where his heart had been.

"It's a miracle he even made it back after that explosion," said Steve. "He was already going into cardiac arrest when he dragged himself to TechCorp's doorstep. But the artificial heart has been accepted by his body. Once the rest of him heals, it will keep him functional."

"And his powers?"

"I've upgraded the wrist cannons as requested. The new heart will feed the cannons with even more electrical energy, so he'll be able to deliver a far stronger discharge. It should also alleviate any interference between the cannons' electrical energy and his body's other systems."

"Ms. Vaas, I just wanted to let you know, I had no idea Pink Punch would do this to him. I thought we'd made the wrist cannons powerful enough to deliver a discharge to take down and retrieve the suit. I know I made a mistake trusting Rachael, but I was worried about her. And she did make it sound like there was something wrong with the suits. But once you set me right... I really did think Thunderclap would be strong enough to recover your assets."

Steve had been terrified when the Boss told him she knew he'd made contact with TechCorp's previous Chief Engineer, Rachael Mahrone, and was intending to pass on classified company information. The Boss could have fired him right there, or worse. But whilst being caught out had made Rachael a greater threat, Steve was smart enough to know when to pull himself back in line. The Boss had allowed him to keep his job, and sent her nephew Greg, a.k.a. Thunderclap, in his place. The trap hadn't functioned as intended, but at least the Boss now knew she shouldn't need to worry about a repeat of the misadventure she'd had with her last Chief Engineer. It was always the smart ones who caused the most trouble. "Relax, Steve. I know you understand where your loyalties lie."

Rachael was in hospital now, in a coma. 'Pink Punch' was no longer a threat. Where the suit itself had gone was of some concern. But as it was no longer operated by a troublesome woman determined to tear down everything TechCorp was working toward, recovering it had become a lesser priority.

"Are you sure Greg's body can handle these upgrades?" Steve pressed. "He was unconscious. He couldn't tell us if this was what he truly wanted."

The Boss lifted Thunderclap's thick set arm and turned it over. "Steve, what does it say here, right here, on this wrist cannon that I gave Thunderclap, at no charge?"

Steve didn't even bother looking. "It says 'TechCorp.'"

"And TechCorp belongs to me. When Greg agreed to the initial upgrade, he became my property. Besides, do your job properly, and he won't come to any harm. It is your job to tell me whether he can handle it."

"Of course."

The Boss' phone chirped; the flashing screen indicated it was her Hiring Manager. At least that was his title on the books. "What is it?"

"We've had a report from the werewolves. They completed their task as requested."

"Excellent. Make sure they are paid according to the agreement."

Her Hiring Manager remained on the phone; the Boss could almost taste his tension.

"But you don't need my permission to proceed with that," she said. "What is it?"

"Ma'am, there was one other thing. The wolves said Pink Punch was there. She was fighting alongside some of the other supers. It looks like she wasn't incapacitated in that explosion."

The Boss' free hand tensed. Either Rachael had an apprentice to whom she'd given the suit, or someone had found themselves a very expensive, and very dangerous, toy. Pink Punch could still be a threat to TechCorp, and now the Boss had no idea who she was. Whoever it was, they were now in possession of TechCorp property. That, the Boss wouldn't allow. "It's not a problem. I'll deal with Pink Punch."

Steve was watching, listening. "Thunderclap didn't take her down."

"He took down Rachael. Not Pink Punch." The Boss hung up, then reached into her jacket and pulled out a small piece of equipment. "It looks like this didn't come too late after all. Your subordinates gave it to me. The EMP generator. It's complete; ready for you to fit to Thunderclap."

"Ah." Steve took the device from her. He turned it over in his hands, inspecting it quickly and expertly. "Technically, it's not a generator. Thunderclap already makes more than enough electricity to create an electromagnetic pulse. This will allow him to generate a pulse at the correct frequency to disrupt the communication between the suit's nanites. I can't be sure whether it will completely shut down Pink's suit. But she won't be able to generate weapons. It will certainly slow her down, and probably make the suit next to useless as armour."

The Boss raised an eyebrow. "Probably?"

Steve held out his hands. "Rachael took the only prototype of the suit she'd been working on. If I had that suit, I could test this and tell you for sure how devastating the effect would be. Heck, if I had that suit, I could reverse engineer her work and we could make a far superior product for the cops. All I can tell you now is that I'm confident it would disrupt it enough for Thunderclap to take her down. But can we trust Greg with this? He can get out of hand. You only want the suit back, right? Whoever this new Pink Punch is; he could kill her."

"You have a problem with my plans?"

"No! I get it; if Pink casts any doubt on the safety of those suits, the cops won't want them. And I know now you have the best interests of the city at heart."

"And that's why she must be stopped. The cops can't, or won't, do their job. And the supers are no better. That's why we have to take charge. It's for the best." She took the device back from Steve. "May I?" Without waiting for an answer, the Boss stepped past him and fitted it to the waiting slot on Thunderclap's wrist cannons. The metal was slick with blood, but it didn't bother her. She drew back and wiped her hands on her lab coat. "We'll try take care of Pink Punch before Thunderclap wakes up. And if I can't get this city's villains to succeed, once Thunderclap wakes up, Pink Punch won't know what hit her."

* * *

The VCU department was based in Northberg's police station main headquarters. The building was an old courthouse, near the center of the city. Big stone pillars stood out front, solid and pale. One of the pillars had a sizable chunk torn out of it, from when a particularly vengeful vigilante with claws the length of dinner knives had taken out his anger on the city's cops. He'd been disabled by one of their larger tase-nets. The cops had been lucky; only the building's facade had suffered his wrath.

John Mahrone's desk, along with the rest of the VCU detectives, was located on the second floor. John strode across the room, and pointedly avoided meeting the gaze of the men and women around him. He could feel the stares of his colleagues on his back, the concerned and sympathetic glances. He'd felt them for the last four days. They could stare all they wanted. He was here because he had a job to do; he had to find out what had happened to Rachael.

Johansson was waiting for him, perched on the edge of her desk beside his with her arms folded. "John, what are you doing back here? You can take a break, you know."

"I don't need a break," John said as he pushed past his partner to access his desk.

"Have you tried telling the Chief that? You know what he said - he doesn't want you working yourself into the ground over this. That doesn't help anybody."

"If Dave doesn't like it, I'm sure he can tell me himself. Besides, he'll understand. It's vigilante crime. Our department. So, finding out who this Pink Punch character is is part of my job."

"Right. And it has nothing whatsoever to do with the fact she was there when you found Rachael."

John shuffled a few folders across his desk, not taking in what they were. He told his partner everything relating to their job. It was the only way to keep each other safe. Or at least he had. He hadn't breathed a word to Johansson about Rachael becoming Pink Punch. Rachael was being highly immature, but that didn't mean he wanted her to get arrested. Heck, he'd be incapable of arresting her even had he wanted to. And not because of the powerful suit. John wasn't going to let Johansson arrest his wife just because he didn't have the guts to do it himself. And he certainly wasn't going to let her know he'd failed at that part of his job. It still felt like a betrayal, and a part of John wondered if she realised he'd been hiding things from her. "Of course it does…"

"… which probably means you shouldn't be working on it."

"It's not just Rachael. That werewolf attack last night was brazen. Something's going on in this city. And I'm certain Pink Punch knows what it is."

Johansson lowered her voice. "But the main reason is Rachael. You're compromised, you know that. You've already worked your shift. Go home and get some rest."

"I need to work. You can't make me leave."

"Damn it, John. I will tie you to your bed myself."

The low level of chatter and shuffle of paperwork behind them dropped dramatically. Someone coughed. The entirety of the police station staff within earshot had stopped what they were doing and were listening, whilst, in varying degrees, pretending to continue with their work. He'd been separated from Rachael for only a few months. Already the damned rumor mill was trying to set him up with his partner. "Bloody hell. What is wrong with you lot? Are all your soap operas on hiatus or something?" John spun around to fix them with a glare that would surely send them scurrying back to where they belonged.

He found himself face to face with the Chief. "Dave..."

Chief Dave Thompson glared at him, arms folded. His red mustache quirked to the side on top of his scowl.

"Chief," John corrected himself. "I didn't realise you'd be here this late." He and Dave had known each other since John started on the force. Along with Johansson, they had practically gotten the VCU off the ground, ever since the Night of the Fallout. The night that the previously easily handled dozen or so vigilantes had multiplied into a hoard. And the same night they'd realised they couldn't depend on vigilantes to keep the city safe, even when dealing with superpowers. But the glare his friend now gave him meant he was very much in boss mode, not John's buddy.

"I bet you didn't. Been avoiding the office during the day, haven't you? You're supposed to be on compassionate leave."

John gritted his teeth. "I'm fine. Rachael's fine. I don't need to be at home."

"My office."

John followed Dave to the glassed-in office at the end of the room. Faded horizontal blinds kept out prying eyes. In the closed ecosystem of the police station, they were needed. Most of the staff had surreptitiously followed the two's movement across the office, and John did not want them snooping. "I'm just trying to do my job," he said, as he closed the office door. "I can't just sit around at home. If you want to give me a lecture about mental health, well, I'm going to be a lot happier if I'm here, actually doing something…"

Dave sat down behind his desk. He was a couple years older than John and Johansson. He was thin, though fairly fit. His pale skin made his red hair and mustache stand out. The role of Chief suited him. He'd be sure to protect and do what was best for 'his' cops. Besides, he wasn't so interested in field work nowadays. Not since his wife had left him and disappeared off the face of the planet. And good riddance. She and her bloody powers had messed Dave up good and proper.

"If that's the case, then tell me what you've been doing. You were at that werewolf attack last night. Tell me what's happening out there, and what you think we need to do."

"I…" The arguments John had been constructing tripped over at the unexpected change of subject.

"John," said Dave, his glare softening. "Sit down."

John sank into the plastic chair opposite and felt his tired muscles relax. He gathered his thoughts. "It's bad. Luckily, they didn't hurt anybody. But they did a lot of damage. People are scared. This was a public place, highly visible. And not only that, but I think it actually wasn't worse because some of the supers showed up and chased them off. Pink Punch was there. And that's the last thing we need. Rick's going to have a field day saying we need their help. We need to deal with these sorts of threats ourselves."

"And how do you propose we do that?"

"Superpowers give them an advantage. What have we got? A few gadgets from TechCorp? Tech-tasers and handcuffs. Tase-nets from GadgetCo, their competitor. Which tend to glitch. And I know - we can't go getting all our resources from one company, else they'll think they own us, but we need better equipment. And we need it to work. It needs to be from TechCorp."

"You want the suits. You know why I'm iffy about it; TechCorp's the reason all these powers started."

"Yeah, but that was decades ago. Vaas Enterprises, as it used to be called. The company's changed. Heck, my wife worked for them. You know they've made heaps of progress making up for the past. I was just saying to Jo, those suits they've been trying to get us to buy - they're starting to sound pretty damned good."

"Funny, you using Rachael working for them as a positive. After she left, she didn't think we should use those suits. You told me so yourself."

"Sure, she told me never to put on one of those things, but..." John could still remember Rachael coming home all flustered the day she'd lost her job. Which was unusual, because she didn't usually get emotional about, well, anything. She'd pegged her keys into the wall, then just stood there, chest heaving, and hands balled into fists. It had taken him nearly ten minutes to get her to put together a rational sentence and tell him what happened. "But they fired her. I think she was just upset."

She'd been a lot more than that. John had wondered where his wife had been for a few nights, when she'd told him she'd rented a small office and was trying to get some engineering consultancy type work running, seeing as she'd probably never get employed after leaving a big company like TechCorp, who, reputation aside, could still drag her name through the mud should they see fit.

Then he'd met Pink Punch. He had thought, *Hey, great, a new vigilante I have to deal with.* She had not given him long to stew over that before the revelation, however. She'd cornered him right after he'd dropped Johansson off home and was alone. He'd briefly thought he was in trouble. Until Pink Punch's helmet had dissolved, and he'd seen his wife smiling back at him.

John didn't want to talk about what Rachael had been doing. He didn't want to lie about it anymore. But he still couldn't let his wife get in trouble. "Besides, you can't tell me you don't trust TechCorp, at least a bit. Otherwise, you wouldn't have sent Penny to their clinic."

Dave's hand went absentmindedly to his side. "I don't want her to end up like her mother."

"Dave..."

The Chief shook himself out of it. "The clinic will look after her. I had no other option. I'm protecting her. And I'm looking out for you guys too; that's my job."

"Then why not armoured suits? That would protect us. They would also help us bring down vigilantes too strong for us to handle. To be able to have the power, the strength, just to pin one of them down and put them in a pair of handcuffs. To get them in jail, where they belong. That would be enough." John bunched his hand to a fist in front of him. Clothed in armour, that would more than be enough to bring down Pink Punch. And get her to tell him what she'd done to Rachael.

Dave eyes drilled into him from across the desk. "Are you sure you're all right? Anything you need, you can let me know."

"You know that goes the same for me, and I'm sure Jo as well. We're here for you too, if you need to talk. You know, about your daughter, or anything."

Dave smiled a lopsided smile, his mustache quirking to the side. "No suits just yet. I still need to be sure they won't cause any issues. I'm not selling us out to some big company if I can help it."

10

Fortitude Hill was the premier suburb in Northberg and over-looked the expansive bay. Open to cool ocean breezes with no unsightly infrastructure blocking a direct line of sight to the scattered islands beyond, it was where many of Northberg's richest residents lived. Stan drove Kris up the winding road lined with well-watered palm trees which had no trouble flourishing in the humid climate. They passed a dozen or so massive houses that grew in opulence as they climbed ever higher. Stan's engine growled as he ate up the steep incline.

The mansion he pulled into was almost at the very top, save for one. It was perched on the side of the hill with a wide balcony hanging out over nothing, facing toward the bay. The driveway dipped down to a wide paved area. Stan rumbled down the incline and came to a gentle stop, perhaps showing a little care for the fancy paving stones. The entrance was impressive. Had the double mahogany doors been any larger, it could have been the entrance to a well-fortified castle. The castle look was softened by ferns and palms planted around the doors and lining the driveway.

The house was familiar to Kris, if only from the precariously perched balcony visible from almost anywhere in Northberg's city. She could remember the first time her father had pointed it out to her, in the middle of one of his vigilante rants. That was where Rick lived, the man who caused all his trouble.

"He's complaining about his rights? Look at the size of that place! Yeah, so he's got powers. He can read emotions, empathic... or whatever he calls it. Barely uses it, never engages in vigilante activity, or so he says. He wants to help 'superheroes' get more recognition, but I bet he's helping them out in other ways too, especially with that much money to cover his tracks. Not that I can prove anything."

Kris smiled faintly. Her father had been right. Why else would Nimbus have invited Pink Punch here?

"All right, Stan. What am I doing?"

"The equipment your mother promised the supers is in the suitcase in the back. Don't worry about explaining it. In fact, the less you say, the less chance you have of stuffing it up. They know what they asked for."

Kris rolled her eyes. "Thanks for the vote of confidence." She collected the suitcase and headed to the mansion's front doors. There were lights on inside, and one of the doors was cracked open, letting a shaft of artificial light strike out across the driveway. Kris tentatively knocked, and her metal clad knuckles boomed on the thick wood. She winced, but though loud it had not done any damage. "Hello?" She pushed the door open all the way and stepped inside.

Pyromaniac leaned against a wall in the big entrance hall with a glass in one hand, chatting to Nimbus as casually as if he was simply here for a cocktail party. Except that he still wore his superhero gear and mask. Nimbus wore a flowing white dress like the one Kris had seen her in the night before. Whether that was her normal attire or her superhero costume, Kris didn't know, but either way, Nimbus was making no attempt to hide her identity. Anyone could see who she was. And when she'd gone out to fight those werewolves, though she hadn't done anything flashy, she'd been identifiable there too. That was, had you been able to see her way up there in the clouds.

Nimbus smiled. It was warm, and despite her caution around letting Pink join them, it seemed genuine. "Pink Punch, you made it."

Kris craned her neck upwards. "This is, um, quite some place you have." The front hall had high ceilings, and off to the right a large staircase stretched both upward and down.

Her inspection of the interior stopped there, as Zero K chose that moment to waltz down the stairs and into the entrance hall. He froze. "Pink Punch, what are you... I mean, hi." He cleared his throat, then straightened and thrust back his shoulders. "What brings you here?"

"Real suave," Pyro said under his breath with a smirk, but unfortunately just loud enough for everyone to hear.

Zero blushed. Under the internal lights, Kris could see under his hood. But now he was wearing a pair of wraparound sunglasses. In brighter light, she supposed that would keep his identity effectively concealed. Just not his embarrassment.

Kris felt herself tensing up. She was still annoyed with Calvin over dinner. But she quickly reminded herself Pink Punch had no reason to be cranky with Zero K. He wouldn't understand why. He obviously thought Pink Punch was cool, and Kris didn't want to shoot him down like she had accidentally at the markets.

"We invited her, Zero." Rick walked into the entrance hall, smiling warmly. The tension in the air, both from Zero's entrance and Pyro's accompanying commentary, immediately evaporated. It was like the man had brought his own personal cloud of comfort and merriment along with him and was all too happy to share.

Kris felt the tension in her shoulders release. She hadn't met Rick in person, nor felt the effect of his powers. But apart from these, he was easily recognisable, and probably would be so to anyone in Northberg who had even a passing interest in the news.

He was wearing a dress shirt and cream slacks. They looked expensive and were neatly pressed. His blond hair was slicked back, and his blue eyes sparkled.

Zero K immediately brightened and did a little fist pump. "Yes..." He cleared his throat and yanked his fist back in.

"Well, it's about time they invited you," Stan grumbled in her ear.

Kris was pretty sure that wasn't something Stan wanted her to repeat. She held up the suitcase. "I brought a present."

"Excellent. So, you finished the equipment we asked for?" Rick cracked open the case.

Zero sidled right up beside him to get a look.

Rick smiled faintly and pulled out a chunky pair of sunglasses. He handed them to Zero. "Why don't you let Pink tell you what this does?"

Kris' stomach lurched.

Rick glanced up at her and frowned. Shoot, his powers. They weren't all warm and fuzzy; rumour had it that was just a byproduct.

Zero dropped his old pair in his excitement. He slipped the new ones on. Then ran to the door and stuck his head outside. Kris needn't have worried about providing an explanation. "Adaptive night vision. Sweet. I won't have to worry about people seeing my eyes when I'm out at night. How do I look?"

Zero's antics had distracted Rick. He smiled faintly. "I'm sure all your fans will think you're super cool. Even at night."

Nimbus cleared her throat. "Zero. What did we say about leaving your stuff in the hall?"

"Sorry." Zero scooped up the dropped pair of sunglasses and slipped them in his pocket.

"So, is that enough to get me in the door?"

"Relax," said Rick. "I'll get X to send the payment we agreed on to your bank account as soon as we're done here. The main device we asked you to design for Elspeth should be very useful. Though I do appreciate you throwing in the shades for Zero."

Well, at least Mum was getting paid. Not that that would make Dad any happier about it. Supplying tech to vigilantes would certainly not go down well.

Kris wasn't concerned about Rick reading those thoughts. It was only the brief bout of panic around explaining tech she had no clue about that Rick had sensed. He wasn't a mind reader, and he couldn't read what had caused the feeling itself, but she would have to watch that she did not display any emotion that he wouldn't expect from the Pink Punch he knew. So, no pressure there.

"I'm glad you've decided to help us. I thought, now that we have these, that showing you around the place would be a good place to start," said Rick.

"I'm sure it's a very nice house…" In truth Kris was a little curious. But she wasn't sure being shown around some mansion would help Pink's mission.

"By which I mean showing you around our Broom Closet. You don't think we do all this super stuff without a lair, do you? I know you've wanted our help on things with TechCorp, and you'll feel better knowing we've got the space you can use to suit your needs."

"Wait, your broom closet?"

Zero grinned. "You'll see."

Rick led Pink and Zero down into the basement of the house. The space was small and dark, only lit by a dim bulb. It was like the architects hadn't bothered to make the laundry as grand as the rest of the place. Rick paused, a hand on a door next to the washing machine. "I shouldn't have to tell you, but I will anyway: you can't tell anyone about this. Even other supers. We've got a very strict policy about who comes in here."

Kris raised an eyebrow and said slowly, "Into your broom closet?"

"Let me show you." Rick opened the door. To a small closet space full of brooms. He stepped inside.

Kris briefly thought of her father, telling her not to follow strange men into small dark spaces. She stepped in behind Rick and pushed a broom aside. The closet space went back and back. Rick put his hand on the back wall. It shimmered, then changed to a solid metal door. He entered a code on a keypad, then pushed open the heavy door.

The door opened on a cavern at least as big as the house upstairs, but completely open. The interior walls were coated in metal. Large computer screens were packed into the far corner. It was big, but the furniture was spread out and sparse. As well as the bank of computer screens, the other main feature was three long benches, strewn with equipment, and situated in the middle of the open space.

"It's a disused bunker," said Rick. "Rumour has it Fortitude Hill is littered with them, though I only know of this one. It was why my mother bought the place. It isn't seeing as much use as I felt she envisioned. But it suits our purposes."

There were two people working at one of the benches. One was a man with goggles on his head, and a leather suit. He picked up what looked like a giant gun. Max Dynamo. Every once in a while, he'd emerge with some new tech he wanted to 'field test.' Which was when he usually got himself in trouble with the VCU. Kris was pretty sure he was currently on parole. Max pulled the goggles down over his eyes and hefted the weapon. "Fire in the hole!"

"Goddamn it, Max," grumbled Rick. "I suggest we duck."

The big gun whined and spluttered. Nothing happened.

"Max!" A woman wearing a green suit crawled out from under the work bench, where she'd cowered when Max produced the gun. "Give us a bit of warning!"

"I said 'fire in the hole,' Elspeth."

Rick waved down at them. He got an exasperated toss of the hands from Elspeth, directed in Max's direction. Max just shrugged. "Well, she'll be happy if you've got her equipment the way she wants it."

Rick headed down the metal staircase that clung to the cavern's wall to meet the two supers. Kris and Zero followed. Kris winced as her heavy boots made the metal clang and ring out with each step.

The other item in the suitcase turned out to be some sort of suit. It was green, similar to the one Elspeth already wore. It looked as if it would be more form fitting, and it sparkled in the light. Kris hadn't been aware her mother was into costumes. She'd never seen her using a sewing machine; a welder was more her style.

Elspeth took the cloth and draped it over one hand. Her features were petite, almost elfin, and she handled the material with great care. On contact, the material faded and disappeared entirely, then reformed into a dull tartan cloth, faded ripped denim, and then bright fluro orange. Elspeth seemed to be controlling it. She frowned in concentration, then nodded. "Oh yes. This will do just nicely. Thank you, Pink Punch."

"I don't know why you didn't let me design something," grumbled Max, crossing his arms. "I'm a tech whiz too."

"Max, this is something I need to wear. At least if I don't want to run around starkers all the time. Also, I don't want it to randomly explode."

Rick shifted his weight. He looked uncomfortable at even the slight expression of antagonism. He moved a few paces across the cavern, just out of earshot of the brewing argument. Max and Elspeth continued, oblivious.

"It gets a bit hectic down here," said Rick, tugging at his shirt. "I've tried to set up a place where supers can test their inventions, come when they're hurt, hang out. A safe house, if they need it." He grinned. "Not everyone is a billionaire and has a disused bunker under their house to use as a lair. So, I figured I'd share mine. I'm not much of an inventor, or anything like that, so I don't need it. I mean, who wants to put together a defensive weapon in their garden shed? The cops would find them out for sure."

Zero grabbed Kris' arm. "I want to introduce her to X. I'm sure they'll like each other."

"Just don't distract her, she's working," Rick called after Zero's retreating back.

Kris allowed herself to be led across the cavern. Zero brought her to the bank of computer screens. A girl of about twelve, her hair in two plaits, stared at the screens in concentration.

"Hey X," said Zero K. The girl ignored him. He poked her shoulder. "Xtrapolate."

X jumped. "Zero! Don't sneak up on me like that."

"I was standing there for like ten seconds."

"Oh."

"X is, well, my sister now, I guess. Rick and Nim have taken her in as well. And X, this is Pink Punch. She's the one I was telling you about. We're going to help her, now that Rick and Nim seem convinced she might be right about all the stuff going on with TechCorp."

X looked at Kris over the top of thick rimmed glasses. The glasses did nothing to deaden her intense gaze. "I thought you may have been on to something. But I didn't have enough data to predict what. It might be okay for you to make assumptions like that based on intuition, or whatever you call it, but I can't."

"X can tell the future," said Zero.

X huffed. "I don't tell the future. I predict outcomes based on precipitating events."

Kris smiled faintly. Tommy would get on well with this kid.

"So, if X tells you to do something, you'd better listen. It could save your life."

"If you don't mind, I'm busy." X turned back to her computer screens. Instead of a computer-generated battlefield like what was usually on Kris' brother's laptop, X's screens were filled with graphs, charts, and spreadsheets.

Kris frowned. "Is that the stock market?"

Rick stepped up behind him. "Somethings going on upstairs. I can feel Nim's anxiety."

"It's the cops," said X. When everyone looked at her, she sighed. "It's obvious, based on the events of last night, and... just trust me."

Rick patted her shoulder. He smiled faintly, the same expression he'd shown toward Zero. Kris could almost feel his pride and wasn't sure if it was an effect of his powers, or simply affection for his foster kids naturally showing through. "Always do."

Kris and Zero followed Rick back upstairs. So, Rick could feel Nim's emotions from all the way down here. That seemed pretty far.

"Yes, I can feel her emotions from all the way down here. My range isn't usually that far. But, well, it's different with Nim," said Rick.

Kris stiffened.

"Relax, I'm not reading your mind. Just getting the gist of what you might be thinking from what you're feeling. I promise not to pry or gather clues about your identity."

"It sounds like an... interesting superpower. How come you hardly ever use it? You're always talking about superhero rights on TV. But you don't actually do anything like help the cops fight crime, or even use your powers in your job."

"I'm too much in the spotlight. If I tried anything 'illegal,'" Rick made air quotes around the word, "I'd be arrested in an instant. And fighting crime is more Nim's forte. To be honest, being an empath feels like a useless superpower sometimes. What am I supposed to do? Try and make someone feel guilty about doing the wrong thing? Pushing emotions onto people is about the best I can do, but I don't like it. It feels rude. And half the time it backfires, and people's emotions have more of an effect on me than I do on them. It's easy to get overloaded, sometimes I can't even tell if it's my emotion or someone else's. So, like I said, you've got nothing to worry about, I'm not going to pry." Rick trailed off, lost in his thoughts, and a little agitated by his own words. Kris could feel it in the air, like a lingering scent.

Zero seemed to sense it too. He tugged at Rick's sleeve, getting his attention. "So, what am I feeling now?" He winked at Pink Punch.

Rick smirked. "Nervous."

Zero faltered, and Kris had to fight down the urge to laugh.

Rick shrugged. "Well, you asked."

They were back in the main house and almost at the entrance hall when Rick drew to a halt. He put a hand to his forehead. "Oh, great. X was right. It is the cops. And it's that damned Detective Mahrone. I've argued with him so much, I can spot his emotions from a mile away." He winced and rubbed at his head with a groan. "He is not usually this intense; must've had a bad day. I am going to get a headache for sure."

Kris swallowed. She didn't need to be an empath to know her father was more stressed than usual. "Well, his wife's in a coma."

"What? Poor guy. That would do it. All right. I know what he's like; I'll be fine. Though I wouldn't mind a bit of backup."

Kris held up her hands. "Woah, wait. Detective Mahrone cannot see me. He thinks I had something to do with his wife getting hurt. He'll flip."

"No worries," said Rick. "And no explanation needed. You ever need protection from the cops, just let us know. I'll deal with this myself." He headed out to the entrance hall.

Zero bumped Kris' shoulder. "We don't have to be there to see what's going on. Come on." He led her up another level of the stairs, to the mansion's second story. It opened to a big lounge room, and he flicked on the massive television screen set in one wall. "Rick has a camera on the door so they can see who's at the door from the Broom Closet. We can watch from here too." Within seconds Zero had the feed set up.

Nimbus was already at the front door. Rick stepped up to her side and put a hand on her shoulder. Dad was outside and he looked like he wanted to put his fist clean through a window. He had his arms folded tightly across the chest, like he was reining that urge in. Detective Johansson stood beside him.

"So, what's this you're harassing my wife about?" Rick asked.

"We're trying to find out if you had anything to do with the werewolf attacks last night," said John.

"Sounds like you should be speaking to werewolves," said Nimbus.

"We have a witness who says she saw Nimbus kicking up a storm. She was there. And so was Pink Punch."

"And werewolves," said Johansson, "Look, this isn't something that happens a lot. We thought you may have noticed an increase in villain activities."

"Vigilante activity," John corrected tersely.

"Just because we entertain a lot of people with superpowers, just because I have them, doesn't mean we're involved with every bit of villain activity," said Rick. "Unless you just want to blame us for everything that goes wrong."

"Yeah, well, you certainly always have something to say when it does," said John, his voice rising in volume. "You're happy to give a statement for the cameras, how about legally helping with an actual police investigation for a change?"

"What, you want our help now?" Rick held up his hands, maybe as much to pacify himself as the detectives. "Look, I get you're upset. I know your wife is in a coma and..."

John bristled. "Who told you that? Get out of my head!"

Rick winced and took a step back.

"Oh, sorry, did I hurt your feelings?"

Johansson grabbed John's arm, holding him back.

"My feelings?" said Rick. His hands tensed at his side, then he drew a breath and relaxed. "You're a mess; trust me. You need to take a break."

Nimbus stepped between them. "Detective Mahrone, I'm sorry someone mistook some inclement weather for me last night. But you know Rick and I don't get involved in what you call vigilante activity. Which, if you want to be accurate, refers to anyone who fights crime outside the law, not people with superpowers. So, unless you have a warrant, I'm going to have to ask you to leave."

John shrugged off Johansson's touch. He pointed a finger and Rick and Nimbus like a gun. "One of these days I will catch you two out. You can't hide behind your money forever. Come on, Jo."

John stomped off down the driveway. Johansson gave Rick and Nimbus a professional nod and followed her partner.

"I wouldn't be too worried about the cops, Pink," said Zero. "They might be sniffing around, and Rick has even said he's a little worried about it. But he's got me handling it."

Kris raised an eyebrow. He really was trying to talk himself up to Pink Punch. "You?" she said teasingly. "But you're just a kid."

Zero was undeterred. He bounced himself around on the couch so he faced Pink. "Maybe. But that's why I'm such a big help. You see, because I'm a kid, Rick and Nim have sent me to Detective Mahrone's daughter's school, so I can make friends with her. And because I'm her friend, I can ask her questions about her dad and what the VCU are up to. I even got to talk to her dad, for a bit, not that I could get much out of him. But his daughter, although she's a bit of a tough one, I'm pretty sure I've got her on our side. I think she might have a crush on me."

Kris' hands started to shake. "Let me get this straight. You only made friends with Detective Mahrone's daughter to get information out of her?"

Zero shrugged. "Well, she's a nice person too. And she's my age. And normal. Which is nice. But yeah, I mean if I can get any information out of her, or Detective Mahrone, it'll help everyone. It's a very important job."

Kris' hands balled into fists, and she was just contemplating whether it was wise to start a punch up with the kid of the supers who had agreed to help her, when an alarm rang.

Zero jumped right up from the sofa in his excitement. His muscles were tensed, and he grinned madly. "X must've picked up something on the police scanners. Come on, I can show you more about how these guys depend on me. It's not just undercover work I do." He grabbed Pink by the arm as he prattled on and dragged her behind him toward the stairs.

Kris snatched her arm away. Pink's suit whirred as it decided the ferocity of the tug meant its wearer needed more power, and Zero stumbled over backwards and crashed back into Pink's chest. Before Kris could shove him off, he stepped back, clutching his wrist, and stared at her wide eyed like he was waiting for her to do something more.

Kris put her hands on her hips. "All right, hands off the armour, kid." Pink's voice modulator made her sound just as authoritative as she'd hoped.

Zero rubbed at his wrist. "Um, sorry." He relaxed a little but made no attempt to touch her again. "Come on."

They found Nimbus, Pyromaniac, and Rick downstairs at the front door.

Rick had his hands on Nimbus' shoulders. "Be careful, honey. Those cops will be keeping an eye out now for anything they can blame on you."

"I'll be fine. Looks like the weather might get a bit foggy anyway."

"I don't know why you two don't just put on a mask," Pyro grumbled. He had his arms folded across his broad chest, and his mouth was twisted into a half frown, half smirk. "You're pretty powerful, Nimbus, and it'd be real helpful if you could get closer to the action instead of hiding in the clouds all the time." He poked Rick in the shoulder. "And you still need to get yourself a proper superhero name."

"If we keep giving ourselves dumb names everyone will always think of people with powers as different. We should be able to use our real names."

"And I'm not hiding my face just because I might offend some cops because I do their job better," said Nimbus.

Pyro held up his hands. "Yeah, yeah, I know. I get it; you shouldn't have to. But it's always worked for me, so..." He gave them a sloppy salute. "I'll see you downtown. And I'll be looking forward to seeing some of your moves up close, Pink." He took to the air and shot out the front door, leaving a fiery blur behind him.

"Can you take Zero with you, Pink?" said Nimbus. "He can help you patch our communications systems into yours." She tossed a small USB looking device to Zero.

Zero fumbled it as he caught it. "I'm not sure..."

"Take Zero? No! I mean, I work better alone. And the car... is a fastback..."

Nimbus raised an eyebrow. "I thought we had an agreement?"

Rick frowned at Kris. Of course, an empath would feel the flash of anger she had at the thought of having to spend a minute more next to Zero. Calvin didn't want to be her friend. He just wanted to use her for her connection to the VCU. Same as Butch had. But Pink still had no reason to be mad at Zero. Kris' position here was precarious enough without Rick discovering she wasn't who she said she was.

"I'm sorry, but I am used to working alone. But all right. Whatever, this is your show."

Nimbus smiled faintly. "Relax, you'll get used to it. And Zero won't break anything. He'll enjoy it; he thinks you're pretty cool."

Zero flushed. "Nim…"

"Coordinates are in the comms unit, Zero. Don't dawdle." Nimbus flew up into the air in a swirl of cloud.

"So, where's your car?" Zero asked. He still wouldn't quite look at her.

Kris walked to the edge of the driveway and looked around. Stan should have been there. He must have done his invisible thing again when the cops rocked up. She looked for a tell-tale shimmer. Pink would look really stupid if she couldn't even find her own car. "Stan?" she whispered harshly.

A beefy roar cut into the air, and Stan materialised meters away in a swirl of pink.

"Whoa," said Zero. "That's your car?" All trace of his previous apprehension vanished as he ran around behind Stan to get a better look.

"Stop looking at my butt," said Stan.

Zero straightened up slowly. "Um, sorry?"

"I should think so." Stan flung open his doors.

Kris climbed into the driver's seat. "Okay, Stan. You're going to have to let me drive."

"I beg your pardon? You're underage, missy. Do you think your father would like you driving without a license?"

"He wouldn't like me running around as a vigilante; I don't think it matters. They think I'm an adult. I can't not drive my own car."

"Fine, you steer. I'll handle the rest. That way it won't look suspicious."

Zero slipped into the passenger seat. He was grinning ear to ear.

"This is so cool. Hang on, I'll set up the comms." He pulled out the USB and poked it at Stan's console.

"Stop poking things in my dash! Just, get out of it! I can pick up the information wirelessly. Put that back in your pocket."

Zero put it back without a word. He tucked his hands in his lap, away from the console. At least Stan seemed to be able to control him.

Kris put her hands on the wheel and Stan floored it, flinging them both back in their seats. His back end skidded out as he turned 180 degrees at the top of the street, and then he thundered back down the hillside. Kris held onto the steering wheel for dear life.

"Wow," said Zero. "You drive so well."

Kris' eyes narrowed. If she wasn't pinned to her seat, she would have gladly punched him. "Of course you think I do."

11

Kris clung to Stan's steering wheel. She wasn't sure how much control she actually had, but she leaned into each corner and tried to look determined. At least it distracted her from Zero's prattle. He seemed to have completely forgotten she'd frightened him earlier.

"This is so cool. Our first proper fight together. You know, except for the werewolves. I wasn't ready for that one."

Kris threw Stan into a corner hard. Zero gripped the door handle, wide-eyed, and shut his mouth. Oh, they were going to have their first proper fight all right.

Stan screeched to a halt at the location Nimbus had given them. They were downtown. Northberg's half dozen skyscrapers towered into the night sky around them, the biggest of which had 'TechCorp' emblazoned in neon blue on the roof. The street was covered in slime.

Kris squared her shoulders. She had to focus on this fight, not Zero. "Where is everyone?"

Flames flared up the street. Pyro darted through the air, weaving his way around something on the ground that looked like a giant log. Except the 'log' was moving.

Zero opened his door and groaned. "Aw man. There's slime everywhere."

"We haven't got all day." Kris gave him a shove, careful to hold back enough that the suit didn't take over and hurt him.

Zero tumbled out and grabbed onto Stan's roof. He almost slipped but pulled himself upright.

Kris hoped Stan would snark at him for touching his bodywork, but instead she heard the car's voice in her ear. "All right, go easy on the poor boy. What's gotten into you?"

"Believe me, I will tell you all about it later."

A burst of flame lit up the night sky as Pyro darted around his assailant. The creature reared up to a nearly three-meter height. It was dark brown and covered in green ooze.

Zero stepped around to Kris' side of the car, where it was relatively clear of slime. He flicked the offending substance from one boot. "Is that a giant slug? Haven't seen that before. But we can take it, right?"

"You mean I can take it. Maybe you'd better hang back here and let a professional handle this." Kris took a step forward, right into the slime.

"You might want to…" Stan started to say.

Her boot lost traction. Pink's suit whirred, attempting to pump extra power into keeping her upright, but the lack of friction was insurmountable. Kris landed on her backside with a metallic clang.

"Careful, that stuff is super slippery," said Zero.

Kris flushed beneath Pink's visor. "Thanks a lot!" She hauled herself upright, but her legs slipped out from under her yet again.

"Sorry… I'll… just attack it first then." Zero made himself a nice safe ice path above the slime. He skated across it with no effort at all, feeding the front end with more ice as he went.

"Seriously, how come you suck at skateboarding?" Kris managed to slide herself over to clear road and stood back to her feet. She shook the remaining goop from each boot.

"Zero is your age, you know," said Stan. "He's bound to be a little difficult to work with. Trust me, I know what that's like."

"It's not him. It's... Calvin... who is also technically him so..." Kris threw her hands in the air. She was still too mad to explain. Not when she had more important things to do, like figuring out how to stay upright.

"You did agree to fight with them, whatever your issues with Calvin might be." Stan huffed. "This is why you don't tell people who you are."

"I agreed to fight with Nimbus and the rest of the supers. Not Calvin. Can we talk about this later? I need to figure out how to walk over to where the actual fight is. I can't fly by any chance, can I?"

"No. You just need more traction. Here."

Kris felt her feet shift up a few centimeters beneath her. She lifted a boot. The sole had grown a bunch of short, sharp studs. She placed it in the slime, then added her weight. The boot gripped. Much better. She broke into a run and stomped after Zero K. No way was she going to let him have all the fun.

The giant slug had crawled up the side of a building. It was surprisingly fast, slithering all over the surface, dodging Pyro's blast of fire, and Zero's ice. It lifted its head to reveal a mouth ringed with teeth. Pyro darted behind its head, and grabbed it in a choke hold. For about a second, then the slug slipped free, screeched, and spat slime all over him.

Pyro stuck to the wall behind him. "Damn it! I'll slime you, you slimeball."

Zero blasted the slug and ice encased its head. It fell from the wall and the ice shattered as it hit the sidewalk. It screeched and slithered away from Zero, toward Pink Punch.

Kris called up a gauntlet and threw a punch. She hit the slug square in the face and her fist sunk into the gooey flash. The slug sprung back like a big elastic ball. It flipped over itself, wailing, and landed on its back.

"Yes, go, Pink!" said Zero.

Kris scowled. She couldn't even enjoy her first fanboy!

The ground shook. A corner of the TechCorp building exploded. Metal and glass blasted outwards, then a boom of displaced air hit them. Zero clapped his hands over his ears. The sound was loud for a second, then cut down a good few decibels.

A creature completely covered in spikes emerged from the smoking hole. It was about the size of a human, but bulkier, and had an array of spikes and plates that covered its body like armour. A mane of wavy red hair blew out behind it.

Zero yelled something at it. For a few seconds he sounded muffled, then his volume returned to a shout. Apparently, Pink's helmet had protected her from that particularly loud blast of sound from the ugly creature. "Hey, what the heck are you doing? Can't you see you're making a great big mess? We're going to take you down."

It looked at Zero and grinned. The teeth were as sharp and pointed as its body armour. "Look at this pretty boy. Must be nice to have powers that don't make you look terrifying. Why don't you lift up that hood and show me your pretty face?"

"What?" Zero shouted back, still a little too loud. He rubbed at the side of his head. He hadn't had anything to protect him from the blast of sound.

Kris stepped up in front of him. She didn't need Zero's help to take down this creature, even had she wanted it. What a jerk. "Yeah, well, you're not exactly pretty."

"Please, what is this high school? I'm done with all that garbage. You can call me Soundwave." The creature shook the spikes on its back. They vibrated in the air and sent out a rumbling wave which set Kris' teeth on edge. "Nice armour. But it doesn't belong to you, so I've been sent to take it back to where it belongs." It jabbed a clawed thumb back over its shoulder at the smoking building.

"Wait, to TechCorp? You just blew a hole in the side of their building!"

Soundwave gave her a toothy grin. Plates and thick skin clacked and shifted across the face to make way for the grimace. "Should keep everyone nice and confused. Shh. Don't tell anyone."

Fire lit up the side of the buildings, and Pyro emerged from the ball of flame, grinning madly. "Guess what? I just figured out if you heat this stuff up above a thousand degrees it's flammable. I love it when stuff is flammable!"

"Pyro, I could use some help over here!" Whatever this thing was, it was certainly more dangerous than something that simply seemed intent on making the street very, very messy. And better Pyro's help than Zero's.

Pyro held up his hands. "Hey, it doesn't feel right for me to take on a lady. I'm old school; it doesn't feel right. You handle her, I'll take the animal."

Kris rolled her eyes. "Seriously, Pyro? That is just so... wait, it's a lady?"

"Yeah, genius. And that slug's not an animal, you idiot, so stop harassing him. Gawd, and I thought they were exaggerating when they told me even guys like you can't accept us." Soundwave tensed and her hands balled into fists. She rushed at Pink Punch.

Zero K pointed a fist at the ground. His arms glowed blue, and a flurry of snow lanced out and smashed into the asphalt. A wall of ice shards snaked across, rearing up between Soundwave and Pink. It halted Soundwave's attack for about one second. She held up a fist. More plates and spikes crawled from the thick flesh on her arm, making her fist bigger and bulkier. Like an organic version of Pink's gauntlet. She slammed the fist into the ground, and a wave of sound rumbled outward. Windows smashed, the ground shook and cracked. Zero's ice wall split apart in seconds, and both Kris and Zero stumbled to the ground. Soundwave stepped through the debris and threw a punch at Pink.

Kris rolled out of the way and slipped on the slug's slime. When she came back up her boots gripped, and at least she'd slid far enough to get out of harm's way.

Soundwave's face split into a wolfish grin. "All right, let's see what you've got."

Kris ran for Soundwave, but she rattled her spikes and the resulting sound wave knocked Kris down yet again.

Kris hauled herself to her feet and flicked off slime. She couldn't get close to Soundwave, and technically, she couldn't do projectiles. She imagined a big ball of metal anyway and hurled it at Soundwave. It exploded on her head in a burst of pink.

"Hey!"

The slug lifted its tooth rimmed mouth to the sky and screeched.

Pyro built a great big fireball in his hands. "Right, here we go." It vibrated like he was barely holding it there, growing, and then he released it right into the slug's belly.

"Pyro," said Zero, "if that's flammable it'll..."

The entire street burst into flames with a crack. The slug let out a horrendous wail. The inferno rolled toward Pink Punch and Zero K. Zero flung up an ice wall, and the fire burst out against it with a sizzling poof. Behind the wall, the slug collapsed into a gooey, smoldering mess.

"No, Harold!" roared Soundwave. A blast of air rolled outwards as she slammed her fists into the ground. "What is wrong with you people? With your pretty superpowers do you not get that some of us don't get glorious bodies? Must be nice to have powers and still look normal. Forget your stupid suit. I'm going to tear you apart."

"I didn't do that... forget it, you want to trash town, lady?" Dad would probably get stuck cleaning all this up. He hated it when vigilantes broke things. "I'll tear you apart!"

Kris held up her fists, and two gauntlets built around them. She rushed Soundwave. Soundwave's spikes grew even bigger, and she rattled them. Kris jumped ten feet into the air. Despite how annoyed she was with Zero, and now this villain, Kris felt a wave of exhilaration. She cleared the vibrating air, and dropped fist first onto Soundwave.

Spikes splintered and broke off. Soundwave roared, then threw a punch back, and her organic gauntlet smashed into Pink's side. Kris fell to the ground and gasped. Pink's armour cracked around where the punch landed, but it slowly repaired.

"Pink's armour isn't completely impenetrable," said Stan. "You need to be careful."

Kris blinked the stars from her eyes. Her side ached, but she forced herself to her feet. She was shaking, but the suit supported her. Her heart pounded, and her fists tensed. "Is that all you got?"

Soundwave grunted. The spikes Pink had smashed slowly grew back. This time it seemed to take Soundwave some effort, and she rolled her shoulders as they fully solidified. Well, good. Soundwave had felt that too. "Nope."

"Pink, it's okay, I'll help," Zero skidded up beside her. He held his arms out to balance himself on the slippery road. His arms glowed blue, and the temperature dropped.

"I can handle this."

"Just let me help. I know I'm new at this, but I can…" Zero built a ball of ice shards as he spoke.

Soundwave let out another burst of sound. The ice ball shattered, and Pink and Zero both slipped back to the ground.

"Stupid slime!" Kris growled. She'd had it. She was taking this villain down.

"Here…" Zero grabbed at Kris' wrist.

"Let me go, I've got this!" Kris swiped Zero's hand away. She forgot to hold back. Pink's armoured hand slapped into Zero's shoulder.

Ice shards flew in all directions as the temperature dropped dramatically. Kris was knocked sideways, sending a jar through her aching side. She drew in a sharp breath and forced herself to look up. Zero lay on the ground beside her; the uncontrolled ice blast had flattened him as much as it had her.

Ice had cut through most of Soundwave's outer layer of spikes and plates. They slipped from her body as she hauled herself upright, and now she appeared smaller. This time, the shattered armour did not rebuild. Her toothy mouth twisted into a scowl, and despite the effort it seemed to cost her, she lumbered toward the two fallen supers.

A shaft of lightning struck the ground in front of her. Soundwave froze.

Electricity crackled through the air. A fog descended and swirled around them, whipped up in a circular motion. Then a faint silhouette appeared in the midst of the swirling tempest. "I'd get out of here if you know what's good for you, Soundwave. I haven't had the pleasure of meeting you before. And you look young. So, I'll let you go, this time, with a warning. I suggest you rethink whatever it is you've gotten yourself into. You don't want to become our problem."

Soundwave backed away slowly. "What about Harold? Were you planning on giving him a warning? Maybe you're the ones who need a warning. You don't know what's coming!"

Nimbus built a ball of crackling electricity in her hands, and casually rolled it between each hand. "And what would that be?"

Soundwave snarled, then disappeared into the mist.

Nimbus settled onto the ground. The fog immediately around

them cleared, but they were still encircled in a wall of thick cloud which cut off all view of anything beyond about ten meters.

Kris hauled herself to her feet, ignoring the twinge in her side. "You took your time. We could've used your help."

Nimbus straightened a crease in her dress. "I don't like to be seen. Besides, I figured three against two was more than fair. You've been taking on villains by yourself for months, Pink. So, what happened? I honestly expected more from you."

How was she supposed to do what her mother had done for months? And Mum didn't have Zero trying to 'help.' Kris glanced across at Zero and her gaze narrowed. "I'll tell you what happened: Zero K got in my way."

Zero rubbed at his shoulder, wincing as he got to his feet. He frowned at her. "Huh? I mean..." he fumbled for a moment. "I tried to help you!"

"Yeah, well, you just ended up making me trip over myself. And then what you did this ice shard blast thing; that didn't help. Can't you even control your powers?"

"Hey! I'm new at this, all right?"

Well, there was the Calvin she knew. Not that suck-up fanboy. "So, I was right. You can't control your powers."

"Only sometimes, I... I didn't even ask for these powers. But now they're branded on me. I'm just trying, okay!?"

Nimbus put a hand on Zero's shoulder. "He is fairly new at this, Pink."

Pink wasn't supposed to be mad at Zero. Not this much. "Just be more careful. You get in the way, and someone could get hurt."

"I'm sorry, but I'm not the only one stuffing up. Pyro..."

Pyro waltzed into the circle of cloud. His orange spandex looked a little singed, but he grinned. "Relax everyone, I'm fine. Luckily, I am not flammable." He glanced around. "What's going on?"

Zero drew in a steadying breath. "Pyro, did that slug say or do anything that made you think it might not be just some animal? Something Soundwave said."

Pyro paled. "Oh no... I didn't mean... He might be right, Nim. What if it was a mutant? You know, like human, not just a mutant slug."

"If it was, they're getting pretty... inhuman."

Pyro's shoulders slumped. "It used to be so easy. Everyone who had powers just had powers. Then the Fallout happened, and there were the mutants too. And now all their kids... what the heck is happening to this city?"

The wail of police sirens cut through the air.

"Well, that's our cue." Nimbus looked around at the rubble, slime, and still smoldering debris scattered about the edges of the encircling cloud. "And the cops are not going to like this one bit. We'd better get out of here." She and Pyro took to the air, and the cloud began to dissipate. Zero made an ice slide and skated off.

Kris was not going to be caught by her father a second time. "Stan!"

The fog parted, and Stan tore to a screeching halt beside her. Kris piled in and let out a deep sigh as she slumped back in the passenger seat. Her eyelids felt heavy. Leading a double life was not going to be easy.

"All right, you're going to tell me what that was all about. And you're going to tell me now," Stan said.

"Huh?"

"With Zero K! Or Calvin. Or whatever you'd like to call him. I let you use the suit to help your mother. If you're going to use it to bully people, I am taking it back."

Kris' eyes narrowed. "I was not bullying him! And I'd like to see you take this suit back."

"He tried to help you. And you just pushed him around."

"He was in my way..."

"I was watching the whole time, remember? You fell over your own two feet, sweetheart."

Kris huffed and folded her arms.

"Is it something about this Calvin boy?" Stan said after a moment. "Why would he be so stupid to tell you who he was? You're not lying to me about not telling him you were Pink Punch, right?"

"Of course not."

"Well, that was a bad decision on his part. You're obviously taking it badly."

"Of course I'm taking it badly! Stan, he pretended to make friends with me because my dad's a cop. Not because he liked me, or because he needed a friend. Just like bloody Butch. Ever since Penny got sent to the clinic... I can't even..." Kris trailed off. Did anyone actually want to be friends with her? Maybe she was better off wearing the stupid suit. A lot more people seemed interested in making friends with Pink Punch.

"What he said in the Richardsons' house, about hanging out with Detective Mahrone's daughter..."

"Yeah."

"I see. Well, he may have made a mistake telling you his identity, but now you're responsible for not letting that interfere with your work as Pink Punch. You can't tangle your agendas from your real life."

"Seriously? Is that what Mum did? She told Dad, and they're constantly fighting." She swallowed. "Were."

"That doesn't mean you should make those same mistakes. You don't know what harm any contention with Zero might cause."

"I can manage my own life. You're my transport; not my conscience."

"Rachael gave me a voice for a reason."

"Did she make you pink for a reason too?"

"Yes. No... I don't know. Forget it. I don't know if you're tired, or just being a teenager. If you don't want my advice, that's fine. But don't ruin the chance we've got here of getting the help from these supers we need."

12

Kris' alarm woke her the next morning. She slapped her hand on the bedside table, but her phone toppled to the floor and continued to screech. Kris got out of bed to search for the offending noise amongst the clothes scattered around her bedroom floor. She eventually located and silenced it. She flopped back on her bed, but by now she was about as awake as she was going to be. No hope of pretending she hadn't really heard the alarm and could drift back off to sleep. Waking up on school mornings was painful enough, even when she hadn't been up half the night.

Kris retrieved her school shirt from the mess and pulled it on. She winced. A faint blueish mark was on her side, where Sound-wave had hit her. She sure packed a hell of a punch. At least Pink had given as good as she'd gotten. Still, the mark made her pause. Stan had said the suit wasn't impenetrable; she could still get hurt. Kris had never pushed people like Butch too far, because despite the fact she knew how to look out for herself, she knew she was still vulnerable. Up until this point she'd somehow thought that fear was irrelevant when she was wearing Pink's armour.

Kris huffed and pulled on the rest of her clothes. It didn't hurt that bad. She's broken her arm skateboarding before, and that had been worse. If she did get hurt any injuries could easily be put down to skateboarding mishaps.

Outside in the hall, Dad's bedroom door was cracked open; he hadn't been home to sleep yet. Kris traipsed downstairs. Tommy nearly bowled her over as he rushed past her for the front door.

"Tommy, where's Dad?" Kris shouted after him.

"I don't know." Then: "Oh, here he is. Hi, Dad."

John slouched into the living area. His hair was a ruffled mess and he had dark circles under his eyes.

Kris looked him up and down. "Did you just get home?"

"Yeah. Big night. You want to have breakfast with me?"

She was already going to be late for school. But her father looked so haggard. It wasn't a difficult decision. "Sure."

John made a bowl of cereal for Kris, but only a coffee for himself. He didn't say anything to her, either in the kitchen, or when he sat down at the table. It seemed he only wanted to stare at his coffee.

Kris poked her cereal, then cleared her throat. "Dad, what happened to you last night?"

John shifted back in his chair. "There was a vigilante attack. Downtown is completely trashed. That's two attacks in two nights. It's a miracle no one was hurt. And guess who had to help clean up the mess?"

"Oh." Kris looked down at her cereal and chewed her lip. "I'm sorry."

"Not your fault, sweetheart."

Well, actually... "Did you catch anybody?"

John shrugged. "There was this giant dead slug thing. I honestly don't know if it's a sentient mutant or not. But we're still going to have to do an investigation."

Kris swallowed. "You didn't see anyone else? Whoever might have hurt the... slug?"

"By the time we got to the scene everyone else had cleared off. Which isn't exactly unusual." John's hands tensed around his coffee cup. "But I know some of the self-declared superheroes must've fought it. Everything was burnt. And there's only one fire vigilante I know of. But we still have to bloody prove something, and no one saw anything. They think they're helping. They just make the whole damn mess worse."

"So, no one saw which supers... vigilantes it was?"

"Kris, this isn't some fun show you can go and tell your friends about! This is serious. It's my job, and it's bloody hard. And it's dangerous. For the whole city."

"I know, Dad. I was just wondering."

John ran his hand through his hair. He'd had some sort of product in it to start with, but by now it was just a sweaty tussled mess. "I know, sweetheart. I shouldn't even be telling you this stuff. I'm just tired."

Kris pressed her lips together and poked her cereal with her spoon. "Do you think maybe it's like Mum was saying? That TechCorp's making villains commit crimes?"

"They put a hole in the TechCorp building. So, I don't see how. Rachael was just upset when she left TechCorp. She's making connections where there were none. She loved her career. Probably why she was out that night. It's all so stupid! This is my job. Not some vigilantes'. Just because they have superpowers, they think they can do what they please. And if they don't, they think they can design their very own superpowers, and still do what they want even though I'm the one who knows how to solve this stuff..."

"Dad, I think you need to go to sleep."

John shook his head. "I haven't seen your Mum yet today."

"So, see her in the afternoon. I can go see her now." Kris stood to her feet. "You go to sleep. She'd kill you if she knew you were working this hard." And his rants were getting dangerously close to talking about Mum being Pink Punch. Kris was pretty sure he didn't want to reveal that, and even though she already knew, she didn't want to have to try and pretend she didn't. Her life had enough complications right now.

"I'm sorry. Ignore me. But you're going to be late for school." He smiled faintly. "Sure that's not the reason you want to go see her?"

"Yeah, I'm sure." Kris squeezed her father around the shoulders. She was tired from last night: but at least she hadn't been up all night like Dad had.

"All right. But you get to school straight after, you hear me? I'll let them know you'll be late."

"And you get some rest."

John grasped her hand. "Deal. But I want you back home as soon as you can be after school. If you want to talk a bit with your friends, that's fine, but I don't want either of you outside near dark. It's getting dangerous, especially late at night. No hanging around outside unnecessarily, okay?"

Kris' mouth felt dry. "Okay, Dad. Deal."

* * *

Kris sat at her mother's bedside, and the soft beeps and clicks of the breathing apparatus filled the room. She wasn't sure why she felt the need to see her mother. She was in a coma, and there was no way she'd hear what her daughter told her. It was pointless. But maybe it was the same reason Dad felt he needed to see her, even though he was dog-tired. It at least felt like they were helping.

Kris reached out and grasped her mother's hand. "Dad's not here. That means I can tell you my secret: I've become Pink Punch. I know you only wanted me to take the suit to protect me that night. But I couldn't sit back and do nothing. I've been trying to find out what's going on with TechCorp, just like you were. But I don't think I'm doing a very good job. At least the other supers have started working with me; I really need their help. Because the more I fight..."

Kris swallowed, and her hand went subconsciously to her side. "Stuff could happen to me. And I'm not sure I could put Dad through that. Or maybe the truth is that I'm just a little scared."

"But I know you weren't afraid. You were always confident, those times I saw you on the news. Like that explosion at that tattoo parlor that you saved that kid from, or that time you beat up a half dozen ninjas robbing a bank. And you weren't scared to fight Thunderclap. But I need to find out what's going on. Whether you're in danger, whether the city is, whether Dad is."

The breathing apparatus continued to click, but her mother's hand stayed limp. "You can't hear me anyway, can you? And you can't help me. But that doesn't matter. Mum, please… just wake up."

* * *

Kris skated from the hospital and headed slowly toward school. She didn't make much of an attempt to do more than roll along at a crawl. Not only because she wasn't exactly keen to get to there, but it was already scorching hot. She passed Northberg's southern shopping center and angled herself up onto the sidewalk and into the center's shadow. The shade would keep some of the building heat off her.

A scream cut through the morning air, and alarms began to blare.

Kris brought herself to a stop, one foot still on her board. The center's sliding doors nearest her opened. She was assaulted by a wall of noise; the alarm increasing in volume. Seconds later a throng of people tumbled from the building, running for their lives.

"Hey!" Kris yelled at anyone and everyone running past her. "What's going on?"

Someone bowled into her. Kris regained her balance and found Amanda staring back at her.

"Shouldn't you be in school?"

Amanda scoffed. "You can talk. I didn't expect to see you

skipping school to buy some decent clothes. Maybe I was wrong about you."

"What the heck's going on?"

Amanda rolled her eyes. "Stupid mutants. I mean, I'm not being racist, I get they've got to buy clothes too. But they have totally trashed everything in there."

Kris' heart rate quickened. Should Pink Punch help? She was supposed to be at school. Why was she thinking about going to school over getting involved in a superfight? Nimbus had said she'd expected Pink Punch to help with this sort of thing anyway. The flow of people from the mall was dwindling. Mum wouldn't be afraid, so neither would she. Kris squared her shoulders, then jumped on her board and propelled herself inside.

"What are you doing?" Amanda yelled after her. "You really are crazy, you know that, right?"

Inside was now empty. The alarms stopped, leaving an eerie silence. The only sound was the clack of Kris' skateboard wheels on the tiles. "Hello?" Her voice echoed. "Is anyone there?"

A crash sounded. Kris' eyes narrowed. "All right. If I'm going to be a superhero, I'd better start acting like it."

She played with the pink cuff on her wrist. She'd always been with Stan when she'd turned on the suit before. Suddenly, she wasn't entirely sure if she'd done it, or if he'd kept control himself so he could fulfill the order from her mother and keep her 'safe.' "I've got to stop relying on that stupid car for everything..." She gave the bracelet a prod, then twisted it. "Come on!" When she activated a weapon, all she had to do was think of it.

Kris thought, firmly and deliberately, of activating the suit. The bracelet let out a spark, and then the wave of pink exploded over her body. "Yes!"

"Hey, Pink Punch!" The booming voice echoed down the corridor.

A big shape moved toward her. At least seven foot tall, with broad shoulders. Dressed in tight jeans and a stretched-out singlet, the mutant's face finally came into view, a big toothy grin spread across his face. Butch cracked his knuckles. "Well, well, well. Pink Punch. Let's see how tough you are when I've got a little back up, huh?"

"Oh, we're going to have a little fight, are we? Look at that suit, it just fits her perfectly, doesn't it?" From behind Butch, another mutant hopped. She bounded right up against the wall, and then skittered across the floor in front of him. She looked like a kangaroo, but one who'd just crashed through the most girlish store in the entire shopping center. She was draped in costume jewelry, three heavy necklaces around her neck. She wore an expensive blouse and carried three handbags, recently liberated, no doubt. "It's not fair! We finally decide to steal what we want, and I still can't find a pair of shoes that fit!" She stomped a big kangaroo foot on the floor.

Kris raised an eyebrow. "I'm not surprised. Your feet must be a size forty, men's. Have you tried the costume store?"

The kangaroo stomped her foot again. "You see, Teeth. This is what I have to put up with!"

Kris raised an eyebrow. "Wait, Teeth? Seriously?"

"Yeah, that's my name. Do you like it? I'm going to show you why they call me Teeth." Butch grinned.

Kris rolled her eyes. "As if it wasn't already glaringly obvious."

A low growl sounded behind her, and Kris spun around. A large dog growled up at her, hackles raised, teeth bared. "You attacked my mama." This wasn't just some mangy mutt. It was the smallest werewolf. Pup.

"Heads up!"

Kris spun around as the kangaroo loomed large in her face and kicked her clean across the shopping mall. She crashed through the display window of a clothing store and slammed into the floor.

Teeth snorted. "Nice one, Belle."

"The frickin kangaroo is Belle? Figures." Kris hauled herself to her feet.

Teeth stood in the shop's doorway, lit up by the flickering overhead lights. He slammed a fist into a big palm. "You think you can tell me what to do, who I can talk to? Let's see how you go against the three of us."

13

"Rawgr!" Clothing racks skittered out of Teeth's way like skittles. Kris rolled from his path and he barreled through, and face planted in the back wall of the shop. The walls shook. Teeth groaned.

This was ridiculous. Only a week ago she'd thought Butch was her friend. Now she wasn't sure if Pink Punch could take on someone his size at full tilt. Mum could, sure. But this Pink Punch? Perhaps the other villains would be easier to take on, then she could deal with Butch one on one. She ran out into the main shopping center, Pink's boots squeaking on the tiles.

"Hey! What are you guys doing, hiding? I thought you wanted to fight?"

A ball of fur crashed into her. Kris slammed into the floor, rolled herself back upright effortlessly, and flung the small werewolf off her.

Pup yelped and landed on all fours, but her paws skidded out from beneath her and her eyes went wide as she flailed about for traction on the shiny tiled floors.

Belle bounded back onto the scene. "Hang on, kid. I've got your back. Why don't you pick on someone your own size?" She now sported a pair of boxing gloves. "Check it out. I even found pink ones."

"Pink's my colour." Kris winced. "Unfortunately."

"Let's see who wears it better." Belle leaned back on her tail and punched the air.

"Wonderful. Now I'm fighting a boxing kangaroo with a shoe fetish."

Kris called up a pair of gauntlets and circled Belle. Belle struck first, shooting a fist at Kris' jaw. Kris dodged backwards, the actuators in Pink's suit whirring and accelerating the movement. The punch went wide.

Kris threw three jabs in quick succession, testing how fast the suit would make them. Belle rocked back on her tail, taking each successive hit on the gloves she held in front of her protectively, then she sprung forward and kicked Kris in the chest.

Once again, Kris found herself hurled through the air. She winced as she hauled herself to her feet. Slamming into a wall hurt a bit more than a glass window. Man, was she thankful for the suit. "Hey, no kicking!"

Belle winked. "Kick boxing, babe."

Pup circled back around beside Belle, down on all fours. She bared her teeth. "I'm gonna bite you for spoiling my family's fun. Mama said I'm not allowed out doing stuff like this anymore, you know how boring that's gonna be?"

"Hey, not my fault she wants to put you on a shorter leash."

Pup bared her teeth.

"She's not a dog, you're the one being a - "

Sirens cut into the air, echoing off the shopping center walls.

Pup yelped and her tail went between her legs. "I can't get arrested! My parents will kill me." She bolted off down the mall, away from the sirens, her claws skittering on the tiles.

"Pup, get back here! You're not going to get paid if we don't finish this off. Don't forget it's a bonus for that suit!"

Kris tensed. These guys wanted her suit too? "Wait, who's paying you?"

Belle's ears flicked backwards. "None of your business."

"It's TechCorp, isn't it, big foot?" It looked like her foray into the shopping center had paid off. Kris didn't understand what TechCorp would want from a shopping mall, but if the whole point was simply to raise the crime rate and get the cops grabbing for their suits, it was starting to make sense. She and Belle circled each other. "It is, isn't it? You get some free clothes and extra-large shoes out of it. All you have to do is create a nice big mess. But why does everyone want this suit?"

"I ain't telling you if you talk to me like that."

"What about if I punch you in the face?"

"Try it."

Kris put up her fists and crouched into a fighting stance.

Tyres chirped across the polished floors. A VCU Commodore slewed around the corner. It narrowly missed a coffee stand and clipped a set of tables and chairs, sending one chair flying. John stepped out.

"You're supposed to be sleeping!" Kris winced and gritted her teeth. Oh, crap. Dad.

John's gaze fell on Pink Punch. "You. I should've known. I'm not even on duty and I still have to deal with you!"

Oh no. Kris knew how most of the cop stuff worked. "You don't have to be here if you're not on duty. You could've let an officer take the call."

"Shut up! Do you see any uniformed officers here? Damned donut eating layabouts! No, it's up to me, and you're under arrest."

Belle snorted. "I seriously doubt you can arrest us, sweetheart." She put up her boxing glove clad fists.

The floor shook as Teeth stomped out of the clothing store. A blue satin dress stuck to his shoulder. He tore it off with a roar and flung it aside.

John tensed, his hands balling to fists at his side. Did he seriously think he could take on Teeth?

"Detective Mahrone, you can't arrest either of these thugs. You need my help."

"Oh no." John said coldly. "I am not working with you. That's the last thing my family needs; you putting me in a coma too."

"We'll do more than that to you," said Teeth. "You heard what that Boss lady said, Belle. So how about we trash this mall, take Pink Punch's suit, and…" He turned to John and his big face split into a toothy grin. "If we can manage a human causality, that'll be extra helpful. And extra cashful. Ha."

Belle punched Teeth in the shoulder. He didn't flinch. "Shut up. Don't mention that in front of the cops. Or Pink. I'm not killing anyone. It's not in my blood."

"Yeah, funny thing," said Teeth. "Ever since I became this thing, I've been craving it."

Kris cautiously moved herself between the villains and her father. "Da-Detective Mahrone, these kids are working for TechCorp. It's like I've been telling you."

"Bull. All three of you are working together. And you're just trying to blame some big bad for your actions. You're all misbehaving, and you think you can get away with it because you're stronger than everyone else. It's typical vigilante behavior."

"What? And your wife was working with us too?"

"You bloody well tell me what you were doing there -"

"Speaking of typical behavior…" Belle muttered with a roll of her eyes.

"I don't care what you think, pig," Teeth snarled. "And no one's going to find out neither, because I'm going to take you down. Sorry, but that's what's in my blood. You know - just typical vigilante behavior." He stomped forward, gaining momentum, his teeth bared.

John backed against his Commodore and fumbled for his Tech-taser, usually at his side. It wasn't there.

Kris threw herself between them. She needed more armour, way more than the suit usually provided. She imagined her arm completely encased in impenetrable steel. It didn't have to be pretty, there just had to be a lot of it. She flung up her forearm.

Teeth bit down hard. The thud of his jaws slammed into her, but apart from that, Kris felt no pain.

Kris slammed her other fist into Teeth's snout. He reeled back, leaving some of his namesake stuck in Pink's armour. The extra metal dissolved in a poof of pink and the teeth plinked onto the floor. Kris called up a sword.

"Where's your taser?" she shouted over her shoulder. "We can take them down if we work together."

John paled. His anger had finally cooled enough that he realised what a bad situation he'd walked into. "I can't, I... the rest of the equipment is in the trunk. I forgot to take out the taser... look, I rushed right out here... And I don't want your help. I can't trust you."

Kris gritted her teeth. After everything that had happened to Mum, it wasn't Dad's fault he was so angry with Pink Punch. Well, she didn't need his permission. What was he going to do? Ground her? "Fine. I'll just protect you then."

"Teeth, this is a mistake," said Belle. "Let's just take down Pink Punch. Hand her over to the Boss. We'll shut the stupid cop in his car and bend the door shut. But if you kill him, they will never leave us alone."

"They don't leave us alone already." Teeth wiped the back of his hand across his jaw, then lunged for Pink Punch.

Kris swiped her sword at him. Teeth slapped it away with a big grey palm. The sword left a faint line of red but cut nowhere near as deep as Kris would have liked.

More sirens filled the air again.

"Damn it, Teeth." Belle bounded past the shark, right past Kris.

Kris' heart rose to her throat. She whirled back around, brandishing her sword. Dad!

Belle bounded right past John, too. She bounced off the side of his car, left a massive dent, and ricocheted back into Kris, narrowly missing the sword. They both slammed back into Teeth and all three fell to the floor.

John stared at the side of his car and his hands balled into fists. "Stop trashing police property!"

"Forget the stupid car. They're trying to kill you!" Kris rolled out of the tangle of fur and sharp skin. "Get in the car where it's safe."

John scowled but did as he was told. The door slammed. Man, she would never get away with speaking to him like that if he knew who she was. Of course, if he knew who Pink was, he wouldn't be trying to arrest her.

Two police vehicles skidded around the corner, followed by a black VCU branded Land Cruiser. Five officers piled out of the cars, and Detective Johansson from the Land Cruiser. When she saw the Commodore, her eyes narrowed. "Heck, what's he even doing here?"

Teeth and Belle untangled themselves.

"Teeth, let's go," said Belle. She'd dropped her boxing gloves on the floor and now clutched two of her handbags possessively to her chest.

Teeth hauled himself to his feet and roared. Spittle flew from his razor-sharp jaws. "If I'm going to get paid, I'm doing this properly!" Teeth charged.

All the cops snatched tasers from their holsters. The weapons discharged, and Teeth grunted as three of them hit home. But he didn't stop. He barreled into the first cop and his jaws clamped down. The man shrieked, and then was silent. Teeth lifted his head and his jaws dripped crimson.

Kris clapped her hands over her mouth. Butch had killed someone. He'd said he would, but somehow, she'd thought it was all talk. She'd gone to school with him, been his friend.

The other cops backed away. Teeth had slowed, but his gaze had become darker, more focused, and decidedly more animalistic. Beady black eyes turned their cold attention to the rest of the cops. He gulped down a chunk of… something… that had lodged between his teeth.

"Get behind me," Johansson said to the other cops. "There's a heavier tase-net in the land cruiser. Pink, if you can distract him long enough for us to get it…"

Kris couldn't tear her gaze away. Teeth's big body blocked the fallen cop from view. But he sure wasn't moving. There was so much blood.

"Pink! We could use some help!"

The woman's voice snapped Kris out of it. Maybe it was because she was used to hearing Johansson bark orders when she used to train in martial arts under her. But by then, Teeth had already lurched for the detective. Kris' heart caught in her throat, even as she built a gauntlet around her fist. She was too far away. Teeth was moving too fast. And he wasn't going to stop at one cop.

Johansson stepped out of his way as he barreled past and threw a punch so quickly Kris' couldn't see where it hit.

Teeth roared and stumbled backwards, clutching at his eye socket. He was bleeding from his beady eye, an impossibly small target. Kris didn't know if Johansson had punched or jabbed him, but she'd hit a critical spot and it was enough to snap some semblance of humanity back into the bloodthirsty beast.

Kris slammed her gauntlet into that side of Teeth's head. He roared again and stumbled back, clutching his swollen eye socket. "You'll pay... For this... But you know what?" And he broke into that toothy grin again. "Guess I'm going to get my bonus." Then he turned and bolted.

Belle, too, had disappeared at some point in all the confusion.

John stepped out of his car and froze as he saw his fallen colleague. He gulped and put a closed fist to his mouth. "Bloody hell."

The other four cops went to the officer's side, though Kris tried not to look right at them. She didn't really want to see what Butch had done.

Johansson rounded on John. Her hands were balled into fists, shaking at her sides. "What the hell were you doing? Where's your taser?"

John tore his gaze away. "I've been up all night..."

"You can't have expected him to fight that thing! He would've just ended up..." Kris glanced quickly at the body, then forced herself to look away with a gulp.

"You stay out of this!" said John. "You're just as much to blame."

"Didn't you hear what he said about getting paid? He's talking about TechCorp!"

"Just cut it out, Pink! This isn't TechCorp." John jabbed a finger at their fallen colleague. "This is because we're letting vigilantes run rampart. It's the middle of the day, and I bet you know exactly what's going on."

"Um, yeah? I just told you!"

"If you want to help," said Johansson. "Go catch that mutant. He can't hurt you."

"Of course he can't. She's got body armour. Which is exactly what we need... what Officer Douglas needed... if he'd just had it. Dave can't pretend that keeping that from us is protecting us anymore."

"Your boss is right; you can't use suits from TechCorp. I'm just trying…"

"Pink!" Johansson snapped, and again the familiar authority in her voice brought Kris to a halt. "I suggest you leave, whether you choose to do something about that creature or not, but if you don't get your butt out of here, we will arrest you."

Kris turned and bolted. She collected her skateboard where she'd dropped it. Her heart pounded. She just had the presence of mind to shut off Pink's suit before she stepped outside. She didn't need someone spotting Pink Punch walking out through the same doors a teenage girl had walked in with the same board minutes before. When she got outside, there was no sign of Butch. She was a lot safer than the cops had been, what with Pink's armour, but Kris was still relieved. She needed to process what he'd done.

Kris walked toward school; board tucked under one arm. Mum had been right. This was dangerous. The cops were in danger. And after what Butch had done, they'd want the TechCorp suits more than ever. She turned over her wrist, looking at the pink cuff. It was small. But her mother had designed it to pack all the power she needed. It didn't matter how scary or dangerous this was, Kris had to use it to fix this mess.

14

Shift rubbed his hands together and chewed his lip. He hated waiting. He was plagued by the constant fear his control would slip and he'd find himself down a sewer, in someone's apartment, or stuck in a wall. Or a hundred years in the future.

Shift wasn't sure whether he could trust TechCorp. But he'd been gone awhile, relatively speaking. The company had changed, along with both its name and management. Perhaps he had more reason to trust TechCorp than he had Vaas Enterprises. Besides, the offer was a good one. Shift was running out of options, along with, ironically, time.

The meeting room door creaked open, and the Boss stood in the open doorway. She was at least forty, she wore an expensive business suit with a skirt, a blue blouse, and high heels, and carried a briefcase.

The Boss didn't falter as she took in Shift's appearance, only smiled faintly as she looked him up and down. There was no hint of fear that she had entered a room, alone, with a man who had the ability to shift his body out of phase and reappear, half solid, with a fist inside her chest. "I've been told you want to speak with me," she said, raising an eyebrow. "I have to admit, I found that rather bold."

"I suppose so." Shift shook her hand as she sat in the chair opposite. The small meeting room in the lower levels of the TechCorp building contained two simple but still plush black chairs separated by a low, small table. Shift had not been taken anywhere by the TechCorp security guard where there were many people. Whether this was because he was here for some of the Boss' less legal business affairs, or because of his unkempt appearance, he wasn't sure. He was well aware that his shabby coat and five o'clock shadow were not the accepted attire to meet a CEO. It was difficult to afford new clothes when you couldn't hold down a job because you kept disappearing.

"It's about the offer I hear you have going around. That you would pay villains to commit brazen crimes."

"You spoke with my Hiring Manager. He told you what the offer was."

Hiring manager. Hell of a name for someone who picked out suitable superpowers for the Boss' needs. Shift was pretty sure the man didn't also hire her admin assistants. "He did." Shift said, as he fiddled with his fingernails. "But surely you know who I am."

The Boss leaned back in her chair. "Shift. One of the originals. Created along with Pyromaniac and Permafrost by Vaas Enterprises. You can shift your body and limited objects out of phase with reality. You can move through time and space in a non-linear fashion, such that you appear to simply disappear and reappear at will. At least, for a while. At some point you lost control. Ever since the night of the Fallout, when you turned against your fellow creations. They blame you for Permafrost's death, you know. Of course, there was also the rumour that Pyromaniac killed you. But here you are. You, and your kind, were created roughly twenty-five years ago. You were a young adult at the time, attending university, I believe. Yet you look like you've barely hit your thirties."

It was a thorough, if brief, description. But not quite accurate. Shift's hands tensed into fists in his lap. "We weren't created. We existed before that. We had normal lives." Now, when he looked back on the decision which had changed his life, Shift realised being in debt over buying stupid things when he should have been concentrating on his studies was a normal problem. Hardly worth signing up for some shonky experiment, vaguely explained, simply because he had been told he would be well paid. They hadn't lied about that, at least. But when you hadn't signed into your bank account for twenty-five years, that cash was impossible to access.

"We were modified. Exposed to a chemical that gave us these powers." A grin crept onto Shift's unshaven face. "And they used to be glorious. I had control of a superpower that practically allowed me to teleport. To go almost anywhere I wanted to. We could have done anything. But Pyro and Frost just wanted to 'use their powers for good.' Like their definition of what that meant was superior to mine. The night of the Fallout, when they turned against me, they ruined everything!"

"You're not the only one who suffered when the Fallout struck. Thousands of people had their lives changed forever. There are still teenagers who are manifesting terrifying powers, whether their parents appeared to be affected by the Fallout or not. And then there were all the casualties caused by those powers in the ensuing chaos. That was the same night my parents, and my brother, were killed."

"Well, that turned out well enough for you. You inherited their company, after all."

"What is it you want?

Shift ran a hand through his greasy hair. "I can't even do normal things anymore, far less wield the power I once held. I can't hold down a job. I can't keep a girlfriend. I can't do anything. I need this to stop. You're TechCorp. You've previously given superpowers. Heck, you run a clinic specifically designed to help kids and their concerned parents safely remove or at least control their powers without having to resort to tossing them over the Triangle radius like some cruel game of roulette, hoping that they'll simply lose their powers, instead of killing them. So, you must know how to give me back control. All I want is to shift at will, without losing months or years at a time."

The Boss reached into her briefcase and pulled out a small metal case. She placed it on the table facing Shift, then opened it. It contained a remote that looked like a small mobile phone, and a steel bracelet, safely tucked into a custom foam insert.

Shift stared at the offering, enthralled, then tentatively reached out a hand.

"You can take the bracelet."

Shift slipped the bracelet onto his grimy wrist. It shut itself with a soft click. He drew in a quick breath.

"Relax." The Boss picked up the remote. "Now, I do have a task in mind for you, but first, I'd like a demonstration. I'll bet with those powers you can scare people real easy. Try and startle me." She smiled faintly. "But not too much. I do have security outside."

Shift grinned at her. His heart pounded in his chest. She was going to help! "You can bet," he said, as his voice seeped into a more sultry, greasy tone, "that looking like this, I can give the ladies quite a scare. But I'll go easy on you." He thought of standing right behind the Boss. No time shift.

Nothing happened. It wasn't the normal loss of control. It was simply nothing. He grabbed at the bracelet as his heart rate rose even higher. "What have you done? I haven't agreed to anything yet."

"It's just a demonstration." The Boss waved the remote. "That was the highest setting. All I've done is bring your powers under control. That was what you wanted, wasn't it?" She pressed the remote's glowing screen.

Shift felt his hold on reality loosen. The room around him changed; he was standing behind the Boss. "Come here often, sweetheart?" Despite the fact he was supposed to be the one giving the scare, Shift's voice held a faint tremor.

"Excellent. And now it's set to allow you to shift at will. I expect that's the setting you're interested in."

Shift allowed himself to rematerialise back in his seat. It seemed easy, like he didn't have to concentrate as hard anymore. He turned the bracelet slowly about his wrist. "You realise I could just shift out of here."

"You could." The Boss held up the remote. "But you know how this works, don't you? I'm not fooled by your current attire; you're a smart man. You could be working as a professional, if not for what was done to you."

Shift gulped as his focus moved to the remote in her hand. "So what's the deal?"

"Two things. First, I need you to take down Pink Punch and recover her suit. The armour she wears is TechCorp property. I'm not fully aware of all its capabilities, because the engineer who stole it from me was responsible for developing most of them." He lips twisted into a scowl. "I should never have trusted her. But, from the files we were able to recover, it is highly likely it has been fitted with something that would stop your abilities from penetrating it. You won't be able to phase inside it."

"That's not a problem. I can use my powers in less direct ways."

"Find her. Take back the suit. You can do with her what you want to after that."

Shift smiled. "I wouldn't mind having a bit of fun. And the second thing?"

"It involves dealing a blow to those self-professed superheroes, including Pyro. They haven't been too much trouble recently, but they have been talking to Pink Punch. I'd prefer to nip any potential problems in the bud."

"The last time I got in a fight with Pyro..." Shift's put a hand to the concealed burn scar splattered across his torso. Pyro had burnt him so badly that night, but Shift wouldn't have survived without him either. Somehow, that made him hate the man even more. Before he'd slipped, Pyro had taken him to the hospital. It was there he'd first lost control, appearing months later in the same bed. When the hospital staff figured out what was happening, they'd kept the bed for him. Checking, as far as Shift was aware, every day, that their time traveling burns patient hadn't reappeared. It had taken him months in linear time to recover enough to leave. In real time, nearly a decade. And bloody Pyro had kept coming to see him, like they were still friends.

Shift had finally regained enough strength to leave and snuck out one night before the hospital staff could alert Pyro he had once again returned. But he still couldn't control his powers. It was all Pyro's fault. The massive shock to Shift's system had been the cause of all this. He'd lost years of his life and he would make Pyro pay.

"You'll have help. My Hiring Manager has located some promising vigilantes who have come through the clinic lately. I'll get one of them to help you. Thunderclap should also be on his feet by then. So, do we have a deal?"

Shift finally tore his gaze away from the remote. "Yes."

The Boss held up one finger. "Be certain. If you say no, I'll remove that bracelet and you can leave. But, if you leave this room and agree to help me, it's yours to keep. I'll give you this," she waved the remote under his nose again, "when you complete both tasks. But if you fail, you'll be back to your normal, ungrounded self. And if you cross me, or let anyone know of my plans," her eyes narrowed. "I will send you to the end of time."

'TechCorp' was stamped boldly across the silver back of the remote. As long as the Boss had that, she'd own him just as surely as Vaas Enterprises had all those years ago. Her threat was not an idle one. Shift did not want to put himself back in TechCorp's thrall.

But, once he finished the job, he'd have the remote, and he'd be free. It was a risk he was willing to take. "It's a deal. I can't keep living like this."

"Excellent. It's been a pleasure doing business with you, Shift."

15

Much to Kris' frustration, her father didn't go out to work that night. He'd been napping most of the day and had only woken up long enough to make sure Kris and Tommy ate dinner, then collapsed back on the couch. It was great he was sleeping. He had certainly been overworking himself, and it would also keep him out of Pink Punch's way. However, it made it that much more difficult for her to leave the house in the first place. No wonder Mum had moved.

Kris decided stuffing a bunch of pillows under her bedspread and hoping for the best would have to do. Dad might check on her, but he'd be unlikely to disturb her if he thought she was sleeping.

If he realised she was gone, he wouldn't guess the truth but he'd certainly be furious. He'd told both kids what had transpired at the shopping center, so they were clear how dangerous it was out there. Despite him leaving out the details, Kris could still see the mutilated body when he told them about Officer Douglas' death. He'd made no mention of Pink Punch.

Before she left, Kris stopped by her father as he slept draped over the couch. She threw a blanket over his chest, partly because he might need it later, partly to see if the movement would wake him. He rolled over with a grumble but grabbed a wad of the material and hugged it tightly. Kris stifled a giggle. He really was dead to the world. She picked up his phone from the coffee table, set it on silent, then shut it in one of the kitchen drawers.

Stan met her at the abandoned parking lot where she'd first found him. "So, I hear you were at that incident at the shopping center this morning. Without me. I'm fairly certain you should have been in school."

Kris settled herself in the driver's seat as they pulled away. "Don't tell me, Stan. Mum would disapprove."

"Your mother would have done the same thing. And it was a good thing you did. Near as I can tell her aim in all this was to protect your father. It was a good thing you were there."

Kris swallowed the lump in her throat. "I didn't help enough. I knew Butch before he got his superpowers. I don't know why he'd do something like that." Kris still didn't know how far Butch would have gone. Maybe one kill would be enough. Or maybe now that he'd had a taste of blood, well, he looked like a shark, after all. "Butch said he was getting paid to trash the place. And he'd get extra for killing someone. They mentioned the Boss. And TechCorp."

Stan's engine grumbled. "You need to tell the other supers. They're stubborn, but by now it must be obvious to them Rachael was right. I can't see them not paying attention after someone was deliberately killed. Even a cop."

"They'll help I… Stan!" Kris sat straight up. There was a man standing in the middle of the road.

Stan slammed on the brakes. The screech overtook the grumble of the engine. The man didn't move. He just stared at them, his face growing in the blinding white glare of Stan's headlights. Then he disappeared. The smell of burnt rubber drifted into the cabin.

Kris craned her neck as she tried to see over the expanse of Stan's hood. "Did we hit him?"

"I detected no impact. I'm not detecting him at all."

"Hello there, love." The man was in the passenger seat. Scruffy and unkempt, he eyed her sideways, then grinned. One of his teeth was missing.

Kris pressed up against the driver's side door. But she had no reason to fear. She had her suit; she was Pink Punch. "What are you doing in my car? Love."

The man laughed. "I like you already. Pity. The name's Shift."

The seatbelt snaked out and latched around Shift. Two more loops of belt shot out of the seat and bound Shift's upper arms, pinning them beside him.

"Whoa. You don't muck around, do you?"

"That was me," said Stan. "I can't have you just jumping into me without my consent."

"What do you want?" Kris demanded.

"Your suit. And then to secure your silence. Sorry." Shift gave her a tight-lipped smile. Then he vanished. The seatbelt clinched up and the extra loops sagged empty.

Kris checked the back seats. There was barely enough room for anyone there anyway. "Where did he go?"

Stan jerked forward and listed to one side. "Son of a... That jerk took my tyre."

Everything changed. One moment Kris sat in Stan. The next she was on a rooftop. She overbalanced. Her body hadn't shifted position with her, and she was sitting in a weird half crouch. It was like someone had snatched a chair out from beneath her. But the suit compensated, and Kris barely pinwheeled her arms before it pulled her into an upright stance.

"Now, this is a bit more intimate, isn't it?"

Kris spun around. Nothing.

"The Boss told me your suit might not let me phase through it. But it doesn't seem to have any problem with me moving it and you in it. Maybe she was wrong." Shift appeared in front of her. Then he faded. Didn't disappear entirely; Kris could see right through him. She felt a faint thud in the center of her chest.

"Ow!" Shift became fully solid again. He pulled back his hand and cradled it.

Kris threw a punch, and Shift went flying across the rooftop. He pulled himself upright and rubbed at his jaw with one hand. Kris stomped toward him as she called up a gauntlet.

Shift phased out. "Right, gametime is over," he said from somewhere behind her. "The Boss was right. You're going to be tough to kill. Nothing I can't handle though."

"Kill? I thought you just wanted to silence me?"

"Killing you would certainly have that effect, darling," the disembodied voice replied.

Kris shook herself. Shift couldn't even penetrate Pink's suit. There were other things that concerned her about this. "You're working for the Boss too?" she pressed. First those mutant teenagers, now this guy. They'd killed someone but Shift specifically wanted her. "Why does she want me dead?"

"Sounds like you've been interfering with her plans. But I think it's mostly because you stole that suit. She seems to be pretty rigid about intellectual property and all that."

Kris spun around. Still no Shift. "So come out and fight me."

"Now where's the fun in that?" Shift whispered, right in her ear.

Kris threw a punch. She saw Shift for a split second before her fist went right through his fading body. "Stan? A little help?"

"I've contacted the other supers. They should be here in minutes. I've..." Stan's voice went to static.

"Stan?"

"Move!"

A horn sounded. The underside of a vehicle loomed directly above her. Kris didn't have time to contemplate what a car might be doing falling out of the sky. She let Pink's gauntlet turn to powder, and created a shield even as she dove to the side. The car slammed into the rooftop. The underside hit the edge of her shield, and the shield cracked and shattered. Kris pushed herself to her knees, the car so close she could reach out and touch it.

"Stan!" Kris jumped to her feet and put a hand on his side. "Are you okay?"

Stan's voice warped a little before gaining some solidity. "I'm... fine. What... you?"

"I'm okay. Where did Shift go?"

"Right here, sweetheart." Shift stood on the low brick wall the surrounded the roof of the building. He waggled his fingers at her, then pointed up.

A mailbox dropped from the sky. Now that, a shield could handle. Kris created another and braced herself. The mailbox bounced off harmlessly.

"Come on," said Shift. Now he was on the opposite side of the roof, behind her, leaning against the low wall. "You want to hit me, right?"

Kris called up a set of gauntlets and rushed him. Shift phased out and Pink's punch slammed into the wall.

"Heads!" said Shift.

Kris didn't even look before she dissolved the gauntlets and called up another shield. A sewer cover bounced off with a clang.

"Kris," said Stan, his voice still mangled. "Careful with... nanites... overload..."

"Come on, Pink, you should be fast in that suit." Now Shift stood on top of Stan, his arms thrown wide. "Hit me!"

That was the last straw. Stan may have been annoying, but she wasn't going to let Shift toss him around and stand all over him. Nanites crackled around Kris' fists as they started to form a pair of gauntlets. They sparked and crackled, but the gauntlets only half formed before the bracelet let out a little whine and flashed. "Wait, what?"

Shift lowered his arms and the maniac grin fell from his face. "Ah, there we go. I didn't think all those weapons came out of hammer space. It was nice to meet you, Pink Punch." He disappeared.

A huge oblong shape materialised above Kris. She dropped to the ground and imagined a shield. Pink's bracelet beeped at her impotently. Kris put her arms over her head.

The impact never came. Instead, the temperature dropped, and cold air rushed past her. "For god's sake, move!" Zero K dragged her to her feet, holding out one hand to shoot a stream of ice into the plummeting shape. The ice attached the mass of metal to the roof at one end and the other end stretched up at a forty-five-degree angle above Kris and Zero's head. Kris' eyes widened and she gripped onto Zero's arm. It was a locomotive. Shift had tried to drop an entire locomotive on her head!

The ice creaked and groaned. Zero dragged Kris to the side. Ice couldn't hold a hundred tonne of metal for very long. The ice cracked free at the lower end, and the locomotive smashed into the rooftop, shards of ice shooting out in all directions.

"Where's Stan?"

Stan rolled from behind the locomotive. His body wobbled like something was wrong with his suspension. He was a more solid pink now; the nanites in his bodywork slowly repairing him. Kris shoulders slumped with relief. Stan would have surely come out second best if that locomotive had hit him.

Zero pulled Kris around so she faced him. "Who's attacking you?"

Kris snatched her arm back as her face flushed. "I don't need your help, Zero!"

Zero threw his hands in the air. "You said you wanted the supers' help. You called us!"

Kris poked him in the chest. "I don't have a problem with the supers, I just don't want help from you!"

"So, you have a friend." Shift appeared again, leaning against the low wall. His shoulders heaved as he drew in deep breaths. "Wish I'd known, I wouldn't have phased something a hundred and twenty tonnes. Guess I'll have to finish this." He faded out again.

"Pink, take three steps to the left and throw a punch." The voice was in her ear, but it wasn't Stan.

Kris stiffened. "Who is this?"

"It's X. Just shut up and do it."

Kris took three steps to the left and threw a punch. She felt a bit stupid, but this freak was trying to kill her, so she gave it everything she had.

Shift phased into existence at the exact moment Pink's fist connected with his jaw. He slammed back against the low wall.

"See!" Kris rounded on Zero as she threw her arms wide. "I don't need your help."

"X told you to do that." Zero tapped the side of his head. "I can hear her too. She's patched herself into your comms."

"Well, at least she's useful then."

Zero huffed and looked away.

Shift grunted and with effort hauled himself to his feet. He leaned heavily against the wall. "I hate to break up this little lovers' tiff but..."

"Well, well, well. If it isn't Shift. You didn't even wait for the hospital to release you. I never got to say goodbye." Pyromaniac drifted down from the sky, hands on his hips. He stepped down lightly onto the rooftop.

Shift shrunk back, the movement accompanied by a sharp intake of breath. "You! You know what you did to me?"

"All I did was protect this city. You have no one to blame but yourself."

"Bla bla bla, yeah that's right, play the hero. We're gods, Pyro. You attacked me for being who I am. You know how many years I lost in that damn hospital?"

Pyro sighed. "If you cause trouble, I'll put you in there again, if I have to. You touch the furnace, Shift, you're gonna get burned." Flames sprung to life in Pyro's hands, but all he did was hold them there and let them flicker above his open palms.

Shift's arms shook at his sides. Then he took a step back and disappeared.

Pyro lowered his hands and the flames snuffed out. "Wow, Shift really made a mess." He winced as his gaze fell on the locomotive. "He can move big stuff now. That's a little worrying. Are you all right?"

"Fine," said Kris. She glared at Zero, and he looked away. "You know what, stuff it. I don't know, okay? Shift just tried to kill me!"

Pyro shrugged. "Yeah, villains will do that on occasion. So, what'd you do to upset Shift? I'd have expected him to come after me."

"I don't know what I did to upset anyone. Someone paid him to kill me. And those teens in the shopping center said they'd been paid to take my suit, same as Soundwave. I've been trying to tell you guys TechCorp was up to something! You're not going to believe me until they kill me, are you?" She'd wanted to help Mum, and Dad. With Pink's suit, she'd thought she could do something to make a difference. It had all started out so exciting. But Kris hadn't signed up to get killed.

"I believe her," said Zero.

"Well, gee, the littlest super Zero believes me. That counts for a lot!"

Zero winced and looked away.

Pyro rubbed at the back of his head. "Look, I'm sorry. I know we haven't been as helpful as you'd like. The villain crime rate is definitely going up, no one can argue with that. It's just no one can agree on why. Cops keep telling us it's these kids popping up with powers recently; the TechCorp's clinic says the same thing. But what happened today at the shopping center, that isn't normal for Northberg.

"Meanwhile, we've all been too busy worrying about how the cops are treating us and our 'rights.' I couldn't care less if I have to fight in a mask, or if the cops get upset when I call myself a hero. I'm still breaking the law. But I guess I've been just as distracted as Rick and Nim."

Kris heart thudded a little less as Pyro's words sunk in. "So, you believe me?" Mum should have been the one to finally hear this admission. She'd put her life on the line to get the supers to believe her and ended up in the hospital for her trouble.

"I think we need to consider all the possibilities," said Pyro. "Not just believe what TechCorp tells us, or the cops. But we'll need Rick and Nim on board. Rick's the worst offender." He rolled his eyes. "He doesn't get out here to fight often enough; thinks his fight is with the media and the cops. Fair enough, I suppose. But I'm pretty certain a corporation with TechCorp's history upping the crime rate is a bigger problem. And now they're willing to kill for it? Tell you what, I'll talk to Rick and Nim. They'll listen to me."

Kris swallowed. "Thanks, Pyro."

"In the meantime, let's get you down off this roof. I can help with the Mustang."

"Wait, we're on a roof?" Stan reversed a little. "I may be afraid of heights."

Zero squinted. "You're afraid of heights?"

"I'm a car. My four wheels are supposed to stay on the ground, thank you."

"Stop picking on him, Zero," said Kris.

"I'm not..."

"It's not a problem," said Pyro. "I'll get him down. I won't drop you, promise."

Stan groaned. "Wonderful."

Pyro hefted the vehicle over his head, like he weighed no more than a toy. He lifted off and carried him toward the edge.

"Just don't look at my undercarriage."

"Don't worry, I'd be more interested what's under your hood."

"Charming."

Zero watched them disappear over the edge. Then he squared his shoulders and rounded on Kris. "Are you going to tell me what your problem is?"

Kris' shoulders slumped and she rolled her eyes. She could not deal with this now. "Let's just get back to the Broom Closet. We're got other things to worry about - villains intent on killing people, including me, remember? And I've still got to figure out how to get down from here." What on earth could she make that would get her down? She thought of something simple. A gauntlet. It appeared around her fist. At least the nanite generator had recovered, but a gauntlet didn't help any.

"I could help, but we all know how you feel about that."

Pyro floated up at the building's side. "What, haven't escorted her down yet, Zero?" He held out a hand to Kris. "Come on. I bet you could jump with that suit, but you'd leave a hell of a crater."

Kris took Pyro's hand, pointedly not looking at Zero. Pyro held her by the wrist and glided down. It should have been uncomfortable, but the suit kept the strain off her arm.

"There," said Pyro as he set her on the ground. "Your Mustang decided it was best he went home to repair himself properly. Made me promise to take you straight to the mansion though."

"Look, Pyro, thanks, but you've done enough already. I really don't want you carrying me there like some damsel in distress."

"I know. I'm sure you can get there yourself."

A skateboard would do for transportation. Kris imagined one, and it appeared under one foot.

Pyro watched it build. "Oh, and one more thing. I don't know what's going on between you and Zero, but go easy on him, all right? He is just a kid."

"Yeah, a very annoying kid." Kris winced at her own words. That sounded childish. I mean, she was a teenager, but she didn't want to give herself away. "He's just a bit clumsy; it's hard to work with. But I'll try."

"Good. He is new at this, and it hasn't been easy for him, but he's been trying really hard. I tell you, when I first got my powers, I couldn't burn anything without singeing off my eyebrows for the first month. Couldn't grow a mustache either. But that kid's already icing up entire locomotives, which just came in pretty handy for you. Pretty remarkable, especially for someone who came by his powers the way he did, poor kid. But you already know all about that."

"Ah, yeah," said Kris. She flashed Pyro a quick smile, like she knew exactly what he was talking about. A few days ago, she might have actually wanted to know.

16

Kris arrived at the mansion without running into anyone else intent on killing her. The knot in her gut made her angry. She felt even more conspicuous than she had those times she'd sneaked out at night before, to go to the skatepark. Pink Punch was supposed to keep her safe, make her invulnerable. Instead, she felt like a bright pink rolling target.

The big mahogany front doors were open, so Kris walked inside and made her way upstairs. Xtrapolate was sprawled out on the biggest couch in the living area, her nose in a book. "They're in the Broom Closet, talking about you," she said, without looking up. "Don't go down there. Pyro has a statistically better chance of convincing them if you don't."

Kris rubbed at her arm. "Can you tell me if they're finally going to help?"

X shrugged. "There are a lot of variables. And unless your life is in direct danger, I'd prefer not to start thinking like that right now. If I do, I'll give away the ending to this book to myself. You'll find out soon enough."

Kris swallowed the urge to snap. X wasn't her personal fortune teller, and she'd already helped her more than enough tonight. "I guess I can wait. Thanks for telling me how to hit Shift."

"No problem. Guys who think they're running circles around you are so easy to predict."

Kris wandered around the big home. She found Max and Elspeth in the kitchen, bickering over some contraption Max seemed to think would peel carrots super efficiently. They were both absorbed in conversation with each other, so Kris left them alone, and wandered out onto the large balcony that overlooked Northberg's bay. Despite the humidity in the air, the wind that whipped up off the ocean was cool and refreshing.

Kris leaned on the railing, arms spread wide, hung her head and let out a deep breath. What was she supposed to do?

The shopping center had shocked her, sure. But she was fairly certain if Pink Punch had not been there, it would have been much worse. It was the cops who'd been in danger; Teeth couldn't chomp through Pink's armour.

Even getting a little hurt fighting Soundwave had not bothered her. Any fight you got into you'd come out with bruises. She'd learned that at Taekwondo. But Shift had rattled her. If Pyro hadn't scared him off, if X hadn't told her how to hit him, if Zero K hadn't caught the locomotive... Kris' hands tightened on the railing. She could be dead right now, or seriously injured. How would that help her parents? What if her father had found her?

Kris looked down at her pink clad hands. Pink Punch was a target, but Kris Mahrone, no one bar a sentient car had any idea she was linked to this.

Kris swallowed hard and blinked back tears. Why couldn't Mum just wake up! Even if she wasn't up to being Pink Punch, she could at least let her know how big a threat TechCorp was. Perhaps it didn't require her daughter putting her life on the line. Perhaps her mother had just been bored. She'd always been proud of her career. Not having a job must've driven her stir crazy.

Even as she thought it, Kris knew it wasn't true. Mum wouldn't have left home if she hadn't thought her quest was important.

"Hey, Pink Punch, I want to talk to you." Zero K stood with his arms folded, a frown twisting his lips beneath the oversized dark glasses Pink had made for him.

"Not now, Zero."

"Look, if you're…" Zero fumbled, then stilled his arms. "Yes, now."

"I nearly got killed. I'm a little bit preoccupied."

"Yeah, I saw that. But I saved your life. So, I think you owe me, but instead you just keep biting my head off."

"Well, you are kind of annoying."

Zero threw out his arms. "I'm just trying to help."

"You're doing a terrible job of it."

Zero swallowed hard and looked away.

Kris felt bad, almost. Zero wasn't a terrible hero. He was bumbling his way through this, just like her. It wouldn't have bothered her, except that he had tried to manipulate her. And then crowed about it to Pink Punch. She wanted to give him a good telling off, but she couldn't. And maybe that was the problem. She sighed and turned back to stare out at the ocean. "I can't explain it to you. So just leave me alone."

Zero leaned on the railing beside her. "I think I understand what's going on." He turned a little away from her, gazing out at the ocean. It made it impossible for her to read his features beneath that hood. "At first, I thought I was just annoying you. I mean, I did trip you up with Soundwave. I know I've still got things to learn. And I am just a kid. But I'm not actually that bad."

"X is helpful. You're not. And you were sucking up to me. Seriously, you live with supers. Why do you need to impress me?"

Zero ran his fingers over the railing, leaving icy trails. "I think you're cool. You have cool powers. I mean, I'm guessing you don't, it's all the suit. But that's cool, you still try and help people, using the suit. Some supers just like showing off their powers, some like the praise. You always seemed to just get on with the job, and you didn't care that the supers here thought you were crazy going on like you did about TechCorp." Zero looked up at her, then frowned. "What?"

"Huh?"

"Why are you smiling?"

Kris had been thinking of her mother. She certainly didn't care what people thought. "Nothing."

"You're not scared of anything and, you did save me."

"You mean the werewolves?"

"No, from the fire at my dad's tattoo parlour." Zero's hands tightened on the railing. "At first, I thought you might not have realised the kid you saved that day was me. But you saw my tattoos, you brought me here, to Rick and Nim. You know who I am. Where I came from, whose kid I was. That's why I've realised you don't like me."

This was something that had happened when Mum was Pink Punch. Why wasn't Stan here? He'd tell her what Zero was on about. "Why wouldn't I like you?"

"Because my dad was a villain," Zero said, forcing the words out. Then they came faster. "For some reason, Nim and Rick don't seem to care, even though I keep stuffing up. But you, you know too, and you're worried I'm going to betray the supers, just cause of where I'm from. But I'm not, I've tried my hardest to prove it, but..."

Kris held up her hands. "Wait, slow down, who was your dad?"

"You don't remember?"

"I... I guess I've saved a lot of people. I'm sure if I thought about it..." And talked to Stan.

"Damn it!" Zero pounded a fist on the railing. "But I'm in this stupid outfit, aren't I? You've only started working with Rick and Nim recently, you didn't know it was that kid they took in…"

"What happened at the tattoo parlour?"

"Forget it, you don't remember. It doesn't matter. It's like you keep telling me, I'm just annoying." Zero rubbed a hand over his tattoos, like he could erase them.

The movement was agitated and distracting and seemed to be upsetting Zero himself. Kris put a hand on his arm, if only to get him to stop. "You're not annoying, it's just…" How could she tell him without giving herself away? But she didn't need to tell him the full truth. "Okay, that first night we were here, after you'd just shown me the Broom Closet, you said you'd been hanging out with Kris Mahrone so you could get to her father."

"Yeah." Zero stilled as he tried to understand the change of subject. "What of it?"

"Look, why do you think Kris was out looking for me that night? I can't tell you who I am, but I know the family. And I don't like people messing with them." Kris' voice rose steadily higher as she spoke. "How could you pretend to be Kris' friend like that? Her mum's in a coma. Her friends are all nonexistent right now. Her best friend's in the TechCorp clinic!"

"The clinic's one of the reasons we need to find out what the cops are doing; I thought she'd understand that. For all we know, they'll decide that being a vigilante means they can send us there without our consent. Take away our superpowers like they're a disease…" Zero rubbed at his tattoos again, but it was less agitated than before. "It's bad enough being given powers without being asked."

"But you're not her friend; you were just pretending. You manipulated her."

"Wait, she said that?"

"Why do you care if you're just using her?"

"I'm not! Sure, it was useful her dad was a cop, and that is what

Rick asked me to do. But that doesn't mean I don't still want her as a friend. I never had any normal friends when I was living with my dad, he wouldn't let me. But I wasn't trying to hurt Kris, or her family, I swear. I only told you because… you're right, I was trying to impress you." His shoulders slumped.

Kris chewed her lip. "Look, I'm sorry. I'm not trying to be mean; I'm just stressed out right now. I didn't think doing this would be dangerous, that someone would want to kill me… I'm…" Scared. The word was on the tip of her tongue, but Kris clamped her mouth shut. Why was she telling Zero this? Maybe because he'd just told her about his father. But he'd also thought Pink knew that information already.

"What happened, Pink?" Zero asked, his voice softer now. "It's like you're a different person. I mean, I never talked to you up close until recently, but I had to save you tonight. You always knew what you were doing before."

Kris swallowed. When she spoke, her voice sounded thin, even through the voice modulator. "Yeah. I could've been hurt. And now I don't know if I can handle that."

"You could take the suit off, if you wanted. You've still got that option."

She could. No one would know. Pink Punch would just disappear.

"Look, I'm sorry about the Mahrones…" Zero began.

Kris held up a hand. "If you want to apologise to someone, apologise to Kris." She turned and headed back into the mansion.

"Wait, where are you going?"

"I'm done talking; I'm done with this whole thing, I'm going home." Kris needed to think. She'd jumped into this headlong, and now she didn't know what she was supposed to do. It would be so much easier if she could just ask Mum.

Zero followed her. "Hey, wait, I wasn't serious about ditching the suit."

"Leave her," said X from the couch, without looking up. "She'll be back."

"You can't quit. You're Pink Punch, you can't..."

Kris flushed. "I don't know, Zero!" She turned her back on him and stomped out of the mansion.

17

John straightened his tie. It wouldn't be right to visit the most prominent woman in the city with a crooked tie. He was glad Dave had made him take the previous night off too. He felt more awake, and probably looked better for it.

To his left in the elevator, Johansson leaned toward him. "Stop fidgeting."

"I actually want to look presentable."

"You do realise you're still wearing your boots."

John cursed softly. Whilst his black, steel-toed combat boots were great for rushing around Northberg keeping tabs on vigilante activity, they weren't what he would have chosen to meet Tech-Corp's CEO. He'd been in a rush. One of the kids had hidden his phone in the kitchen drawer and he'd missed the alarm. They both should have been too old for something like that.

"You look fine," said Dave. "Now can you both please behave? This is serious. I'm sure she'll try show us some fancy pictures of the suit. But keep your heads, okay? I need to make sure those things are safe."

After Officer Douglas' death, Dave had announced he would be looking more thoroughly into the TechCorp suits. They could not afford to be overcautious any longer. The Chief had brought John and Johansson along on his visit to TechCorp as the two detectives who had the most experience with vigilantes. Whilst this was true, and what he had announced to the rest of the VCU, John knew it wasn't simply professional trust that meant they were the backup he'd chosen.

The VCU would have never gotten off the ground if all three of them hadn't pushed for it after the Fallout. And, he and Johansson had also been there the night the Chief's wife left him.

The young, broad shouldered security officer who escorted them led them out of the elevator and down the white walled corridor to the first door. John wondered if the boy had any training to back up all that muscle, or if he'd just been hired because he looked intimidating. "Please step inside. Ms. Vaas will be with you shortly." The escort waited as the three cops entered, and then shut the door behind them.

This wasn't a meeting room. They were on the floor with the engineering labs. John had visited a couple times when Rachael had worked here. When Rachael had been in charge of all these labs. "I think she might want to show us more than pictures, Chief."

"Wow, this is really... something..." said Johansson.

A glass panel separated them from the main lab. Behind it was a hodgepodge of equipment and mechanical and electrical projects. Robotic arms with half-finished soldered wires lay on metal tables. Drawing cabinets lined the back wall, one with a drawer cracked open and a curled-up wisp of paper, evidently crammed back in with little care, sticking out. Laptops and scattered paperwork populated the bench tops at random intervals, as well as a few employees working on those laptops, or deciphering a drawing.

But it wasn't the expansive workspace that had elicited Jo's response. It was the dark grey suit that dominated the entrance area. Its head hung, slumped against its chest. Across the torso in bright blue, in the same colours as those used for the VCU unit, was stamped 'VCU.'

Dave's mustache quirked to the side. "She's getting ahead of herself."

The door behind them opened. Ms. Vaas entered, followed by a shorter balding man in a lab coat. It was clear she was in her domain. She held herself straight, but comfortably. In contrast, the older man looked anything but confident. He pushed his glasses up his nose and fidgeted with the folder he held in his hands.

"Chief Thompson," Ms. Vaas smiled. The greeting wasn't warm. It was crisp and business-like. But she did seem pleased to see him. Unsurprising, as she was about to sell them what had to be some pretty expensive tech. She gestured behind her. "This is my chief engineer, Steve Blakey."

Chief Engineer. The position Rachael had held. John was quite certain his wife would not have been so nervous about showing off her mechanical creations.

Dave introduced the two detectives. Ms. Vaas shook both their hands. "I recognise you from TV, Detective Mahrone. Quite a dedicated campaign you have against those villains. I'm sure you'll see the value in these suits." She made no mention of Rachael, although she had to recognise the surname.

John smiled faintly. "Vigilantes, Ms. Vaas. We'll see."

Dave waved a hand at the suit that dominated the end of the room. "So, this is it?"

It looked like Pink's suit, although perhaps most body armour of the type was similar. The only visible difference, save for the colour and branding, was that the helmet fully covered the head, protecting the jaw better than Pink's. John had pointed that flaw out to Rachael when she'd first declared her intentions as Pink Punch. Though, admittedly, that had largely been because he'd been looking for ways to pick at her already outrageous plan. Stupid vigilantes! If they'd lived anywhere else something like this would have never entered her head.

"The suit itself," said Steve, "is comprised of nanites. Tiny machines that we can program to build, well, almost anything. The suit doesn't always have to be deployed. You wear a mechanical cuff that contains the nanite generator. If you get yourself in trouble with a villain, um, vigilante, you can power it up. And back down again, so you're not always running around in bulky armour."

Steve grasped the machine's wrist. The suit hummed, then turned to powder. The powder rolled over itself like a small, billowing cloud, back to the wrist, where it was sucked into the only remaining bit of solid metal. Steve held the cuff up. It was no bigger than an oversized watch.

"The suit also increases your strength. Sensors detect your movements and amplify them. You throw a punch however you normally would, and you'll hit just like you have superstrength."

"It's not enough to just be stronger," said Jo.

"It'll also make your movements faster. Far faster."

She nodded.

"Would any of you like to try it on?"

John's guts tightened. He wanted it. He wanted to feel it making him strong enough to pin down whoever had taken Rachael's suit. But still he hesitated, and Rachael's words came back to him like a sledgehammer.

"You take those suits, and it'll destroy everything you've built with the VCU. You might even get yourself killed."

John had pointed out becoming a vigilante could get her killed too. But she hadn't listened. Now, he wished he had tried harder to get Dave to help. But at that stage, had TechCorp been up to anything, it was well in the realm of corporate crime. Not vigilante. And that was why, Rachael told him, she was taking things into her own hands. A day of arguing later, when both had calmed enough to realise the other was too stubborn to budge, they'd decided it was best if Rachael, temporarily, moved out. Only now could John admit to himself that he simply hadn't wanted the stress of deciding whether he would do his job and arrest his wife every time she sneakily left the house.

"No one's trying it on," said Dave. "Just show us what it can do. And the cost. We're stretched thin as it is trying to keep up with paying for our tase-nets getting torn by the bigger mutants."

"The cost will be that TechCorp gets to test my new body armour out in a real-world situation," said Ms. Vaas.

Dave bristled. "They're untested?"

"What she means," said Steve. "Is that they haven't been field tested. We've already run every laboratory test we can. Any faults have been rectified. I'm confident they'll perform splendidly."

"We're aware the VCU is on a tight budget," said Ms. Vaas. "Particularly with the rising vigilante crime rate. Taking that into account, a deal like this makes sense. And as for those tase-nets, whilst GadgetCo's models might be cheaper, they are inferior to our product. We'll throw in a few for free. It's a win-win situation."

"How does the suit compare to Pink's?" John asked.

"Unfortunately, the prototype was mysteriously stolen," said Ms. Vaas. "The weapon building capabilities it has are not present in this model. Steve is still working out some bugs with those."

John swallowed. Mysteriously stolen. How the heck Rachael had gotten the suit out without her boss twigging it was her, he didn't know. Even if she hadn't decided to wear it for her vigilante escapades, her actions could have got her in mountains of trouble.

"So, some vigilantes might still be strong enough to crack these suits," said Dave. "I've already got overconfident detectives. I don't need them putting themselves in danger just because they suddenly feel invincible."

"There's a built-in safety protocol," said Steve. "When the suit gets in a pickle, or if the user gets injured, or is unconscious, you'll be able to remote control the suit and walk them back to safety."

"And we're to believe only the cops will have access to that?" said Dave. "On the suits you're offering us for free?"

"Of course," Ms. Vaas said with a smile. "There are also protocols in place which make them impossible to hack."

Johansson folded her arms, but before she could say anything, John's phone rang.

Dave rolled his eyes. "Your ring tone is police sirens? Seriously?"

"Yeah, my wife hates it..." John froze. It was the hospital. "I'm sorry, I, ah, have to take this. Hello?" He walked to the other side of the room, listening as his jaw tensed with each passing second. "Yeah, I'll be there in half an hour." He clicked off the call and stared down at the phone screen. The picture of the kids and Rachael, posing in front of the Christmas tree last year, glowed back at him. He ran a thumb over the screen just as it timed out and faded to black. "They, ah, they said there might be complications. I need to go."

"Of course," said Dave, "go."

Ms. Vaas put a hand on his arm. "Detective Mahrone, I heard about what happened to your wife. I hope it's not serious."

John swallowed. "She's in a coma. I really need to go..."

Ms. Vaas handed him a business card. "TechCorp also manufactures quite advanced medical equipment. If anything does go wrong, and you find the government medical treatment lacking, please feel free to give me a call."

18

"Kris, slow down, wait!" Outside the front gates at school, Calvin caught up with her. "Kris, please don't ignore me."

Kris picked her skateboard back up. She had been about to take off, and then Calvin would have had no chance of catching her up. "Sorry, I wasn't," she said, lamely.

As confused as she was about Calvin, ignoring him for the whole day had been entirely unintentional. Kris had barely been able to concentrate on schoolwork, even though that wasn't so big of a deal. She'd been replaying the fight with Shift in her head.

Calvin gulped a couple of deep breaths. "Oh, good. Listen, I wanted to talk to you. I... I have a confession to make."

"I actually haven't been very nice to you. You know how I told you I had superpowers? And that my parents are Rick and Nim? Well, I kind of told them about making friends with you and who your dad was. And they asked me if I found out anything about what the VCU were up to, to let them know. And I kind of agreed. But I just want you to know I wasn't using you. I really did want to hang out with someone normal. I'm sorry. I was just doing what I thought I had to protect my family but... well, someone pointed out to me I might not have been being that nice." He chewed his lip and looked at his feet. "It wasn't that I didn't want to hang out with you. It just worked out to be useful. But I know I shouldn't have done it.

I'm not going to tell them anything else or ply you or your dad for information. Just, please don't be mad at me."

"I'm not."

"Really?"

Kris shrugged. "Yeah, I guess." The words had been out of her mouth before she'd thought about it. Calvin had had no reason to tell her. It was Pink who had confronted him, not her. For the briefest of seconds, Kris wished she could tell him she was Pink Punch. It would make things so much easier. "I guess I'm having trouble making friends at the moment too. So, I understand."

Calvin grinned at her. "Yeah?"

"Don't give me that face."

"What face?" His blonde locks didn't help. Too bad they were hidden under that hood when he was Zero K.

Kris rolled her eyes. "Look, I'm going to the skatepark. Why don't you come, and I can teach you a few things?"

"Teach me? Kris, I already know how to skateboard."

Kris raised an eyebrow.

* * *

The clack of rolling skateboard wheels on concrete and wood scraping metal was strangely absent as Kris and Calvin approached the skate park. They arrived to find most of the kids standing off to the side on the grass, fidgeting nervously. A grumbling roar echoed off the concrete surface, and the ground shook. Teeth stood at the edge of the park, and he wanted on. At least he was making an effort to clear the other kids off first. Otherwise, he would have surely crushed them.

Kris stiffened. "Calvin, we need to call the cops."

"Kris, come on, I thought better of you. I'm sure the big guy just wants to skate. I don't know how he's going to and if it's safe for anyone else to be on there. But just because he has big ugly superpowers…"

"Calvin, that's Butch."

"Your friend?"

"Not anymore. He killed a cop. Dad told me."

Calvin put a hand on his sleeve, ready to reef it up.

Kris grabbed his arm. "Calvin!"

"I don't have time to change into my outfit. I've already told you my identify right? Some things are more important."

"No, not that. You'll just make him angry. If he wanted to chomp kids, he would've done it already. I'm going to go talk to him."

"Talk? Kris, he'll hurt you."

"So, back me up." Pink Punch and Zero K together would be able to subdue Butch. But despite how blasé Calvin was about his own powers, it would be better if neither of them revealed them.

"Hey, Butch. How do you plan on skating without breaking anything?"

The big shark turned to her with his toothy grin. "Kris, I was wondering when you'd show your face again. But I'm not particularly impressed with the protector you brought this time."

Calvin bristled beside her. "Hey!"

Kris held Calvin back with a hand to his chest. "Come on, Butch. That night you called me here, you know you were being a jerk. But I'll forgive you. Turning into… that, must've freaked you out a bit. I just wanted to check out your new board."

Butch held up a slab of wood the size of a small surfboard. Someone had made a decent attempt to attach oversized trucks like a regular skateboard. The wheels were the size of a child's trike. "Not too many of these around, you know. Dad knows a guy who does 'em." The board had a picture of a shark, mouth open, flecks of blood from its last meal exploding outwards.

Kris swallowed. "Print's a bit tacky."

"You calling the cops?!" Butch roared.

Calvin lowered his phone. He had not been too subtle about dialing. "Nope. Just my parents."

"Well, you can scram. Along with the rest of you!" Butch roared at the rest of the kids who were trying to sneak back on the far end of the skate park. A grouchy but not immediately violent mutant didn't scare Northberg's teenagers as much as it did their parents. Still, they weren't stupid enough to ignore a direct threat. Most of them scattered. "Go on! Get!" he snarled at some of the older ones who had stopped once they'd reached the grass. "I need all this space. Unless you want to get chomped."

Kris moved herself around in front of Butch again, careful to keep her distance. "Come on, Butch. There's no need for that. Everyone gets to have a go."

Calvin placed himself subtly in front of Kris. "Unless you want to be a big baby about it. Then I think it's you who needs to clear off."

Butch roared again. "That's it. You, I might put up with," he jabbed a big fat finger at Kris. "But this little punk doesn't tell me what to do!"

Calvin gripped one sleeve. "Yeah, we'll just see about..."

Butch opened his jaws and lunged.

Calvin raised his arms, his hands glowing blue, and ice crystals formed in the air. But he wasn't going to be in time.

Kris leapt between them and executed an upward block even as she willed the nanites to build. All she needed was a sleeve.

The jaws hit her with a jolt. Without the weight of Pink's suit Butch lifted her up like a ragdoll and flung her into the grass.

"Kris!" Calvin's voice cracked.

Kris groaned and rolled herself upright. Her arm was covered in a thin sleeve of pink metal. She shook it. The armour dissolved and a single shark tooth fell into the grass beneath her.

Butch worked his jaw. "What the heck are you packing?"

Most of the kids had scattered for real this time, back to the edge of the road, accurately estimating the safe distance from this particular superfight. They were too far away to notice the flash of pink.

"Don't. Bite. Girls!" Calvin screamed, as he hurled a wad of ice crystals with each word. They hit Butch's feet, and ice stalagmites grew up around his legs.

Butch roared and tugged, but he couldn't free himself. He snapped his jaws in frustration. "So, this is your boyfriend now? At least I know where you've been all week. So much for your real friends."

Kris rushed back to Calvin's side, and they both stood barely out of snapping range, much to Butch's frustration. "You were never my friend, Butch. All you wanted to do was ask stuff about the cops. And you always got way too snarky whenever I talked to anyone else. Seriously, even girls. But you know what, seeing as we were kinda close for a bit, I'll tell you one thing about the cops. They're going to come here, and they're going to arrest you. And I don't think they're going to be too happy about what you did to their friend."

Butch stopped snapping and glared at her. "They'll put me in the clinic. They'll take away my powers!"

Sirens grew in the distance. One of the kids must have called them.

Calvin tugged his sleeves back down. "Tough. You know, normally I might think about letting you go. But you can't go around killing people, and that includes cops. You'll give us all a bad name. So sorry. I really don't think they're going to be too happy." He built another blast of ice and flung it in Butch's face. It encased his jaws and head. He overbalanced and his nose plonked into the grass.

Kris watched him long enough to determine he wasn't suffocating. His gills were flapping in a rush, so he must be okay. "We should go before they get here and start asking where all that ice came from."

"Yeah," said Calvin. "By the way, how is your arm is still attached to you?"

"He didn't actually bite me. Just hit me with his big nose. Lucky huh?"

Calvin's eyes narrowed. "Yeah. Lucky."

They jogged off, past where the other kids had gathered at a safe distance, and only slowed when they reached the nearby corner shops. Calvin grabbed her arm. "Are you sure you're okay?"

"I'm fine." Kris snatched it back, putting a hand over Pink's cuff.

"I still don't see how you…"

Kris' phone rang and she pulled it out, holding up a hand to tell Calvin to be quiet. "Hello?"

Calvin stopped talking, but he folded his arms and glared at her.

"Kris, what took you so long to answer, where are you?" Her father's voice was flustered.

"The skate park…" Kris began. She winced. He could've been with the cops who had just arrived on the scene. "But I'm okay. I didn't go anywhere near…"

"That's okay, sweetheart. Can you just come home now? I want to talk to you and Tommy."

"Sure, I'll be fifteen minutes."

"Okay, I'll, ah, I love you, sweetie. See you soon."

Kris frowned down at the phone. "Dad sounds weird."

"Is your mum okay?" asked Calvin. If anything, at least the call had served to distract him from his previous line of questioning.

Oh no. Mum. "I don't know," Kris gulped. "Dad said he wants me to come home so he can talk to me and Tommy."

"Oh." Calvin rubbed at his arm. "I guess he's still mad at me."

"Yeah, better wait until… well, he's pretty stressed at the moment.

Maybe you can come over when you can meet Mum, when she's back at home." Assuming she decided to move back in. She had to.

A grin tugged at Calvin's lips. "So, I am invited, you know, at some stage? Sweet."

"Maybe." Kris gave him a quick punch in the shoulder. "I need to go."

* * *

Kris skateboarded home by the quickest route, cutting through the deserted parking lot where she'd first found Stan. At least she'd made up with Calvin. But what was she supposed to do about Zero K? He probably though Pink had been a jerk to him. And on top of which, she couldn't even remember saving him.

Not that he could think much of her now anyway. Pink Punch, suddenly too scared of getting killed in the line of duty to fight. Mum wouldn't have been scared. She was definitely better suited to being a superhero.

Kris pulled open the front door and tossed her skateboard under the stairs. Dad and Tommy were sitting in the living room. Tommy was sniffing, his eyes red. Dad had an arm around his shoulder, pulling him into his side.

Kris' chest tightened. "What's happened? Is it Mum?"

"Not exactly," said John, looking up. "I mean, nothing's happened to her. I was going to wait for you, but Tommy was getting worried it was something bad, so I told him."

Tommy sniffed and pulled away from his father. He wiped the back of a hand angrily across his eyes. "I'm fine. Dad just wouldn't tell me right away and I thought..." He sat up a little straighter. "I'm fine."

Kris sat down on the single seater beside them. "So, what's going on?"

John gave Tommy's shoulder one last squeeze, then leaned

forward and drew a deep breath. "Okay. Look, Mum's fine, for now. But I spoke with her doctor. First he'd told me she was going to wake up and make a full recovery, now he's telling me there might be complications."

"Like what?"

John ran a hand through his hair. "He wasn't specific. He just said it might be more difficult for her to wake up than they first thought." He forced a smile. "I don't want you kids to worry; I just want to be honest with you. Nothing's definitely wrong, it's just..."

"It's just there might be something wrong," Kris finished for him. "But she's still going to wake up, right?"

John stared at the floor. His twisted his wedding ring around his finger a few times before he finally replied. "Yeah, sweetheart. She's going to wake up. She has to."

John's phone rang. He cursed softly. "Sorry, kids, it's work." He went into the front hall to take the call.

Tommy's gaze followed his father, then fell on Kris. "I'm going to go play some video games," he blurted out. He rushed out of the living room and upstairs.

John returned, looked about, and patted his pockets. "Kris, I'm sorry, I have to go. Where are my keys?" He spotted them on the dining room table and scooped them up. "There should still be fried rice in the fridge, you know how to use the microwave..."

"Dad," Kris grabbed at his sleeve. "Is there something else going on with Mum? You can tell me, even if you don't want to upset Tommy."

John aborted the escape attempt, and his shoulders slumped. "Kris, I'm just worried about her head. They're certain there was some damage now, but the brain's 'funny' as our doctor puts it. It could affect nothing at all, or anything. She was always so sharp and smart, and, I mean, she worked for TechCorp. She was their chief engineer! If she lost any of that, if she realised, it'd upset her so much." John cleared his throat and blinked. Then he reached out and ruffled Kris' hair. "But that's not going to happen; she's tougher than that. You don't need to worry."

"Dad, how can I not worry when you..."

John's phone started wailing again. "Damn it. I really have to go."

Kris guts knotted again. "What's happened?" If it was about Butch, she wanted to know. If he blurted something about her confronting him - heck, she'd basically stuck her hand in his mouth - her father would never let her out of the house again.

John paused. He wasn't fighting with his inner demons now, but with protocol. "You know where Rick Richardson and his wife have that great big house? The bloody expensive one that practically hangs off the cliff face? Well, it sounds like someone took a crack at blowing it up. Vigilantes no doubt. I guess Rick finally got involved with the wrong ones. Whoever it is is still at it."

"What do you mean still at it? What did they do? Is anyone hurt?"

"I can't tell you anymore; I've got to go. Stay inside. I'm serious." John stomped out toward the door. "Bloody Rick, I knew he was up to something." The front door slammed.

It took every ounce of Kris' willpower to stay put, at least until she heard Dad's Commodore start up. The wail of sirens sliced the air, and she waited a few seconds more, until they started to move away. She grabbed her skateboard and rushed for the door. She'd call Stan and meet him on the way.

Tommy stood at the bottom of the stairs. "Kris, where are you going?"

"Just out to the shed. Are you okay?"

"Yes!" Tommy snapped and rubbed at his eyes.

Kris winced. "Tommy, did you hear what Dad said to me? I'm sure Mum will be okay."

"Yeah, but that's not why I'm, ugh!" Tommy stomped his foot

on the bottom stair. "Kris, you're not going to the shed with your skateboard. I know you've been sneaking out at night, all right?"

Kris' stomach lurched. "I don't know what you're talking about."

"Yes, you do! You think I'm an idiot because I sit on my computer all day. But that doesn't mean I don't notice things. You've been going out at night, and it's too dangerous. Mum's already in hospital, Dad's hardly ever home because he's out doing dangerous police work, and now you? Are you sneaking out to see some boy, or something?"

"Seriously? Why do you immediately assume I'm out to see a boy? Girls have other priorities, you know."

Tommy smirked. "So, you are sneaking out. Just not for boys."

Kris rolled her eyes. "Okay, fine, I've been going to the skate park."

"Well, you can't. It's too dangerous. And I'll tell Dad."

"Tommy, you can't do that!"

"I don't want anything to happen to you. I can't do anything about Dad."

Kris' shoulders slumped. This wasn't her little brother just being a pain and trying to dob her in. "Tommy, I won't get hurt, I promise. I've got… protection."

Tommy squinted.

Kris groaned. "Not like that. I mean…"

"What if some villain finds you and hurts you? Like they hurt Dad's friend at work?"

Officer Douglas' mangled body flashed across Kris' vision again. "Yeah, believe me I get it, it's dangerous," she said, throat dry. "But what if I could prove to you I'd be safe?"

Tommy eyed her suspiciously, arms still crossed. "Go on."

Kris put her hands on his shoulders. "Can you keep a secret, little brother?"

Tommy snorted. "I don't talk to anyone in this house unless Mum threatens to blow up my computer."

"All right." Kris stepped back. "You tell Dad, and I'll break your computer myself, got it?"

Tommy chewed his lip. "Okay. Tell me."

Kris put her hand on her wrist, drew in a deep breath, and activated Pink Punch's armour. The suit enveloped her body.

Tommy jaw swung open. He looked her up and down, then gulped and took a step back. "You're Pink Punch. Since when?"

"Since Mum went into a coma. She took this suit from TechCorp."

"Wait, Mum was Pink Punch?"

"Yup. That's why she moved out. Dad knew. I don't think he made her leave; I think they just decided it was safer for us that way."

Tommy stared some more, then he threw his arms wide. "That's why she moved out? That makes so much sense now. Why didn't they just tell us?"

Kris mirrored her brother's movement. "I know, right?" Her metal clad hand hit the fan. The blade bent and continued to wobble. "Oops."

"Can you show me how she makes weapons?"

"Tommy, this isn't a game. Mum was looking into some very serious stuff with TechCorp. That's why she got hurt. And they could be trying to hurt my friends now. That's what Dad's call was about. I have to go."

"He'll kill you, you know."

"Yeah, but my friends might be killed for real. This is my job now, and..." Kris looked down at Pink's hands. She'd put on the suit, decided to help, without a second thought. She clenched her fists, then looked up to meet her little brother's gaze. "Tommy, I'm Pink Punch now. I have to go."

Tommy nodded, then reached out and squeezed her arm. "So go help them. Don't worry, big sis, I've got your back.

19

Calvin cursed as the board scooted out from underneath him. He landed on his feet and stumbled on the sidewalk, then looked around to see if anyone had seen him stack it. He'd been thinking too hard to concentrate on his balance. He was distracted.

Kris shouldn't have pushed him out of the way like that. She could have been hurt! He had superpowers, he could deal with it. But Kris hadn't been hurt. And Teeth hadn't just nose-butted her out of the way as she'd protested; Calvin had clearly heard the crunch of his jaws on her arm. But it had been the clang of metal, not the crunch of bone, and Kris had been left without a scratch. Calvin had barely seen the sliver of pink metal shimmer in the sunlight before it dissolved to grey dust.

Kris Mahrone was Pink Punch. And the thought made Calvin grin, because she had no clue he knew. She'd let him tell her he was Zero K but had said not a word about her own secret endeavors. Of course, she'd been doing the superhero stuff longer than he had. She would never make such a rookie error.

Calvin picked up his board and started to climb the road that wound its way up to the expensive houses on the hill overlooking the bay. He ran the thought over in his mind again: Kris was Pink Punch. He was so glad he hadn't properly ticked her off. Kris was awesome. He had to find some way to let her know he knew her secret. He'd been such an idiot. First telling her he'd had powers straight off the bat. And then using her friendship, a friendship that was a new concept to him, valuable, and something he had truly been excited about. No wonder Pink Punch had laid into him.

A crack rent the air. A stream of smoke rose from up the hill, right near the Richardson's mansion. Calvin groaned. "What have you done now, Max?"

There was a boom and a pressure wave rumbled down the hillside, blowing back Calvin's hair and shattering some windows in a nearby house. A bolt of lightning shot into the air, followed almost immediately be a crack of thunder.

That wasn't any of Max's misadventures. Calvin ducked behind the wall enclosing the nearest house. He glanced about furtively. Then he stripped off his long-sleeved shirt and dug in his bag for his sleeveless hoody. He grabbed out his shades, specially designed by Pink Punch so that he could see in all light conditions. He paused. When had Kris got the skills to make these? She certainly didn't come across as some kind of science nerd. But right now, he had far more pressing concerns.

Calvin jogged up to the mansion, arms tingling as his powers tensed in response to the adrenaline in his veins. There was a hole the size of a car in their front door, splintered mahogany and crumbling concrete dripping from the edges. The air crackled with electricity and storm clouds brewed overhead.

Calvin dashed upstairs to find Nim facing off against two villains. She stood in the center of the vast living area, her arms spread wide as faint tendrils of electricity crackled around her. Rick and X were behind her, but they were letting Nim tackle the situation. Their powers were probably not going to help.

Soundwave stood across from Nim. Her legs were apart, fists bunched, her ragged red hair trailing behind her. The spikes and plates that covered her body vibrated with a low hum.

The second villain was a bulky young man Calvin didn't recognise. He wore a trench coat with sleeves that ended at thick metal manacles that bound his wrists. "Aw, that's cute," he said. "I can do that too." He flexed his fingers and a big fat ball of electricity appeared in his hands.

Nim smiled faintly. "Oh good. You brought more for me to play with."

Calvin rushed to Nim's side and fully activated his powers. "I can take Soundwave if you want the electricity guy. I'm ready for her this time, I promise."

A flash of orange shot into the living room. Calvin felt the telltale rise in air temperature that clashed against his own powers. Pyro emerged from the blur and dropped the heat, just a little. On more than one occasion Rick had made it quite clear he did not want any fires spontaneously starting inside. "I usually like an even fight but break into our house and I'm willing to make an exception."

"Oh, we'll be even." Shift materialised behind Pyro and clapped a hand heavily on his shoulder. They both disappeared.

"All right, Zero," said Nim. "Take Soundwave but be careful. X, Rick, get out of here and make sure everyone else is clear."

"I can help..." X said.

Nimbus just looked at her.

X's face blanked for a split second. "You're right, I'll probably die. I'll look out for Rick."

Calvin wasn't sure if X had actually seen the probability of her getting hurt, or if she was just being sarcastic. Sometimes it was hard to tell.

Rick rolled his eyes and dragged X out by the hand.

"So, you think you can take me?" said the big man. He struck his wrists together and a wave of electricity rolled toward them.

Nim effortlessly took control of the energy and pushed it aside. "You were saying?"

Soundwave let out a short laugh. "Well done, Thunderclap. You picked the one who can control the element your gear runs off."

"Shut up! Where's Pink Punch? I know she's been hanging out with you guys."

Calvin's guts clenched, his fists tensed, and a flush of heat rose inside him. "What do you want with her?"

"Just give her to me." Thunderclap generated a ball of electricity, this time pulling it from one of his wrist cannons and rolling it in his hands before he tossed it. It shot over Nim's shoulder and smashed a hole clean through the wall.

Soundwave slammed both fists into the floor. The spikes on her arms rattled and blasted a wall of sound into the surrounding infrastructure. The house rumbled and groaned, and a crack appeared in the floor. Calvin lost his balance. The roof cracked and splintered down on the mansion's topmost floor.

* * *

X and Rick made it downstairs just as Soundwave's pressure wave tore through the house. X froze, then tugged Rick's arm. "Here."

Rick let her lead him to the doorframe that linked the entrance hall and the stairwell, and they pressed against its side. Rick wrapped his arms around her. He trusted X's instincts, but he could sense the low-level fear, unreadable from her usual blank expression to anyone else, emanating from her.

The splinter and crack of concrete and timber came from overhead. A beam tilted down and lodged into the floor of the entrance hall as the top floor collapsed. But the doorframe stood firm. X tugged at his arm and Rick let her lead him outside.

X's fingers dug into Rick's arm. "Pyro. We need to find him." Flames shot up into the air from down the street. X tugged Rick toward them.

This time, Rick resisted her pull. "We need to be careful, X."

"I'll know if something is going to go wrong."

"You can't predict everything. Just slow down. Pyro can look after himself." Rick wasn't going to let X put herself in danger. She might have been able to predict when things were going to go wrong, but in some situations that made her even more bold.

They'd tried to put X in a normal school when she'd first come to live with them, but it hadn't worked out. Not that that was abnormal for kids with powers; Rick's own school years hadn't been that great. He was already the sensitive kid. And then the Fallout had given him his powers. Suddenly he'd had everyone else's emotions to deal with as well. Coupled with his mother's death on that same night, with everyone's emotions pressing in on him, fighting his for dominance like they had more of a right than his own grief and confusion to be there. It had been too much. Up until the day he'd lost control and let those pent-up emotions explode out over his classmates, giving them an intense, concentrated lesson in what he had to put up with every day. His entire class had needed counseling. The bullying stopped, not because they understood, but because now they feared him. It had hung in the air of the school corridors like a thick fog. Since then, Rick had learned to shut that particular aspect of his powers off so he didn't hurt anyone else.

X's school experience hadn't been nearly so bad. She'd simply found it boring. She could predict all the answers and was better at teaching herself. She hadn't had much trouble with bullies, not after the first one attempted to harass her, and she told him if he did what he had in mind he'd just trip over and snap an ankle.

It had been impossible to convince the school that the fact that X's powers had predicted the outcome did not mean they had directly caused it.

"This fight is going to be dangerous," X said. Then added when Rick frowned: "For Pyro. I might be able to help him."

"All right. But we keep our distance. Understood?"

X nodded.

Pyro was at the bottom of the street, hovering about three feet off the ground. He was alert, but not overly perturbed.

Rick gripped onto X and held her back. "Pyro, where's Shift?"

Rick felt Shift's presence a second before he struck. Shift grabbed Rick's shoulder, yanked him back, and wrapped an arm around his throat. "Hold back, Pyro. Or I tear out his heart."

Shift was wiry, and he couldn't have been a great deal physically stronger than Rick. But the wave of anger and broiling hate that emanated from the man sent a shudder through Rick, and he couldn't work up the willpower to tear himself free. He had a splitting headache in an instant. He winced, and mentally cursed his all but useless powers.

"Whoa, hang on," said Pyro. "This is between you and me, Shift."

"Like it was that night? You ganged up on me. You burnt me!"

"That was your own damn fault!"

Rick drew in a breath as he tried to force the other man's emotions out of his head and reassert his own. "I get you're angry at Pyro, Shift. But you need to calm down." He tried to emanate a controlled feeling of calm, but it bounced off Shift's wall of hate like a bullet off a tank.

Shift laughed. "Is that all you've got, empath? At least your mother put up a fight. You must be a real disappointment. Good thing she didn't live long enough to see the useless powers her sniveling brat ended up with."

Rick felt his stomach knot. It was all he could do to stop himself flinging out the guilt and hurt, and the anger over what had been torn away from him, back at Shift. Shift deserved it, but he was just as likely to catch Pyro and X in the wave.

Pyro cupped a ball of flames in his hands, but he didn't throw it. "X?"

X backed away from Shift. Her powers weren't physical either, but at least she could be useful. "I'm thinking!"

"Hey, Pyro? Do you still like playing catch?" Shift asked.

The street disappeared, and Rick found himself a thousand meters up in the air, the lights of Northberg winking up at him. A faint line of smoke wove its way up from the hill, catching in the city lights, and the blue flicker of bolts of electricity flashed below. Then gravity took over. Shift's arms let him go, as did the emotional pressure of his anger, leaving Rick's mind, at the least, free. Shift vanished before the laws of physics took hold of him too.

Rick squeezed his eyes shut. A roar approached, and then warm arms were around him. Not just warm, but hot. "Damn it, Pyro!" Rick grabbed onto the other man when he saw how high they still were. "Turn the heat down!"

"I thought it was down." Pyro's body temperature dropped a few degrees, but at least it was now bearable, as opposed to being carried by an open oven. "This is why I can't have a girlfriend."

"Just get me down, you stupid..." Rick winced. "Sorry. Shift is really angry with you. I guess it rubbed off. I should've been able to help but all I've done is get in the way."

"He dropped you from a thousand feet. It's fine." Pyro paused briefly. "Your powers aren't useless, you know. Frost was never anything but proud of you, and she'd be even prouder with everything you've done for the superhero community since she's been gone."

"Yeah, I know. I'm the perfect poster boy for the charming, harmless superhero. Thanks. But I don't need a pep talk."

Pyro carried Rick back down to the ground. A few meters up, he let Rick slip out of his grip, feet first.

Rick crashed to his knees as a wave of terror and pain hit him. He gasped and wrapped his arms around his chest. He knew the emotional signature, though he had never felt such a strong jolt of fear from Pyro before. Rick fought back the nausea and forced himself to look over his shoulder.

Shift had phased onto Pyro's back and ridden him the last few feet to the ground. He'd also phased his fist right through Pyro and out the front of the man's orange clad chest.

"I figured you'd have to cool down the furnace to grab your buddy," Shift said. He faded and pulled his arm back out, then re-solidified. "You won't be sending me reeling through time this time round." Pyro fell to his knees, Shift still clutching his shoulder. "Bye, Pyro." Shift put a boot to the man's back and pushed him over. Then he phased out.

"Pyro!" X's wave of grief hit Rick like a punch to the gut.

Rick felt the exact moment Pyro died. The man's soul leaving his mortal body, carrying every emotion and thought that had defined him, hit Rick like a sledgehammer. It was too much for the empath to take. He passed out.

* * *

Nimbus floated above Thunderclap as he stood atop the most intact portion of their roof. She couldn't help the faint smile that played at her lips as she parried his attacks again and again. The man was getting angrier, but he still couldn't land a hit.

"Not having much luck, are you?"

"Your fancy house is trashed, lady," Thunderclap shot back. "I wouldn't gloat too much."

"But you still haven't found Pink Punch. What do you want with her, anyway?" Maybe it had been a mistake to let Pink into the Broom Closet. No one had dared attack their home up until now. And Rick had certainly ticked off his share of villains. But Rick had insisted. His instincts were almost always right when it came to people, and Nim trusted them. But Pink Punch was a wild card. She had first contacted them a few months ago with her theories. But she'd barely been on the scene for a month before that, so they were hardly going to take her word on TechCorp's plans. They'd asked for more evidence. And, as she apparently had technical skills that were better, or at least safer, than Max's, that she make them some tech to prove she would contribute.

Pink had become irritated at the perceived lack of support, although she'd gone and made the tech anyway. Nim suspected she had simply wanted the funds. She hadn't seemed interested in being a team player, until recently.

But despite all that it seemed Pink Punch had been right about TechCorp. Pyro thought so. And these villains surely wouldn't be so keen to get to her if they didn't want to silence her.

"My orders are to knock her dead," said Thunderclap, convincing Nimbus still further. First Shift, now this upstart. You had to either be pretty powerful, or have a good reason to want another super dead, to go this far. Dealing with the VCU just wasn't worth it otherwise. He flung another bolt of electricity at her.

Nim sighed. This one was not too bright. The electricity swirled around her body, and she calmly flung it back.

Thunderclap staggered as the bolt slammed into his chest. Something had been done to his body to allow him to absorb more electricity, but it was still hurting him, though far less than a normal human. Nim was starting to think his powers were not a result of the Fallout, else the electricity would be as harmless to him as it was her. The powers seemed to come from these cannons grafted to his arms, which were undoubtedly TechCorp. Yet another point for Pink's theories.

Were they playing at modifying humans? Again.

The wail of sirens filled the air.

For once, Nimbus felt relief at the familiar sound. "Sounds like it's time for you to leave."

"The cops? They'll arrest you too."

"This is my home. You're breaking and entering."

Thunderclap shrugged. "Well, Soundwave sure did a lot of breaking. I hope there's nothing down there you don't want the cops to see."

Nim stiffened. Would Soundwave's assault be enough to crack open the Broom Closet? The VCU had waited long enough to catch them out, it didn't matter how little was revealed. They'd take any excuse to make a thorough search.

"Make sure you let Pink know I'm looking for her." Thunderclap sent a blast of electricity into the roofing at his feet. It turned the materials to a powder that engulfed him. Nim blew the dust and debris away with a rush of wind, but Thunderclap was gone.

Nim smoothed down her dress and sent out a feeling of calm. Rick would want to know she was okay. Though she wasn't an empath, because of her connection with Rick, she found that she could usually sense his 'reply.' She felt nothing.

* * *

Calvin picked himself up at the bottom of the ice slide he'd made to carry himself to safety. He'd ended up halfway down the stair-well, near the basement. Above him was clogged with debris. He felt a rush of air and stepped to the side as three slivers of scale shot past him and embedded in the wall. Calvin's arms glowed blue and ice crystals swirled around them. "Where are you?"

Soundwave laughed. "Down here. I've found a really interesting looking door. Wonder what's inside?"

Calvin moved cautiously down the stairs. The floor shook, and he clapped his hands over his ears as a rush of wind slammed him back against the wall. Dirt and mortar rained down. Calvin moved forward again, then dropped as the next pressure wave hit. When he pulled his hands away from the side of his head, his ears rung.

What the hell was Soundwave doing? She'd bring the house down on both their heads.

The front door of the Broom Closet was torn off. The concealed doorway behind the actual closet was no longer concealed. The thick metal was exposed, and the surrounding frame was cracked. It hadn't yet succumbed to Soundwave's attacks, but Calvin wasn't entirely sure if it was built to withstand a battering, or if his foster parents' intent had been that it simply stay hidden.

"Right, this is going to take a bit of effort," said Soundwave. She squeezed her eyes shut in her ugly plated face and strained like she was trying to lift something really heavy. The spikes and plates on her body grew, elongating, perhaps better suited to generate a large wall of sound. Whatever she was doing, it seemed to take tremendous effort. She stopped, panting. "I am seriously going to need a burger after this."

Calvin hit her with an ice blast.

Soundwave roared as the ice encased the lower part of her body. "You little rat!" She lifted an arm and hurled one of the bigger plates like a discus. It embedded itself in the wall above Calvin's head.

Calvin dropped to one knee and continued to blast her with ice. It wasn't enough to block up her feet. He had to get all of her. Every inch of her body was a sharp weapon, and she could fling it at will.

Soundwave was having none of it. She vibrated her plates, and the ice started to crack.

Calvin kept up the stream as long as he could, then drew in a sharp breath and dropped his arms. His powers were fine for short spurts, but whenever he used them for a while, they made the ink stains on his arms ache. His father would have slapped him for calling his art 'ink stains.'

Soundwave blasted spikes in all directions and tore through the ice anchoring her to the floor.

Calvin stood up shakily. He built an ice ball in his hands, but his arms shook. That was all he had in him. But Soundwave didn't know that. He hefted the ice ball to his shoulder and stared her down.

Almost all of Soundwave's spikes were gone, embedded in the walls around them. A few plates hung onto her thick hide like dinner plate sized flakes of dry skin. She looked smaller, minus all that armour. No bigger than Calvin. She panted. It didn't seem she had the energy to regrow any of it.

Calvin faltered, and his ice plinked to the ground.

"Zero!" Nim's voice echoed down the staircase.

Soundwave snarled. She launched herself at a hole in the basement roof, caught its edge on her long nails, then pulled herself out and was gone.

Nim breezed down beside him. "Zero, are you okay?"

"I'm... I'm fine. I just... I think I used up all my ice. I... bit tired."

Nim patted his shoulder. "You'll be fine. Now you know where empty is." Her expression darkened. "We need to find Rick."

"Is he okay?"

"I don't know. But something's wrong."

Nim had blown herself a path through the rubble in the stairwell on the way down, and they easily picked their way over the remainder to the outside. The wail of sirens was on the night air.

"The cops are coming," said Calvin. "What do we do?"

"We find Rick," Nim said firmly. She cupped her hands to her mouth. "Rick!" She waited, then drew in a sharp breath and blinked. "He's down the street. I just felt him."

"Is he hurt?"

Nim squared her shoulders. "No. He's upset. Someone else must be."

They found Rick crouched down in the middle of the road, hugging himself. His shoulders shook. X stood upright beside him, staring blankly. Nim knelt at Rick's side and put an arm around him.

Pyro lay on his back in the road with a smoking black hole in the centre of his chest.

Calvin's stomach caught in his throat. "Pyro?"

20

Stan roared through Northberg's city streets. The lightning arcing into the sky was visible as soon as they left home. It crackled and flashed, shooting up into the clouds, instead of down from them. And all from a single point, atop Fortitude Hill. All of Northberg had to have seen it.

"We're ahead of the police," said Stan. "And your father. That Commodore he has is never going to outrun me, I don't care if they left first."

Kris rolled her eyes. "I don't think Dad's police car is sentient like you."

"Well, the police scanners say they're still a few minutes away. Which is great for everyone; they'll only get in the way."

Stan ripped around the final corner and climbed the winding street. "I just hope we're in time to help..." He cursed and slammed on the brakes. They skidded sideways, tyres squealing, and stopped barely meters from Rick, Nimbus, X, and Zero. And Pyro.

Zero knelt beside Pyro. Pyro's chest was smoking, a big black mark splattered across the bright orange of his suit. He wasn't moving.

Kris climbed out of Stan and swallowed hard. "What happened?"

Zero rose to his feet. He drew in a sharp breath and swiped at his cheek. "Pyro's dead."

X stood beside Zero, still as a statue, her expression blank. Kris wasn't sure she even blinked.

"We were attacked by villains," said Nimbus. "And at least one of them was looking for you." She knelt on the pavement beside Rick, arms around him. Rick was visibly shaking, his face buried against Nim's chest.

"Me?" It was no longer a surprise that some villain wanted her. But they hadn't come after her. They'd come after these guys - she barely knew them! Up the street the mansion was smoking, trashed. And Pyro. Kris' fists tensed at her side as she looked at his lifeless body. "Is Rick okay?"

"He's an empath," said Nim. "One of his oldest friends just died right beside him. He's not going to be much good to anyone for a while and he's the only reason I'm not in your face right now demanding an explanation."

"Nimbus, I'm not even sure why they're after me. How is this my fault?"

Nim squeezed Rick a little tighter. "Can you keep the emotion down, please?"

"But you just..." Kris wanted to defend herself, but she didn't want to hurt Rick. So, she just swallowed the lump in her throat, and forced her reaction back deep down inside her.

Nimbus fought to keep her own voice steady. "They destroyed our house. Barely days after we let you in. And Thunderclap asked for you, specifically."

Kris' guts tightened. "Wait, Thunderclap? Big guy in a trench coat with electrical powers?" The guy who'd put her mother in hospital. "He should be dead. I'm sorry. I had no idea this was going to happen. I didn't even think they'd want me dead until a few days ago, and now..."

"Look, I know this isn't your fault. It's just, if we hadn't let you in… But maybe this isn't just about you. Maybe they want us out of the way for a reason."

Zero cleared his throat. "Um, Nim? We have to go. The cops…"

"I'm not leaving Rick."

"Soundwave cracked open the Broom Closet. I don't know how bad. When the cops see it…"

"I'm staying with Rick."

"What about X?" Zero poked her shoulder. The girl didn't respond. "She's probably still trying to calculate how to save Pyro, even though she knows she can't. You want her to get arrested too?"

"Nimbus," said Kris, "if you want to stay, Stan and I can get Zero K and X out of here."

"No," said Nim. "Your fault or not, I still barely know you. And I'm not trusting you with the kids. I'd rather the cops."

"I trust her," said Zero.

Nim sighed. "Zero, I know you look up to her, but that doesn't mean…"

"I know who she is! The real her, under that suit. So, I know I can trust her. Please, Nim, trust me on this."

Kris' heart rate quickened. "No, you don't…"

Zero smiled faintly, the expression sadder than his usual cheeky grin. "And she knows who I am." He stepped over to X and scooped the girl up in his arms. "It'll be fine, I promise."

How the hell did Calvin know? Maybe he was making it up to get Nimbus to cooperate.

Calvin put X in Stan's back seat. "Come on, Pink. Before your, er, detective buddy is all over this place."

Detective buddy. Her father. Calvin knew. He wasn't playing games.

"All right, go," said Nimbus. "I'll stall the cops. And Pink? Zero better be right about you, or I'll come after you myself."

Kris nodded dumbly and climbed into Stan. "Zero… Calvin… I

don't know where to take you guys. I guess you know where I live but I can't take you there. Dad will kill me. And I don't know how I'd explain..."

"I've already thought of that," Stan cut in. "I'll take you to where your mother was staying. It's about time I showed it to you anyway."

They passed four police vehicles on the way down the hill. Stan swerved to the side to avoid one coming right at them, but they didn't stop.

"He's got camouflage," said Kris, when Calvin looked momentarily startled. She squared her shoulders. "All right, spill, how do you know who I am?"

Calvin leaned against passenger window, his chin resting on one hand. He gave a half-hearted shrug but didn't turn to face her.

"I'm sorry about Pyro."

"Shift must've got him," said Calvin quietly. "He was all..." He gestured around his chest area, and then cleared his throat. "Well, he would've died quickly anyway."

"I'm sorry."

"It's not your fault. I don't think you were the only reason those villains were there. We harass them all enough, some of them were bound to come for payback sooner or later. Nim's just upset about Pyro. And Rick."

"Will Rick be okay?"

"I hope so."

Kris nodded to the back of the car. "What about X?"

Calvin smiled faintly. "X will be fine; she's tough. She's just stuck in her calculating mode. That happens sometimes when she tries to predict something that's impossible. You know, like how to save someone who's already dead." His next words came out shaky. "But once she snaps out of it, she'll be fine. She'll miss Pyro though."

"So, how'd you figure it out? I never did anything stupid like tell someone I'd just met I had superpowers."

"Well, you did decide to stop Butch chomping you with Pink's armour."

Kris groaned. "You saw that? It was an accident."

"Accident? He could've torn your arm off. You really scared me, you know, jumping in front of me like that. I didn't know what you were thinking. You're lucky none of the other kids saw, seeing as you seem intent on keeping it to yourself."

"It wasn't that I didn't trust you..."

"You shouldn't have. We barely know each other."

"But you trust me."

Calvin pulled off his shades and turned them over in his hands. "I like you." He cleared his throat. "You know, you're a good friend. I trust Pink Punch. She, you, saved my life."

"That was my mum. Calvin, I've only been wearing this suit for like, a week."

Calvin's jaw dropped. "Wait, what? But then how are you so good at all the superhero stuff?"

* * *

Kris fidgeted in her seat as they approached the dilapidated warehouse. "Mum lived here?"

"It was one of TechCorp's old storage warehouses. This section of the port hasn't been used much recently." There was no one around. Many of the nearby buildings were in poor condition. Most had broken windows, and loose iron sheeting. A sheet banged in the night breeze, the only sound above the distant hum of traffic and far away clunks of ships and rigging from the nearby active port.

Stan activated a roller-door that creaked and groaned as it was raised and drove inside. Dim lights flicked on as he entered. The open space within was littered with junk, mostly scrap metal. There were worktables set up with equipment. A welder off to the side. And a Toughbook type laptop open on one of the work benches.

There was a boxing bag and mats set up in one corner. On one table sat a helmet like Pink's, with the face shield off.

When her mother had said she was staying somewhere she didn't want the kids to see, Kris had assumed it was a shady neighbourhood. But this place would raise too many questions. Mum had always been a tinkerer, but she wasn't crazy enough to devout her entire living space to the endeavor. Neither could she have passed this place off as the only thing she could afford and that was available.

What she was working on here, perhaps it could be explained away as the 'engineering consultancy' she proclaimed she'd been working on. Except it was far too hands-on for that. It was a vigilante lair, as her father would have called it. Had she invited her kids here, it likely wouldn't have taken them long, especially Tommy with his overactive imagination, to connect the dots. This was clearly Pink Punch's lair.

"Her sleeping quarters are in the leading hand's office," said Stan. He flashed his lights into the corner of the building, at an enclosed office space within the warehouse. "You can put X there."

Calvin lifted her out of the vehicle and carried her over.

Kris stayed in the main area, her eyes roving over what her mother had been working on. She'd been busy. Kris picked up the helmet on the bench and turned it over in her hands. Was this a newer helmet for Pink? A prototype? Or simply a model? Unlike the current helmet, the jawline was fully encased in metal.

Calvin stepped up beside her. "X is still out of it. She'll be fine though, once she's finished processing. So, this is all your mum's stuff?"

Kris replaced the helmet. "Yeah, I guess."

Calvin was quiet for a long moment. "This must've been where your mum was living when she rescued me. I suppose that's why she gave me to Rick and Nim." Calvin moved around in front of her and sat up on the work bench in one of the relatively clear spaces, next to the laptop. He'd already taken off his shades, but now he flipped down his hood. "Guess I don't need these anymore. Seeing as I told Kris Mahrone who I am."

Kris paused, and then powered down Pink's suit.

Calvin smiled briefly, then looked down at his hands. "You know, my father wouldn't even let me out of the house, because he thought I'd get hurt. Or that I'd just hang out with normal kids, and apparently, they were weak and would just make me worse. I never had any actual powers until he gave them to me."

"Your father gave you superpowers? I mean, like, you didn't just get them from him, or the Fallout?"

"His power was that he produced this ink; he could give people powers with it. Hence the tattoo parlor. He said it wasn't an exact science, more like an art. Sometimes he got it wrong. One of his clients wasn't too happy with what he got; I think he started the fire your mother saved me from. My father died in it. I can't say I was that upset, apart from then being without a home."

He drew in a breath and ran a hand over the tats on his arm. And froze, staring at them for a long moment. The only sound was the clank of distant machinery, and the plink of Stan's cooling engine. Eventually, he spoke again, and, at first, it seemed a struggle for him to get the words out. "Right before the tattoo parlor was destroyed, my father gave me these. I guess he eventually decided I needed a power to defend myself, and I obviously wasn't developing any. So, one night he said he wanted to try something. And I let him strap me down to the chair. And he gave me these. I asked him to stop, that I didn't need powers, that it was hurting. He didn't listen. He just said I needed to suck it up and stop being a wuss. I figure he probably meant well. But I must've passed out at some stage, because then I woke up and the place was trashed and burning, and you were there..."

"Only I guess it wasn't you. I still have nightmares sometimes. About needles. For some reason, fire doesn't really bother me."

Kris sat beside him on the bench. She hesitated briefly, then put a hand on his arm. "Why are you telling me this?"

"I'm not entirely sure." Calvin folded his arms over his chest, hugging himself. "You know, you're the first person I've told besides Rick? Rick's easy to talk to about those sorts of things. He's about the most opposite of my dad. He doesn't think expressing an emotion makes you a wuss. I guess he can sense them even if you're hiding them anyway. As for you..." Calvin shrugged. And then he smiled at her. "I guess it's just nice to finally have a normal friend."

* * *

John slammed the door to his car. Rick caused enough trouble with the media as it was. Whatever this incident was, he'd make a big deal about it and how he, the poor guy with powers, was being discriminated against. It was ridiculous. Discrimination certainly hadn't stopped him getting a house bigger than John had ever had, even with his wife's previous salary. Maybe this would make Rick think twice about whatever vigilante activity he was involved with.

There were a number of emergency vehicles already on the scene, and with the winding road crammed onto the precarious hillside amongst oversized houses, John had to walk a short distance to get up to Rick and Nimbus' place.

It was worse than he'd expected. The big house was smoking, half of the roof caved in. John winced and felt a faint twinge in his guts at his previous thought that Rick deserved whatever had befallen him.

Dave was at the back of an ambulance, speaking with a paramedic. That brought John to a halt. The Chief was here. "Dave, what's happened?"

Dave's expression was grim. "Pyromaniac's dead."

John's jaw dropped. "Pyro? You're sure?" He'd been around forever. Though they'd certainly had their differences, John had assumed he'd always be there with his terrible sense of humour. As well as the hint of grief he felt at the man's passing, this was Pyro. The man was a ball of flame. A weapon. He couldn't be easy to kill.

"He's got a great big hole in his chest. I'm no expert, but I'm pretty sure that's fatal." Dave swallowed. "First Officer Douglas, now this. It's been years since a super was killed in a fight, John. I thought the VCU had things under control, or at least the vigilantes were behaving themselves. I'm really worried. We've got to get on top of this."

"We'll figure it out."

"Jo's inside the house, downstairs. There's something there you should see."

John made his way inside, carefully stepping around bits of rubble. Rick had never been foolish enough to let him in, so it took him a few moments to find his way down into the basement, where Detective Johansson was waiting.

There wasn't much of the basement remaining, and the creaking roof made John nervous. The walls and washing machine were littered with spikes, some embedded a good few inches in. But it wasn't these his partner seemed interested in. Johansson chewed her lip, arms folded, cautiously eying a jagged tear in the wall beside the washing machine.

"You'll like this, John," she said. "You always thought Rick was up to something. Well, I can bet you it's right behind that door."

The jagged tear in the wall revealed a thick metal door, hidden at what would have been the back of a deep closet. It was dented in the center, but still shut fast.

"We can't open it. And Rick and Nimbus sure aren't cooperating."

John's eyes narrowed as he focused on the door, and his heart rate quickened at the prospect of what might lie behind something so obviously intended to keep people out. "They aren't, are they? Well, maybe we can convince them to talk. They cannot explain this away."

"You be gentle with them," Johansson warned. "Rick's pretty upset about Pyro. If there are some villains that have it in for them, perhaps it would be a better strategy to help them. Then they might be more willing to share what they know. And you know that's technically part of our job anyway - to help them - they're the victims here, don't forget that."

"Maybe this is the wakeup call they need, and I'll be able to shake some answers out of them." John stomped back up the stairs.

"Damn it, John, wait."

John found Nimbus and Rick in the custody of a couple of officers outside, sitting on the curbing. Nim had an arm around Rick as Rick stared listlessly at the ground, his head in one hand.

"All right, tell me what happened," John demanded.

"Pyro died..." Rick said faintly, but he offered nothing more. His eyes were red.

"Look, something is going on in this city," John said, his voice softening. "And I'm sorry about Pyro. But we have to figure out what, before it gets out of hand."

Nimbus glared up at him. "You think? If you hadn't noticed, half our house is gone."

"Whoever these vigilantes are, they're getting more brazen. If they're targeting you too, you have to know why. We'll be going after whoever did this to you, so if you know anything that would help..."

Nim raised an eyebrow. "Now you want our help? I thought that was considered vigilante activity?"

"No, it would be considered aiding an investigation."

"When it suits you, you label us a nuisance. But now things are getting bad, you want our help. Tell me, do you want me to help you take out these bad guys with a few lightning bolts?"

"Is that what you did? Because I saw lightning coming over here."

"Oh, here we go. If I did, it would've been self-defense. But no, because I used a superpower, it's illegal."

"That's not how it works, it…" John cut himself off with a huff. "All I'm asking you for is information."

"Just tell him what happened, Nim," said Rick. He squeezed her arm without looking up. "They can't arrest us for getting attacked."

Nimbus sighed. "They called themselves Soundwave, Thunderclap… and Shift."

"Shift?" The name sent a chill up John's spine. "I thought he was dead?" If Permafrost had been the polar opposite of Pyro's powers, Shift had been his opposite in temperament. He'd been more than happy to see the Fallout, bringing him many more comrades he envisioned would fight alongside him for his freedom. The last time John had seen him, he'd picked up a cop car and phased it into the side of a building. He'd been going to do the same to a cop next. He would have if Pyro and Permafrost hadn't fought him off.

"No. Pyro took him to hospital. Not that he would have told you lot that. Maybe that wasn't such a good idea on his part. It was Shift who killed him."

John's fists tensed. "He didn't just let him burn? That seems immensely stupid." If all he'd done so far was kill the man who'd been fool enough to save him, the city had gotten off light.

Nimbus paused, mulling over what she was going to say next. John hoped she was seriously considering whether they could trust the VCU. "They could have been working for the Boss, for TechCorp. At least, that's what Pink Punch thought."

"Pink Punch was here? Did she cause any trouble?"

"Not for us. Not directly anyway."

Rachael had never mentioned a thing about being on good terms with Rick or Nimbus. After telling him she was the newest, most garishly dressed vigilante in town, she'd left the house, and whilst they had run into each other both in uniform and out of it, they had argued, but hadn't shared detailed information about their activities. John felt his stomach knot at yet another act of betrayal from his wife. "How long has she been... are you saying you're housing active vigilantes? Is that who's hiding in your basement?"

Nimbus' eyes narrowed. "That's just my broom closet."

"Seriously?" John ran a hand through his hair. "All right, you want to play games? I'm taking you both in for questioning. And that armoured door is enough for a warrant, so don't expect it to hide your 'brooms' forever."

Nim drew her arm tighter around Rick. "Well, look at that. I guess you can arrest us for getting attacked."

21

Kris woke to her phone chirping. She rolled over with a groan and looked at the screen. She didn't have to get up for school for another half hour. She threw the phone on the bed beside her and pulled her covers over her head.

The phone chirped again and then it clicked on all by itself. "Kris, it's Stan. I need to talk to you."

"It's not even six!" Kris threw off her covers and glared at the ceiling. "How'd you get through anyway?"

"Pink got an email late last night from her contact at TechCorp. The one whom Thunderclap said he was coming in his place, that night in the alleyway. I had assumed Steve had pulled his head in after that, before the Boss took it off for him, but perhaps now he feels it's safe to speak with us again. He still works for TechCorp; he could have very useful information for us."

Kris' guts tightened. "Thunderclap is alive, Stan. How do you know it's not another trick?"

"He's asked to meet someplace safe. Plenty of people about, plenty of supers about, in fact. Not a dark alley. That makes me a little more comfortable."

Five minutes later, Kris had slipped into her clothes and was out the front door. She slowed as she approached the driveway and checked her father was not nearby.

"Kris."

"Tommy! Don't sneak up on me like that."

"I practically slammed the front door!" Tommy's eyes narrowed as he looked her up and down. "You're not in your school uniform. Are you doing Pink Punch stuff?"

"Yeah…"

Her brother's face brightened. "Can I come?"

Kris rolled her eyes. Maybe telling her little brother had not been the best idea. "No. You have school." And there was no way she was going to let Tommy help with anything dangerous.

"So do you!"

"Look, you can still help me. If Dad asks, tell him I went to the skatepark early, then I'm going to school. And if anyone at school asks, say I'm off sick."

"Okay, but if they find out…"

"Then I'll just say I skipped school."

Tommy raised an eyebrow. "You'd tell Dad you skipped? You know how he is about rules. Plus, he's a cop."

"He can't arrest me for not going to school." He'd probably be less upset about it than if he found her sneaking out near dark. And it was by far preferable to him finding out she was Pink Punch; he'd freak. He hadn't been able to do anything about Mum, but he could ground his daughter for the rest of her life. "Can you do this for me?"

Tommy's lips pulled into a thin line, and he squinted like he was making a tremendously important and onerous decision. "Okay, big sis," he finally said. "But you owe me big time."

* * *

John woke groggy and with a headache, to the sound of sirens blaring. He threw back his covers, glared at the ceiling, and groaned. He seriously had to change that ring tone. He rolled over and picked up his phone. If it was the Chief, he couldn't complain about his detectives not getting enough sleep if he called so early.

It wasn't the Chief. It was Rachael's doctor. John's heart caught in his throat. "Hello?"

"John, you should probably get here right now, your..."

"What is it? What's happened?" John barked, then he winced. He kept his eyes squeezed shut, heart hammering in his chest. "Sorry."

The doctor waited a moment that felt like an eternity, making sure John was listening. Then: "It's your wife. We're picking up increased brain activity. She's waking up."

John called the school before he drove down so the kids would be waiting for him when he arrived. He desperately wanted to tear down to the hospital right away, but they'd want to see their mother too. When he pulled up Tommy stood at the curb outside the school gate, fidgeting. Kris wasn't there.

John rolled down the window. "Where's your sister? We need to hurry up, I..."

Tommy fumbled with his schoolbag. He looked at the sidewalk, the trees, everywhere but at his father. The signs of guilt were not difficult for the detective to spot.

"She's not here, is she?"

"Um..."

"All right, get in the car." His son climbed in, and they pulled off. "So, if your sister isn't at school, where is she?"

"I don't know!" Tommy exploded without any further prompting. Well, at least if his kids were lying to him, it didn't take much for them to crack. "She said she was going to the skatepark, and then, I don't know."

John scowled. Anger and concern fought somewhere down in his guts. He'd thought his daughter had pulled her head in after he'd caught her out at night. He'd warned them about the rising vigilante activity! Maybe Kris was just being a teenager and had decided school was boring. But it was the skatepark. That was where they'd picked up the shark. At least that meant he wouldn't turn up there. He was currently packed off in the corner of a reinforced cell. The only thing keeping half the force from paying him a visit because of what he'd done to Officer Douglas, was the Chief specifically ordering them not to. John was pretty sure that was because the Chief didn't want the mutant hurting anyone else, rather than the cops hurting him.

"Dad, has something happened to Mum?"

John blinked himself back to reality. "Oh god, Tommy, I'm sorry, no. The doctors said she was waking up. I thought we should all go see her as a family."

Tommy's face lit up. "Yeah?"

John sighed. Pressure was not the way to get answers from his son. "Yeah. Tell you what? I'll give you two a free pass today, all right? Your sister should be here to see Mum, though. You sure you don't know where she is?"

Tommy shook his head.

"Okay. I'll talk to her when she does turn up, but I'm not mad at her. Or you. It's just things are kind of dangerous right now."

Tommy grasped his father's arm. "Dad, she'll be okay. She understands it's dangerous, but she knows how to look out for herself. Trust me."

John swallowed. When had his twelve-year-old son become so mature? Okay, ignoring the fact he'd just tried to lie for his sister. But John needed the encouragement right now. He should have tried to spend more time with his son, whether he could understand the video game obsession or not. Sure, the kid spent most of his time on the computer, but that was no excuse on his father's part.

John put his hand over Tommy's and squeezed it briefly. "I'll text her, tell her to come see Mum. If she's a little late, that's her fault for skipping. And your Mum will be awake anyway..." Despite the apprehension he felt for his daughter, John found himself smiling faintly. Rachael was waking up. Everything was going to be okay.

* * *

When they arrived at the hospital, the doctor was in Rachael's room. The door was partially closed. John ground to a halt, suddenly feeling out of place.

"Come on, Dad." Tommy dragged at his hand and pushed open the door.

Rachael was sitting up in bed. She still had a drip in her arm and dark bags under her eyes, but she was awake. John's shoulders slumped and his vision blurred.

The doctor sat at his wife's bedside. "And you're sure you can't remember anything beyond that?"

"Mum!" Tommy burst from John's side and threw his arms around his mother's neck.

"Tommy!" Rachael grinned and ruffled her son's hair. "I missed you, sweetheart."

"Remarkable," muttered the doctor. He stood to his feet and took John aside.

It was with a slight twinge that John allowed himself to be led away. Rachael's attention was on her son, listening to the impossibly fast string of words pouring out of his mouth. Something about video games, and something he'd programmed at school. John could wait a moment to talk to his wife. "She's okay?" he blurted out.

"More or less," said the doctor. "I'm pretty pleased with her recovery. However, there may be some memory loss."

John's jaw worked for a moment. "She looks fine."

"She's got amnesia. She can't remember what happened to put her in the coma. And I'm still trying to assess exactly how far it extends..."

"So, she doesn't remember what happened to her?" Plenty of

people John had interviewed who'd had violent run ins with vigilantes could not tell him what had happened. The trauma had blacked it out of their mind. The thought that whatever this new Pink Punch had done to Rachael being bad enough to make her blank out the incident caused John's hands to tense at his sides.

"No, she doesn't. But it's not just that. How long have you been married?"

"Huh? Seventeen years."

"Well, then it would seem the amnesia extends back the last seventeen years, at the least."

Seventeen years? John's mind churned. "What, but..." Rachael and Tommy were talking, though Tommy had a faint frown on his face. "But she knows who Tommy is."

"It's not a complete loss of everything over that period of time. Just certain bits of information. When I questioned her about her children, she remembers them. She knows she's an engineer, and that she worked for TechCorp. But she doesn't remember she's unemployed, and..." the doctor squeezed John's shoulder. "I'm sorry, when I asked her about you, she didn't remember you."

John's head spun. The room seemed to tilt around him. "But..."

The doctor gripped his shoulder a little tighter. "Are you okay?"

"No!"

"I meant, are you going to pass out on me?"

"No," John pulled his arm away, and ran a hand through his hair. "How could this happen?"

"Are you up to speaking to her? I only told her your name. Seeing you in person could trigger an entirely different synaptic response."

"Of course I want to talk to her." John moved to step past the doctor.

The doctor grabbed his arm again. "Don't make her uncomfortable. Remember, she may not know you, so don't get close to her like you normally would. Just let her get a good look at you and say hi."

John guts tightened. 'Say hi.' He wanted to do so much more. To take Rachael up in his arms, hold her. He swallowed, and when he spoke, his voice wavered. "Rachael?"

Rachael looked up. "Yes?"

"Do you know who I am?" Rachael squinted, then her face brightened. "You're a cop." She pointed to his belt.

His badge. John had it clipped there. He could feel his stomach sink, and the back of his eyes started to burn.

"Are you here to help me? I already told the doctor; I can't remember what happened. I've got amnesia. It's like half my hard drive has been wiped."

He'd refused to help her before, when she'd chosen to become Pink Punch. Remember him or not, John was going to make it up to her. "Of course I'll help you. I'm going to find out what happened to you, and who's responsible. You can trust me."

"Thanks so much. Not remembering how I got here is so frustrating." Rachael turned to Tommy and smiled. "At least I've remembered all the important bits."

Tommy smiled faintly at his mother, then looked up imploringly at his father. "Dad, aren't you going to tell her?"

Rachael frowned. "Dad?"

"I, um, I'll come back and talk to you shortly... I need to... coffee..." John cleared his throat, then turned on his heel and retreated from the room. He sunk into one of the nearby plastic chairs that sporadically lined the hospital hallways and put his head in his hands.

* * *

The café consisted of a half dozen small tables, interspersed with a few crates and cable spools. A hissing and spitting coffee machine was crammed into a cut-out in the alley wall no bigger than a store-room. Kris, Calvin, and X had reached the café through a winding course of alleyways, too small to fit a vehicle down, and through a short section of what looked like someone's cramped backyard. You couldn't have found the place if you didn't know it was there.

What differed from the average hipster hangout was that ninety percent of the patrons hanging around had powers, some more obviously than others. The more obvious were those in bright getup. There was a young woman with purple hair, and purple Converses. Which wasn't a giveaway in itself except that she had just dumped a third sugar sachet into her coffee, and she hadn't touched any of them. The sachets floated up, opened, and emptied themselves out of their own accord. She sat with a young man all decked out in denim. His left arm from the elbow down was completely made of metal.

"Some of these guys are kinda bright," Kris whispered as they sat down at one of the vacant cable spools.

Calvin smirked at her from beneath his hood. "You're wearing pink, remember?"

Kris turned over her pink-gloved hands and groaned.

"Why'd your Mum pick pink anyway?"

"I honestly have no idea. When she wakes up, I'll ask her."

"He's here," said X. She'd picked up a menu from their table but didn't look up from her inspection of it as she spoke.

A man appeared at the end of the alley, glanced around furtively, then made his way toward them. He was balding, wore glasses, and looked nervous as hell. He slipped onto the modified crate next to Calvin and dumped the folder he carried on the table.

"I take it you're our contact?" Calvin said.

"Yes, my name's Steve," said the man. He drew in a breath, squared his shoulders, and looked Kris right in the eye. "But first things first, who are you?"

Kris stiffened. "Pink Punch. The person you arranged to meet, remember, genius?"

"Yes," said Steve, lowering his voice. "But I know you're not Rachael Mahrone. She's the person I originally arranged to meet with, and now she's in hospital. So, forgive me if I'm a little wary of the, presumably, woman who is now wearing her suit."

This man was supposed to give her answers. Not interrogate her. "You expect me to just tell you my identity? I don't even know you."

"But you knew Rachael?"

Kris chewed her lip. "Yeah. That's why I took her suit after she was caught in the explosion. And I want to figure out why someone had to put her in a coma as much as I'm guessing you do."

Steve's shoulders slumped. His moment of assertiveness seemed to have cost him a great deal of energy. "I'm sorry. I have to be sure you're someone I can trust. But TechCorp does seem a little annoyed at what you've been up to lately, so I guess that speaks for itself."

Kris snorted. "Annoyed? They're trying to kill me!" She cringed as she realised how loud she'd spoken. None of the other patrons seemed perturbed. Maybe death threats were a normal thing for supers.

"Yes, well, no one knows who you are. Rachael was useful to TechCorp. But the Boss just sees you as some unknown running around wearing her property. She wants it back; I think she cares very little what happens to the person wearing it. And I'm sorry about what happened to Rachael; I feel partly responsible." Steve fiddled with the folder in front of him, a faint tremor in his hands. "They intercepted my email. I had to convince them that Rachael had tricked me, and when I heard the 'real' story from them, I'd realised what a fool I'd been. That's why Thunderclap was sent.

It was a trap. I've been too scared to try help since. They were watching me."

His gaze hardened. "They might still be, but I can't let my fear guide me any longer. Rachael was right to be worried. Especially now the Boss has accelerated her plans. I need to let you know, and we need to convince the cops what's going on before it's too late."

"Too late for what?" said Calvin.

Steve drew in a breath. "If the cops accept those suits, if they put them on, then she'll have what she wants."

Kris' jaw tensed. The cops. Her dad. "I don't think the cops want supersuits. I mean, they hate supers."

"Vigilantes," Calvin reminded her. "And the VCU practically giving themselves superpowers would really send mixed messages."

"That's why the Boss has been paying villains to raise the crime rate," Steve continued. "And the Boss has recently had a meeting with the cops. The VCU have always been suspicious, they've always been wary about letting any single company 'buy' them out with tech, though they desperately need it. But with one of their officers recently killed by a vigilante, no doubt under TechCorp's order, I fear they may be close to taking her up on the offer."

"So, what happens if they put them on? Mu…" Kris hastily cleared her throat. "Rachael thought it'd hurt them somehow."

Steve pushed his glasses up his nose, and opened his folder, glancing cautiously over his shoulder.

Calvin smiled reassuringly. "Just supers here, mate. They're not going to get you in trouble."

"Yes, that's why I picked this place. Okay." Steve pulled out a sheet of paper with a schematic on it. It showed a suit, with blue lines and tiny little numbers and figures and notes pointing to it. "They're supersuits, just like the one you're wearing, Pink, or at least fairly similar. Like yours, the cops' suits build full body armour from a nanite generator worn on the wrist and can also repair the armour back to its original specifications if it has been damaged." He smiled faintly. "When Rachael stole the prototype, she also took most of the designs for its functions. I've seen Pink Punch do things this iteration can't, like make weapons. But it's the extra function these suits have that's the problem. Unlike your suit, which will always be controlled by you, these suits have a bypass.

"The Boss has told the cops it's simply there so if one of their cops passes out in the middle of a dangerous situation, they can be brought back home safely. But the Boss plans to retain access. If she wanted to, she could take over any one of those suits, and make the people wearing them do whatever she wants. I wouldn't put it past her to use it as leverage against them too, to get them to cooperate with her plans."

"She could make them her own personal law enforcement," said Calvin.

"They would never agree to that," said Kris. Her father would never let anyone control him like a puppet.

"The Boss has assured them they will be the only ones with access, and they have no reason not to believe her. She's had enough trouble pulling TechCorp's name out of the mud. As far as they or anyone knows, since she took over TechCorp, the company has behaved itself. They're still suspicious, but with things so dangerous and the extra safety the suits offer on the surface, she may convince them.

"And when Rachael figured out that's what they were planning, she stole the suit and left TechCorp. Her husband's a cop. But if you do know her, I guess you already know that."

No wonder Mum had become Pink Punch. Kris gulped. "I have a feeling you didn't need to go to all this trouble, putting yourself in danger again, Steve. We already knew the suits were dangerous for the cops to use; we just weren't sure exactly why."

"I know. Don't worry, I'm well aware of the risk I'm taking, and as comfortable as I'll ever be with it. But, telling you that wasn't the only reason I wanted to meet.

"First, I wanted to warn you. You may run into Thunderclap again. I've given him upgrades, made him stronger. And that includes fitting him with an EMP. It's a device designed to interrupt the control signal for your nanites, Pink."

Kris tensed. "Which means?"

"He could make your suit stop responding to your commands, and it would also significantly affect its self-repair capabilities."

"And you gave him this?" Even with Pink's voice modulator warping her voice, Kris felt she'd squeaked far more than she intended to.

"I had no other choice! I made the EMP as ineffectual as I could get away with, but he could still significantly weaken your suit."

"Thanks a lot," Kris huffed. She wanted to clobber Thunderclap after what he'd done to Mum. But if he was stronger than before, and he had the ability to destroy her suit, how was she to fight him? She'd had enough trouble with Shift.

"I'm sorry," said Steve. "But I also have something you should find far more helpful." He reached into his pocket, pulled out a device, and placed it on the table. "Rachael asked me to get this to her. She needed TechCorp resources to have it produced."

It looked like a small remote. Calvin picked it up and turned it over in his hands.

"It gives off a jamming signal," Steve explained. "Similar to what I fitted to Thunderclap, except it's designed to interrupt the control signal to the cops' suits. If you run into a cop with a suit, and someone is controlling them, use that. It'll block the signal and free them. Unfortunately, if you run into a cop in a suit just doing his civic duty, it won't help you one bit. But, I suppose, at least they'd still follow the law."

Calvin snorted. "Sorry," he muttered, when Kris glared at him.

Kris took the remote off Calvin. "I guess this will help, but I don't want them getting those suits in the first place."

Steve pushed the thick folder across the table to her. "Then give them this. It explains everything I've just told you and contains as much evidence as I could gather. I'm not sure they could build a case against TechCorp with it. But it's enough to stop them doing anything stupid."

"Show it to the cops?" Calvin balked. "You expect us to just waltz in there like this?" He gestured to his own outfit, and then at Pink Punch.

"That's your problem. I go anywhere near them, and the Boss will find out. Luckily, I don't think she cares too much where I go for lunch."

X looked up from her menu. "You're right. If you took this to the cops yourself, you'd be dead already."

"X can tell the future, sort of," said Calvin.

"You should quit now too," X added.

Steve smiled faintly. "Believe me, I would if I could. And when this is done, I plan to."

X looked him in the eye for a long time, unblinking. "Okay," she finally said. "But I can't tell you if that's going to be soon enough."

22

The TechCorp building was the tallest in Northberg and dwarfed its nearest rival by at least ten stories. John stood on the sidewalk below and questioned what he was doing here for the umpteenth time. He pulled out the card Ms. Vaas had given him and swallowed hard. The card layout was simple, but the card stock it was made from was thick and glossy, expensive. It did not simply note a number for the company, but the CEO herself. Sure, he, Jo, and Dave had spoken to her previously, but that had been at her invitation. Would she even want to talk to him? Would he even get through? Still, she'd given him her contact details with the expectation that he call if Rachael needed help. Surely this qualified. John steeled himself and dialed the number on the card.

Fifteen minutes later he was escorted to the personal offices of Victoria Vaas. They took up the entirety of TechCorp's top floor, a wide-open space leading up to a battleship sized black desk. Behind the desk, ceiling to floor glass windows looked out over the city. John's guts clenched. Marrying a woman who, up until recently, worked at one of the top paying engineering jobs in the city had been intimidating enough. Rachael had overseen an entire floor at TechCorp, but she hadn't had it all to herself.

"Ah, Detective Mahrone." Ms. Vaas stepped from behind her desk and took his hand. "I hope your wife is well."

John smiled faintly. "Actually, she just woke up."

Ms. Vaas' handshake was already firm, but John could swear her grip tightened. "Oh?"

"Yeah. She's got amnesia though. Can't remember anything about what happened, or how she got there." And she didn't remember him. It was silly, but John felt that now even her subconscious mind was punishing him. "I haven't helped her as much as I could have in the past. But coming to see you, this is something I can actually do."

"I'm sorry to hear that. Unfortunately, we don't have any technologies that would help memory recovery in that area."

"She's got a good doctor. I'm sure he knows how to handle it. She's awake and not in physical danger anymore, which is a miracle in itself. What I wanted to talk to you about, to help her, well, it's not exactly medical. It's about those suits you had on offer. I'm sure they'll be of use to the VCU. And I'm sure the Chief will agree to their use, eventually. But there's still going to be procedures, and paperwork, and I can't wait that long."

John started to pace but forced himself to confine it to the area in front of Ms. Vaas' desk. "Pink Punch was there on the night Rachael got hurt. She knows what happened. She may even have hurt Rachael herself. But I can't pin her down, and I can't get answers out of her. If I had one of those suits arresting her would be a cinch."

"I see," said Ms. Vaas. "Pink Punch is a problem for us too. Her suit incorporates technology stolen from TechCorp. The technology is my property and I'd like it back."

John swallowed. Why had Rachael stolen the damned thing in the first place?

"So, your Chief has decided he's interested?"

"Yeah, that's the problem. The Chief is overcautious. He won't accept something he's afraid will hurt those working under him. If I can show him they're safe, that they'll help us stop someone like Pink Punch, he'll be on side."

"You want me to give you one," Ms. Vaas said. The corner of her lip curled up slightly.

"Yes. I mean, if it's not too much trouble. I plan to tell the Chief I'll be his guinea pig myself. I'm willing to take that risk."

"There is no risk."

"That's what I figure. I just need to convince the Chief of that."

Ms. Vaas reached behind her desk and pulled out a plastic suitcase. She opened it and placed it on the desk. Inside, contained in a fitted foam insert, was the nanite generator the new Chief Engineer had shown them the day before. "Go on. You can take it."

John carefully extricated the device from its foam casing and turned it over in his hands. "It's light."

"It will give you the power to catch Pink Punch."

John swallowed. Dave was going to be really ticked when he told him he'd taken a suit without his permission. "Thanks for this. I still need the Chief's permission before I can put it on. But just having it in my hand, that'll help. I'll convince him, and we'll all be wearing your suits in no time."

* * *

Stan located her father's police vehicle parked outside the Tech-Corp building. Just him; no other cops in the vicinity. Kris figured he was the best person to give the evidence to. On his own, he'd have no other cops to help arrest her. And he was so desperate to get answers out of the new Pink Punch that he'd hardly dismiss an entire folder full of them.

Kris and Calvin crouched on the roof of one of the buildings across the street from TechCorp. About six stories up, they could see the TechCorp entrance, and through the windows of the sixth and seventh stories, but not much else. They'd left X in Stan. She wasn't very good at climbing.

"This is stupid," said Kris. "We can't see anything. And someone in the building will see us."

Calvin snorted. "I'm sure they're all too busy pushing paper around their meter square of desk to notice. But I'll say it again; you are bright pink."

"I think I liked you better when you didn't know who I was."

"Hey, who's fault was that?"

"You can talk."

"So, what are we doing? If your dad is inside, maybe we can sneak in."

Kris raised an eyebrow. "In bright pink?"

"No, I mean, we go undercover. Like, as ourselves. Seeing as we know who each other is..."

"TechCorp won't let a couple of kids in. I could barely get in to visit Mum when she worked here."

Calvin nodded, his expression serious. "So, we wait."

He didn't quite pull off the super-serious super, and Kris was just thinking up something cheeky to point this out to him, when movement below caught her eye. "There he is."

Her father had just exited the big glass sliding doors of the TechCorp building. He fiddled with something on his wrist.

"What is he doing at TechCorp by himself anyway?" Kris leaned a little further out.

"Your visor has binoculars in it," said Stan, in her ear.

"How do I... wait..." Kris thought of seeing her father closer. It worked. An overlay appeared on the inside of the reinforced plastic, showing a closer view of her father. "Why can't you just tell me everything this suit does straight up, Stan?"

"Would you sit still for long enough?"

John adjusted the thing strapped to his wrist. Kris zoomed closer. It looked like her nanite generator, though bulkier, and it wasn't pink. Man, Pink's binoculars were good. She could even see writing embossed on the device's side: 'property of TechCorp.'

Kris stiffened and grabbed Calvin's arm. "He's got it already."

"Ow!" Calvin pulled his arm away and rubbed at his wrist. "What already?"

"The suit. I need to warn him."

"What? How? Kris!"

Kris stood to her feet and cupped both hands to her mouth. "Detective Mahrone!" Her voice boomed. Looked like Pink's suit boosted that too.

John looked left and right, and then finally skywards. He tensed.

"I need to talk to you!" Kris spotted a fire escape clinging to the building's side. She jumped halfway down the structure and the escape rattled and shook. She swung herself over the side and dropped down the last three stories to the alley below. Her boots chipped up the concrete beneath her.

John jogged to the alley entrance. His hand went to the taser at his side, but it just rested there, and he made no further move. "You want to talk to me? About what?"

"About that." Kris pointed to the device on his wrist. ""You can't wear it. It's a trap. If you activate it, TechCorp, the Boss, she'll be able to control you."

John snorted. "The Boss?"

"She's the CEO of TechCorp."

"You mean Victoria Vass? Yeah, she gave this to me."

"You have to take it off. I've got a whole folder of stuff I can show you. If you just let me get -"

"Why? Apparently, this is going to even the playing field between people like you, and us cops."

"What do you mean people like me?"

"Vigilantes."

"I'm just trying to help you. What difference does a suit make?"

"Then why don't you take off that helmet, huh?"

"I can't."

"... And while you're at it, why don't you tell me what the hell you did to my wife!" John's last words echoed in the enclosed alleyway.

Kris held her hands out in front of her, palms down, trying to calm him. "I'm sorry, I can't. All you need to know is if you activate that thing, you'll be putting into motion the very thing your wife was trying to stop."

John ran a head through his hair. "Rachael overreacted. She was upset about losing her job. Maybe she thought... TechCorp said these things could be remote-controlled, and that was probably all it was. But they would hardly tell us straight out if they intended to use it against us. Rachael, she... she just... I don't know why she did something so stupid..."

"I'm sure she'll wake up soon. She'll be okay."

"Stop talking about my wife like you care. Besides, she's already woken up, but don't stress. She can't tell me about who you are, or even why you did what you did. She has amnesia. So, she doesn't remember being you; she doesn't even remember me!"

Relief flooded Kris' chest. Mum was awake. She could finally talk to her. Then her father's words fully registered. "Wait, who doesn't she remember? She's okay?"

"No! That leaves you as the only person who can tell me what happened that night." His eyes narrowed. "But I'm going to give you one last chance, Pink. Tell me who you are and why you took that suit from my wife. Then maybe I'll believe you and I won't have to use this." He jabbed a finger at the device on his wrist.

Kris swallowed hard. She'd had to get out of the stupid car and see what was happening. She'd yelled at Pink Punch and distracted her. How could she tell her father Mum being in hospital really was all her fault?

"You're scared, aren't you? Don't want the cops to have the same technology as you do, huh? That would make things a bit hard. You won't be able to do whatever you want, trash the place, put people in hospital, and then disappear, because we'll be able to catch you?" John stood almost nose to nose with her now. "For gods sakes answer me, or I swear I will arrest you, and I will make you tell me."

"I... I can't."

John grabbed her upper arm, his knuckles turning white. Kris didn't feel anything through the suit, but she didn't pull away. He couldn't hold her if she didn't want him to, but he gripped her so tight that if she pulled away, she'd more than likely hurt him.

"Screw this." John slapped his free hand on the nanite generator, tried to manipulate it, then let out a frustrated growl.

He was having as much trouble with the initial activation as Kris had. But she still wasn't taking any chances. She grabbed at his hand. "Don't!"

"Hey!" John winced as Pink's powered gloves bit into his wrist. The nanite generator whirred and spat out a blue grey wave that swept up his arm, over his body. It solidified, and her father stood there in a suit like her own. It was a dark grey colour, strips of bright blue defining edges, and had 'VCU' stamped across its chest. And, stretched over the imposing figure of her father's broad torso, the armoured suit that stared down at her was much, much, bigger than Pink Punch.

"Whoa..." This didn't necessarily mean the suit had taken him over. Steve had said it was only if someone at TechCorp decided to take control. "Detective Mahrone," Kris said, a waver coming into her voice. "Is it... what's it doing? Can you still hear me?"

John turned his free hand over, inspecting the blue edged glove that enclosed it. He turned to her, his helmet whirring, and then tightened his grip on Kris' arm. Kris drew in a sharp breath. Pink's suit let out a faint crack as the armour-clad fingers dug into her.

John's voice boomed from the suit. "All right, Pink Punch. Start talking. What did you do to Rachael?"

Kris couldn't find her voice. She jerked her arm but couldn't pull it free. A gauntlet. The thick beefy weapon built itself around her free hand.

John grabbed her wrist with his other hand before the gauntlet could fully form. Motors whirred as both suits fought to out-do the other. "No, not this time. You're not going to get out of this because of your superpowers. You see? This is what these suits are going to do for us. No more getting away with murder just because you've got an advantage. No pun intended."

She couldn't break free. Kris' heart pounded in her chest, her breath coming in short gasps.

"Tell me what happened!" John barked. He leaned a little closer, until the visors of both suits touched. "Or I'll take you down to the station, and we'll discuss it there. You won't be able to resist arrest this time."

Kris did the only thing she could, the first thing her father had taught her before she'd learned any more complicated self-defence. She slammed her knee straight up.

John's armour let out an audible crack and he staggered back, releasing his grip on her with a grunt.

Kris bolted down the alleyway.

"No don't... run away... damn it..." John leaned against the alley wall, one hand gripping his crotch.

Kris wasn't waiting for him to catch his breath. She skidded to a halt at the side of the street. Stan materialised and swung open a door.

"It's okay, sweetheart, let's get out of here."

Kris threw herself into the passenger seat and Stan tore off.

"You okay?" Calvin asked from the driver's seat. He had his shades off and looked at her with concern.

"Fine." Kris felt her cheeks flush, and her eyes burned. But at least Calvin couldn't see past Pink's visor.

* * *

Dave paced behind the desk in his office like a caged tiger. He flexed his fingers and held his hands out in front of him, like he wanted to strangle something. "John, what the hell were you thinking?"

John was too annoyed to sit down either, although the Chief hadn't even offered the chair on the other side of his desk to him on his arrival. "I'm sorry, I got carried away. Pink Punch was right there, and she wouldn't talk to me, she was going to get away, so I just, I just activated it."

The object of their discussion lay unbuckled on the chief's desk.

"And why was the damned thing on your wrist in the first place? You had no intention of asking me. You didn't even wait for my okay before you went and got it."

"Dave, yeah, I tried it on. I just wanted to see how well it fit. But I swear, I intended to check with you before I ever activated it."

"Well, that's not what happened, is it? And now someone's got footage of it all over the Internet." Dave reached for his laptop and spun it around. The screen showed a video of John, still in the suit, staggering out of the alleyway. "So not only is one of my top detectives in a suit he's not supposed to have, but he's also doing... what are you even doing?"

"She kicked me in the nuts!" John shifted his weight. He still felt a bit uncomfortable. Sure, he'd been wearing armour, but Pink had an armoured boot. Ironically, if he'd been trying to arrest someone that size and neither of them had suits, he wouldn't have made such a rookie error. In the suit he'd felt invincible.

Dave snorted. "I wish she'd kicked you harder."

"Chief, I know I made a mistake. But we need these suits. You can't keep holding off on this. We need to get familiar with them before things really blow..."

The caged tiger broke its bonds; Dave whirled and jabbed a finger across the desk. "Don't think I don't know why you went behind my back! You think I sit behind this desk because I'm scared of vigilantes. Just because my wife put me in hospital when she left me, it does not mean I've lost my edge. I may not run around making arrests anymore like you and Jo, but if I wasn't here, I couldn't make the decisions that keep the VCU effectual. And I couldn't stop you lot thinking you can bloody well do whatever you want without risking getting yourselves killed!"

John blinked at the outburst. His desire to defend himself waned. "Dave," he said, his voice softening, "she damn near killed you."

The night Trisha had left, both John and Johansson had been on duty. John could still remember getting the call, and the chill as he recognised the address. They both knew Dave's marriage was in trouble, much of it due to Trisha's powers. Neither of them had thought she'd become violent.

They've arrived to find Dave slumped over in the entrance hall, bleeding out. Spines that looked like they'd been thrown from a giant echidna peppered the walls, and a set of deep claw marks marred the family photos hung on the hall. They'll called an ambulance. Dave had just laid there, sobbing, and begged them to check she hadn't hurt Penny.

John had found Penny fast asleep in her bed, a stuffed Ankylosaurus hugged tight to her chest. After that, Trisha had disappeared, and no one had seen her since. No wonder Dave hadn't wanted his daughter going down the same path. When she manifested her powers, so similar to Trisha's, it must have terrified him. "No one blames you for being cautious. I'm sorry I screwed up. But it has nothing to do with a lack of confidence in you."

The outburst had sucked all the energy from Dave's pacing. He rubbed a hand across his face, stroking his mustache, and wouldn't make eye contact. "And yet, you put on that suit. I should take you off duty. But if the whole city knows you went behind my back, then they'll doubt that I'm - that the VCU is in control of the situation.

"So, guess what, John? You get your way; you get to be the VCU's prototype for TechCorp's suit. Go, arrest Pink Punch, if that's what it takes to stop you acting out like this. I'll tell the media you were acting on my orders, and at least the VCU won't look stupid because my detectives can't do what they're bloody well told."

The Chief slumped back into his chair with a huff. "Now get the hell out of my office."

23

They'd retreated to Mum's warehouse hideout. It had taken Pink's suit a few minutes to repair the cracked armour where Dad had grabbed her. Kris tried to resist rubbing at her arm, mostly because it seemed to upset Calvin.

"Are you sure you're all right?" Calvin asked, for the umpteenth time. "I didn't think your dad was that kind of dad."

"I'm fine. And he's not. He didn't know it was me. He has to grab people sometimes, if he wants to arrest him. It's part of his job." But the suit TechCorp had given him was strong enough to hurt her, even with Pink Punch's armour. "I'll just be more careful next time."

"Staying out of his way might be the best option at the moment," said Stan. "Your mother never picked fights with him if it was unnecessary."

"I'm not going to pick a fight. I just want to warn him."

"You tried." Calvin pointed out. "He pinned you to a wall."

Kris straightened in her chair. "No, Pink Punch tried. I didn't. I know what I have to do: I'll talk to him myself."

"Your mother already tried that," grumbled Stan.

"But it's me. He's been worried enough about me and Tommy through all this. If he thinks mucking about with the suits or Pink Punch will hurt us, he just might stop."

Kris' phone buzzed; Tommy was ringing her. That was strange, because if he ever did decide to communicate with her via phone, he'd text. "Shouldn't you be at school?" Kris immediately said on picking up.

"Kris, Mum woke up."

"I know. I saw Dad this morning. At least, Pink Punch did." She rubbed at her arm. "He said she doesn't remember being Pink Punch."

"Well, that might not be good. Dad's mad."

"About Pink Punch, yeah, believe me, I know…"

"And at you. He came and picked me up and you weren't at school, and he'll want to know why. And I think he's upset because Mum doesn't remember him either. You should get home soon, or he'll really flip."

Kris gulped. The pending conversation with her father would be more difficult than she'd thought.

* * *

Dad's car wasn't in the driveway when Kris got home. She'd barely sat down on the sofa when she heard it rumble up. Her father walked in and tossed his keys onto the counter, hard enough they skated clean across and clattered into the back of one of the dining room chairs. John's body was tense, but he relaxed as he noticed his daughter. When he spoke his voice still held a faint growl. "Kris, where have you been?"

"Tommy said Mum woke up."

"Don't change the subject. You weren't at school when I went for Tommy. And after I told you not to go running around outside when you don't need to be. You know how many vigilantes are out there right now…"

"It's the middle of the day!"

"That's not the point. First, you're out in the middle of the night after what happened to your mother, and you promised me you wouldn't do that again. Then you're not going to school..."

"It's Friday..."

"Damn it, Kris! I don't care." John drew in a breath, and his shoulders slumped. "Your mother just woke up. She can't even remember me. And you weren't there. It would've been nice to have a bit of backup."

Some of Kris' apprehension evaporated. Without the supersuit, her father wasn't quite as intimidating. "I'm sorry, Dad. What else doesn't she remember?"

"Don't worry. She remembers you." John ran a hand through his hair. "Everything's just going wrong right now, and I needed to know you were safe. Where were you, Kris?"

"Just at the skate park. Listen, I need to talk to you about something important."

"Don't change the subject."

"Why won't you listen to me! You want to know where I've been? Why I went out that night? It's because of that." Kris pointed at the grey metal cuff, still on her father's wrist. "That's one of those supersuits Mum was talking about, isn't it? The one she said you should never wear."

"Yeah. But I'm not so certain I shouldn't wear it. Your mother has amnesia. She doesn't know what happened to her that night. The only way I can find out is to arrest Pink Punch. Unfortunately, she has made it clear I'm going to have to do so by force. And this gives me enough force."

"Dad, it's dangerous."

"My job is always dangerous. And how would you know? You'd better not have been talking to Pink Punch!"

"I haven't! I know because that's what Mum's been saying for the past few months. Isn't that enough?"

"So, you weren't at the skate park?"

"Dad!" Kris stepped forward and pointed at his arm. "Look at it! It's got 'property of TechCorp' written on it and everything."

John turned his arm over, and the light caught the faint blue etched words. "The suit belongs to them, Kris. They're giving them to the police force, to trial."

"Giving? Aren't you the person that told me nothing ever comes for free?"

"I'm also the guy who told you to stay in at night, and who expects you to go to school, because I'm your father!" John snapped, his voice rising. "But that didn't happen, did it?"

"I'm just trying to protect you; you have to believe me."

"Protecting you is my job, Kris. Not the other way around. Sweetheart, what's going on with you?" He reached out a hand and brushed her shoulder.

Kris whipped her arm up and slapped his hand away. "Don't touch me."

John shifted his weight back. "Kris, what is going on?"

Kris cheeks flushed. What was going on? She'd tried everything to get through to her father. He'd pinned her to a wall. And he still wouldn't listen. She balled her hands into fists. "That thing could kill you."

"You don't know that."

"What, because I'm a teenager? I have proof! But I shouldn't need it. Mum shouldn't have needed it. But you didn't listen to her either. The only reason she's in hospital now is because she was trying to protect you."

"Kris!" John barked.

Kris took a step back.

John shook his head and looked at the floor. "I have to do this," he said, his voice quieter now. "And if you can't be honest with me, don't expect me to listen to you. Go and see your mother, all right?

But don't you dare go anywhere else or I will ground you for the rest of your life."

Kris swallowed the lump in her throat. "Dad..."

He stepped past her and picked up his keys. "I need to take a nap before I look for Pink Punch again. Go see your mother." Without another look in her direction, John headed upstairs.

* * *

Rachael was awake and sitting up in bed. She grinned and threw her arms wide. "Kris."

Kris barreled into her mother's arms and buried her face against her shoulder. "Mum, I'm so glad you're okay. When I saw you get..." Her words choked off, and she had to squeeze her eyes shut tight and gather herself.

Rachael held her for a moment. "I'm fine now, Kris. What about you?"

Kris rubbed at the corner of her eye, and then grinned. "I think I am now. We were all worried about you."

Rachael watched her carefully, her lips flattening into a faint frown. "Do you know what happened to me?"

Kris chewed her lip. Tommy and Dad both said she'd completely forgotten. But maybe she'd been lying to them to hide her identity as Pink Punch. "Don't you?" she finally asked. "You don't remember when I last saw you, before, you know, you got hurt?"

Rachael shook her head. "I've been wracking my brain, but I can't remember details about much of anything for... I don't know how long." She reached out and pushed a strand of her daughter's hair back. "At least I remember you and Tommy."

Kris squeezed her eyes shut briefly. "Then I don't know either. I'm sorry."

"That man, the one the doctor said was my husband. He kept

asking what happened, until the doctor chased him out. What was his name?"

Kris' guts tightened. At least she could talk to her Mum like she always had, despite the memory loss. But Dad had to see her looking at him like a stranger. "John. You don't remember Dad at all? But you remember us?"

Rachael shrugged. "Yeah. I mean, obviously, if I have kids, they must have a father. But I don't recognise him. Is he a good man? He treats you all right? He did tell me we had separated, although it wasn't over anything important, and that now we had the chance we should try again. But he sounded like he may have been hiding something."

"Dad loves you, Mum. He's probably just trying to figure out what he should tell you without giving you too much to process."

Rachael rubbed a hand over her sheets, smoothing out a crease. "I can barely remember the last few years. But I remember you kids. I remember most of my engineering. I work at TechCorp. Or I did; apparently, I got fired. I hope that was for a good reason; I used to enjoy it. But I don't remember... John. I thought there might have been a reason. If I loved him, I shouldn't have forgotten him."

Kris swallowed hard, but Mum didn't seem upset in the slightest. It was like she was simply sounding out a problem to see how it might be solved. "You got fired because you thought the suit TechCorp was making for the cops would hurt Dad. That's what I wanted to talk to you about. I tried to tell him it'd hurt him, I tried to explain it to him, but he wouldn't listen. That's why I need your help. You need to tell me anything you can remember about it."

"I remember the suit. It was armour, designed to protect the wearer. It also made them stronger and faster. It was an interesting project."

"Yeah, but it's got this programming that means the Boss can take the suits over if the cops don't do what she wants."

"Who's the Boss?"

"The CEO of TechCorp. It doesn't really matter; the point is you were convinced it'd hurt him." Kris grabbed her mother's arm. "I know you don't remember him, but he remembers you, and he's got to listen to you now. You have to tell him to take it off." Sure, Mum had already tried. But maybe asking from a hospital bed would finally knock it through Dad's head.

"Kris, I'm not sure I can. If you've tried to convince him already… I can't remember half of this stuff. It feels like I barely know him."

A lump rose in Kris' throat. Mum was Pink Punch. Even with some of her memory gone, she was supposed to be able to fix this! "I've tried everything I can think of. He's going to get hurt. And I know you don't remember, but you started this whole thing. I've been trying to keep going after you went into the coma. But I'm doing a lousy job. And I thought once you were awake you could help me, but I still have to do this on my own…"

"Okay," said Rachael, taking Kris by the arm. "It's okay, slow down. You don't have to do anything on your own. Let me help you think through it. Do you know why he's so determined to use this supersuit?"

Kris drew in a breath. "He wants to find out what happened to you. He found you unconscious in the middle of the night when he was on duty. You'd been caught an explosion. Pink Punch was there."

"Pink Punch?"

"Yeah. She's a vigilante. Dad works in the vigilante crimes unit, so he hates Pink already. But now he thinks she's responsible for what happened to you."

"Is she?"

"No. Not exactly. Pink Punch is good guy. But," Kris stalled for a moment, then plunged ahead in a rush, "I think she feels bad about you getting hurt that night. You were there with her, because you were worried about the TechCorp suits. I think she did something stupid, she didn't mean to, but you got hurt because of it. She doesn't want Dad to know she screwed up."

Rachael thought for a moment. "Is that why she won't talk to him properly? She feels guilty? It sounds like he realises she's hiding something, and that would make anyone suspicious, especially a cop. But if she didn't actually try to hurt me, surely it wouldn't hurt her to tell the truth?" She shrugged. "Trust me, it's really frustrating only having half the story and trying to piece together the rest. If he gets his answers, he won't think he needs a dangerous suit to get them."

Kris swallowed at the lump in her throat. She'd known it in the alleyway, when her father had grabbed her. If she'd given him some sort of answer, he might have listened. She just couldn't bring herself to admit it was her distraction that had put Mum in here. But if that was what it took, she could suck it up. At least it would be Pink Punch admitting it; Kris wouldn't technically have to tell her father she'd screwed up.

Kris steeled herself and forced a smile. "You know what, Mum? I think Pink Punch can do that."

24

John arrived at the police station with plenty of time to start his shift. He should have just clocked on and got out to work as fast as he could. He was now stuck in the parking lot with Johansson, and they would have been ready to head out. But the rest of the cops, who should also have starting shifts, or who were finishing and returning vehicles, seemed more interested in the device on his wrist than work.

"It's not a toy, you know." John huffed as he dragged back his wrist from an overenthusiastic young officer.

Johansson was a little more subdued, but even she eyed the device with a twinkle in her eye. "I wonder how much force I could get out of a punch in that."

John fixed his partner with a glare. "Not you, too."

"Hey, I'm not the one who went behind the Chief's back to get that thing."

The roar of a powerful engine interrupted them. A vehicle skidded around the corner, its tyres squealing across the road surface. The acrid smell of burnt rubber filled the air. This in itself was enough to grab the attention of every cop outside the station. Never mind the vehicle was Pink Punch's garish Mustang.

The Mustang rumbled to a halt, and Pink Punch stepped out. She held a thick folder in her hand.

Beside him, Johansson tensed. "What the heck?"

It was a bold move, right outside the police station. Pink Punch had already confronted him outside TechCorp. Was this more of the same? She'd gotten violent with him there, and he'd attempted to restrain her. He hadn't succeeded, but he was certain he'd given her a shock. Maybe she wouldn't try something like that again. Maybe this was her attempt to do things above board. As above board as a vigilante could, anyway.

Still, John's hand hovered over the device. It didn't need touch to activate; he only had to think about it. But physically touching it seemed to help trigger the mental energy required.

"Wait!" Pink Punch held up her free hand. "I just want to talk to Detective Mahrone."

"You already had your chance."

"Yeah, I know. And I haven't been fair to you. You deserve to know what happened to your wife."

"Damn right I do."

Pink nodded. "Then I'll tell you. But I also came here to give you some evidence to prove what TechCorp's been doing. I'll give you your answers if you promise to look at it. And you've got to promise me not to use that suit too."

John lowered his hand. Was she serious? A nagging doubt over what he'd believed for the last week, that this woman had hurt his wife because she'd wanted to take her suit, started in the back of his mind. She was a vigilante, and he was on the VCU. Their mistrust could be down to that fact alone, and perhaps this was all a misunderstanding. Maybe he would get his answers.

But if this was a trap, at least he could now defend himself. "All right, Pink. Tell me what happened to Rachael. Give us the evidence and we'll look it over. If I believe you, I'll take this thing off. How does that sound?"

Pink Punch chewed her lip. "All right," she finally said, "you've got a deal."

John's heart started to hammer in his chest, though he fought to keep his voice steady and his arms still. "So, tell me."

Pink Punch glanced around at the other cops. They were all staring at her, wide-eyed like a 'roo in the headlights, trying to figure out what to do with a vigilante rocking up on their very doorstep. And speaking to them so politely. "You might want to do this in private," she said. "You might not like what your wife was involved in, given your, um, occupation."

That his wife had been Pink Punch. No, he did not want that said in front of his colleagues. Nor that he'd failed to arrest her. "Okay," he opened the door to his Commodore. "Let's go for a ride."

Pink shifted her weight back. Probably iffy about going in his car, but he certainly wasn't climbing in that Mustang. Pink steeled herself and handed the folder over to Johansson. Then she got in the car.

All John wanted was to find out what had happened to Rachael. If Pink told him, if she were truthful, they could slow down on this whole suit thing. He could tell Dave he was sorry, again, and then maybe he wouldn't be so mad at him. The least he could do was hear Pink Punch out.

Johansson held up the folder. "John, if this tells us what we need to know about TechCorp, you don't need to go with her."

"You know it's not TechCorp I'm interested in right now."

"You can't run off with her. Not by yourself."

"I've got the suit. I'll be safe."

"I'm your partner, and…"

"Relax, I'll call for help if I need it." John slammed the car door behind him. Screw procedure. He had the suit. And he was getting his answers one way or another. He didn't look at Pink but put the vehicle in gear and pulled out.

* * *

Kris forced her hands to stay in her lap. She was a superhero. She didn't fidget. Seated in the passenger seat of her father's VCU vehicle should not have made her uncomfortable. She'd been here many times before. But this was different.

Her father drove deliberately, his gaze fixed outside the windshield. He drove them a half dozen streets away from the police station, pulled down an alleyway, and there he stopped. He switched off the engine and faced Kris, brows lowered. "This better not be a trap."

"You drove us here, detective. And I'm a good guy, remember?"

"You're a vigilante."

Kris threw herself back in her seat and rolled her eyes skyward. "Yes, I know how you feel about vigilantes! Everyone knows!"

"You said you'd tell me what happened to Rachael. So, spill."

Kris got out of the car and stepped around the hood. Her father followed. She didn't want to sit in the car, so close to him. He'd made it plenty clear he was ready to grab Pink Punch if she did something he didn't like, and she wanted a bit of space. "Please just hear me out. And at least keep that suit off until I'm done. You won't need it."

John held up his hands. "Fine. I'm too tired to fight you anyway; I just want answers. In all fairness, you should power down yours too. But I'm not even going to bother asking."

"You know I've only been Pink Punch for a week now."

"I know that already. You stole the suit from my wife!"

"I didn't steal it! I was working with Rachael. I was there that night, in the alleyway. She was attacked by a villain named Thunderclap. He said he had information, but it was a trap. His wrist cannons were what destroyed the alleyway and hurt her. I..." Kris swallowed. "I accidentally distracted her. If I hadn't, she would've taken him down. After the explosion, she gave me the suit to protect me from Thunderclap. When I found out she was in a coma, I kept it, and I've been trying to continue her work ever since." She'd rehearsed the almost-truth all that afternoon. It was the closest to the truth she could get without revealing who she was.

"That's it? Why couldn't you just tell me that earlier?"

"I felt... I felt bad, all right? She wouldn't be in a coma if it wasn't for me." Kris sniffed and drew herself up a little straighter. "I'm really sorry. But that's it, I've done my part of the deal. Now take off that suit."

John turned his arm over, examining the device strapped to his wrist. "You're Rachael's friend, huh? Okay, so who are you? Tell me, and I'll take this off."

Kris' heart began to pound in her chest. "You wanted to know what happened to your wife. I said nothing about revealing my identity."

"Who you are will tell me if I can trust you or not. If you are a friend, then yeah, accidents happen."

Kris gritted her teeth, hands balling at her sides. He was supposed to listen! "I can't..."

"Exactly!" John jabbed a finger at her. "You're still hiding things from me. There's only one way I'm going to find out the truth. Pink Punch - you're under arrest." John slapped his hand over his wrist. The suit crawled up his arm and encased his body.

Kris stepped back. "Detective, I don't want to fight you."

"Of course you don't, not now the odds are a little more even. But I can arrest you without any fuss. It's completely up to you." He began to walk toward her. "Come quietly, and we can talk."

"We are talking! I just told you what you needed to know. I gave you evidence. So, you know what?" Kris threw her arms wide. "Go on, arrest me. All that come quietly stuff is just a bunch of bull, or you wouldn't have pinned me to the wall before."

"Didn't expect that, did you?"

"No. I just didn't think you were that kind of guy."

John halted in his advance.

She had to try, just one more time. "Detective, listen. I know you're a good guy. I know you're just trying to do what you think is right. The only thing I'm keeping to myself is my identity, you have to understand that. But both your wife and I were worried about you wearing that suit. If something bad happens because you wore that suit trying to help her, don't you think she'd blame herself? At least go back and read the evidence I gave to your partner."

John stared at her; his face impossible to read behind the opaque visor. Then his shoulders slumped. "I just want to help her. You know how hard it was, being in my position in the VCU and knowing Rachael was breaking the law? We couldn't even stay in the same house it was so uncomfortable. I should have done something when she first told me why she'd left TechCorp, but it didn't seem that big a deal at the time. Every corporation is dodgy in some way, that's why the VCU buys equipment from more than one.

"But then she got hurt, and I didn't even know whether she would wake up. I had to make it up to her, I had to try find out what happened in that alleyway. I guess I thought it'd make up for ignoring what she'd tried to tell me about TechCorp in the first place.

"So maybe you're right. Maybe I should stop running around like a hothead and do some real detective work, and just sit down and read through your folder." He trailed off, lost in thought. He stood there so long and so still, he almost appeared frozen to the spot.

Kris waited. She was so close to getting him to believe her, but something told her that now what she needed to do was shut up and let him figure it out for himself. Even if all he did was go through the evidence with his partner, the folder was so thick it would take them ages. It might give Mum time to remember things. John still hadn't moved. "It's okay," Kris eventually said, "I'm not trying to trick you."

"Pink," John said, his voice strained. "I can't move."

A chuckle emerged from the darkened end of the alleyway. "Looks like your suit's working just like I was told it would. You see, like Pink's been saying, it's got this little bit of programming that allows TechCorp to issue it commands." From the shadows of the alleyway, a large shape emerged. Broad shouldered, with a trench coat swinging down by his feet. The man lifted his head and broke into a grin.

Kris' guts tightened. "Thunderclap."

Thunderclap held up his arms. Thick metal shackles encircled his wrists, similar to the ones he'd had before, when he'd attacked Mum. These were bigger. "I've got some upgrades."

"Detective," Kris said, her voice wavering, "this is the man responsible for putting your wife in a coma. He lured her out into the alleyway that night, offering information on these suits, and then nearly killed her."

"She was the one who nearly killed us," Thunderclap snorted. "Yet we're both still here. I wonder if I'll be ordered to do something about that? Rachael Mahrone knows too much."

John's suit made little whirs and clicks as it fought to contain the struggling man inside. "No, you can't. She's got amnesia. She doesn't remember a thing about Pink Punch, or these bloody suits."

Kris powered up a gauntlet. Mum had struggled to fight this guy, and that was without his upgrades. How dare he hurt her! Kris had been scared of the thought of fighting him before, and still was, a little. But now she had backup. "Detective, if we work together, we can take him down."

Thunderclap laughed. "Pink, sweetheart, you are not as smart as your predecessor, are you? Don't you get it?" He stepped up next to

John and clapped a hand on the man's shoulder. "He doesn't have control of the suit anymore."

"Get your hands off me."

"Should've listened to wifey, huh? Bit late for that now." Thunderclap put an arm around John's shoulder, like they were best buds, and shook him a bit.

"Leave him alone!" Kris raised her gauntlet. Screw this. She didn't care how big Thunderclap was, she couldn't let him hurt her family again.

Thunderclap stepped back and held up his hands. "Relax, I'm not going to hurt him. Not yet anyway."

"You said you might be ordered to… hurt Rachael. Whose orders are those?" John asked through gritted teeth.

"The Boss'. You'd know her as Victoria Vaas, CEO of TechCorp."

John drew in a sharp breath.

"Yeah, sorry, buddy. But no one is going to believe you after tonight."

"They will if I tell them too," said Kris.

"Sorry, but you'll be dead. Let me explain how this is going to work. The Boss needs you cops to use her suits. I was hoping you'd man up and fight Pink all by yourself. That would've made things easier, and you would've got this Pink Punch off the streets for us as well. But now we have to do this the hard way. The override is the bit you're all worried about. So, we're going to have a cop go rogue, and kill a vigilante. Your wife has amnesia, detective. Because of her," he pointed at Pink Punch. "It's not that big a stretch, is it?"

"None of my friends will believe that!" John's chest heaved. "If you do something like this the Chief will freak out, he'll never want the suits."

"We'll see," said Thunderclap. "Maybe you'll just have to destroy yourself too so there'll be no one to tell them any different. Yeah, that sounds like a plan."

Kris hands balled into fists. "Why the heck does TechCorp need this much control? You know, if you want them to buy your stuff maybe you should just make decent tech, with no strings attached."

"These bastards can't do their bloody jobs!" Thunderclap exploded. "The VCU is a joke. All they care about is…" He turned away and shook his head. "I'm not supposed to talk about this. It's nothing they don't deserve, and you should be happy. They harass people like us all the time. If you really want to know you can ask the Boss yourself. Unfortunately, you're not going to get the chance."

Kris slammed her fist into the side of Thunderclap's head. He crashed back into the wall. Bricks cracked.

Kris threw herself at him again, but Thunderclap darted out of the way. He slapped his hand on a button on his wrist canon. The full weight of Pink's suit bore down upon her, and Kris gasped and dropped to one knee. She shakily lifted her arms in front of her, though it felt like she was hefting a great weight. Pink's suit had gone a crackling grey, fizzling like a television that couldn't get good reception.

Kris gulped. Thunderclap had just used the EMP Steve had told her about. Pink's suit was next to useless.

Thunderclap laughed. "You don't know how much I wish I could take you down myself. Guess I'll just have to settle for watching." He turned to John. "Well, detective. She's all yours. Make sure you do lots of damage." He turned and leaned against the alley wall, arms folded, a grin plastered across his face.

The invisible chains holding John back snapped, and he stomped forward, the pistons in his suit humming overtime. They weren't moving with the muscles of the human inside anymore; they were fighting him. "Pink, I can't… It's doing this all by itself. I can't fight it… I'm sorry."

Kris just managed to haul herself upright when John threw his first punch.

25

John hauled Kris to her feet by the collar, then slammed a punch into her that knocked her to the ground. Kris' heart pounded in her chest, and her head spun from the blow. Dad could throw a punch, and he had the suit's power behind him too. Pink's armour still provided some resistance, despite the interruption Thunderclap had caused. But where the harder hits landed, the suit struggled to repair.

John dragged her up again, and the next blow knocked her into the alleyway wall. This time, Kris was able to haul herself upright. The suit felt like it was helping her again, though it still wasn't quite enough. She held her arms up, fists up in front of her face; the next punch shied off her forearms. "Detective, you have to fight it."

"I'm trying!"

"I can't fight you like this. My suit won't protect me."

John's suit vibrated, pistons humming, and then he pinned an arm across Kris' throat. Kris grasped his wrist and fought to push him off.

"Your suit? My suit is just doing its own thing, I can't, I can't fight it..." John strained, like he was using every muscle in his body to try and stop the powered prison that encased him. He hung his head, whilst his suit continued to press its attack. Kris could smell his sweat. "Damn it, Pink. I'm sorry."

Pink's suit whirred. Kris' fingers became solid pink again. She pushed back, getting John's arm back enough that she could breathe again. Finally!

John sensed the shift in power. "Are you strong enough to fight me?"

Kris chest heaved as she struggled to breath. "I think... I might. My suit's recovering."

"Then fight me!"

"I don't want to hurt you!"

"Well, I am going to kill you, and there's nothing I can do to stop it. I know I've been hunting you down, but I never wanted to hurt you. I don't want to do this!"

Thunderclap shifted his weight from the alley wall. "This is just pathetic. This stupid cop can't even defeat you quick with the Boss pulling the strings. And this stupid thing that that stupid engineer gave him doesn't seem to last very long. But it'll still do the job. Much as I like a fair fight, I've got orders." He put a hand to the EMP on his wrist cannon.

A stream of ice shot from the alley opening. The ice completely encased Thunderclap's arm and stuck it against the wall. Thunderclap snarled, yanked his arm once, twice, and then broke free. He shook off the ice and winced.

Calvin stepped into the alleyway, put his hands on his hips, and thrust out his shoulders. "I'm afraid I like a fair fight too, so I can't let you play with that."

"Zero!" Kris ducked as her father threw a punch. Bricks cracked as his fist slammed into the wall. She backed up a few steps. Her speed was back, her suit now fully functioning. "Zero, keep Thunderclap busy. I can't fight him; he might mess with my suit again. I'll take..." Dad.

Calvin nodded. "Got it." He flung a series of ice shards at Thunderclap.

Thunderclap threw up his arm and the ice plinked off the metal of his wrist cannon. He shot a blast of electricity at Calvin.

Calvin stepped to the side. "Hey, sparky. Catch me before I get the rest of the cops. That'll mess up your plan good, won't it?" He flashed the man a cheeky grin, then turned tail and ran out of the alley.

"Get back here, you little runt!" Thunderclap ran after Calvin, his gait heavy.

"Move!" John threw a punch. Kris caught it in both hands, her boots gripping the asphalt, skidding back a little. Her father was still that little bit stronger, and now she had her hands full.

"Detective, fight it."

"God damn it, I can't!" John drew in shaky breaths, gasping for air, almost in tears. "You got your suit back, so take me down before I hurt you or someone else."

Kris grappled with her father's arm, then twisted his wrist to the side. He stumbled away.

With Zero K distracting Thunderclap, she'd have the time to jam the signal to her father's suit with the device Steve had given her. She unclipped the jammer from the spot she'd put it on Pink's nanite generator and held it up for her father to see. "It's okay, you don't have to fight it for long. This will jam the signal TechCorp is using to control you; then you need to get that suit right off. I just need you to hold back for a second, so I have a chance to..."

John yelled, like he'd just exerted some tremendous amount of willpower. And failed. He spun around, and slapped the jammer clean out of Pink's hands. It rocketed across the alleyway and exploded with a spark of circuitry against the wall.

Kris spread her arms wide and stared at her empty hands. The stomp of the police suit brought her back to the fight, and she jumped back as John swung for her head. He continued to move toward her, but slowly, like he was underwater.

"Kris!" said Stan in her ear, "you're going to have to take him down yourself."

Stan's voice brought a flood of relief. "He broke the jammer, how am I supposed to do that?"

"His suit operates much like yours. If you do enough damage the nanites won't be able repair, then it'll either shut down, or you can get it off him. That's the only way you'll stop him now."

"If I destroy his armour it's going to hurt him too! I can't do that."

"Yes, you can," John growled, though he'd only heard her half of the conversation. "I think I'm slowing it down, just a little, but I can't keep this up forever."

"No, I'll hurt you."

John grunted, and the suit jerked forward. He grabbed Kris by the shoulder, then froze as he held the suit back again. "That doesn't matter. I'm going to kill you if you don't. And then Thunderclap will kill me. I can't do that to my family. I screwed up. I couldn't back up my wife, I didn't believe her because I wanted damn proof. I haven't been there for my kids, and they think we hate each other and are going to get a divorce. And now I'm going to do this... I don't care how bad you hurt me, please!" His suit whirred, pushed harder into Kris, then jerked to a halt again. John whimpered and he hung his head. "Please, get me out of this."

Kris looked into her father's face, though she couldn't see it behind the visor, and her guts clenched. "It's okay, Detective. Hold on."

Kris whirled from her father's grip and sent him stumbling. Then she slammed a fist into his chest. She felt the impact, felt it vibrating her suit. John stumbled back, then threw a punch at her like a drunk man. Kris stepped aside. She powered up two big gauntlets. They'd do more damage, but they'd also get this over with quicker. Kris aimed for panels of her father's chest armour and avoided his head. She was attacking the armour. Not her father. At least that's what she told herself. Her punches left craters of damage, blue energy playing at the edges. But within seconds John's armour repaired. He went for her again.

Kris dodged one blow, blocked another. Then she slammed the gauntlets into her father's body again and again, and only when she was panting for breath did she let up.

John stumbled back. The front of his suit was covered with cracks, but now it struggled to repair. Static played at the edges of the biggest impact mark, lit up like a crater over his stomach.

Kris threw a punch, and John caught her fist. Then he grabbed at Kris' throat.

Kris gasped, and the gauntlets turned to powder as the air to her lungs cut down dramatically. A choke hold: she had mere seconds. She grabbed her father's arm and her fingers closed over the nanite generator on his wrist. She thought of appendages like knives and spikes, and they sprouted from Pink's gloves. They wrapped right around her father's arm and dug into the nanite generator in a series of sparks. Kris pulled her hands down, dragging the appendages like overlong nails over John's wrist. His nanite generator let out a crack and a pop, and then split into pieces.

John let her go. The police suit faltered, fizzled, then turned to powder, blowing away in a grey haze. John swayed on his feet, and his sweat-soaked body slumped into Kris' arms.

Kris dropped to her knees, slowing her father's descent as she did. She wrapped her arms around him, holding him to her chest, and fought the tears that sprung to her eyes. Even through Pink's suit, she could feel him trembling in her arms.

"Detective," Kris said, when she felt her voice was steady enough to speak again, "are you okay?"

John didn't reply, but reached up and squeezed her arm, barely perceptible through Pink's armour.

The wail of sirens cut the air, and a police car skidded to

a halt beside the alleyway. Detective Johansson stepped out, and then froze, eyes wide. She grabbed her taser. "All right, get away from him!"

John grunted and sat up in Kris' arms. "It's okay, Jo. She saved me."

Johansson tucked the taser back in its holster and dropped down beside him. "Holy crap, John. What happened to you?"

"Pink was right. About the suits."

"The TechCorp suit that the Boss gave him," said Kris. "It started doing its own thing. They were controlling it. Trying to get him to kill me. I had to rip it apart to get it off him."

"They accessed the control override. They said they wouldn't. We're idiots." Johansson's eyes narrowed. "Wait, you did this to him?"

"You don't need to get all protective. It was the only way to get me out. She didn't have a choice. I couldn't control it anymore. I barely managed to slow it down."

Johansson put an arm around John's shoulder. "All right. I'll take your word for it. Just take it easy. I think you've had enough excitement for today."

Kris' fingers lingered on her father's shirt sleeve as the detective pulled him away. She wanted him to stay with her, but he didn't know who Pink was. Of course he'd rather his partner support him.

"We cannot take these suits," John said.

"Yeah, I know. Don't worry. This will scare the crap out of Dave." Johansson looked up at Pink. "He'll be okay. But I need to know…"

"Hey!" The shout rang out from the rooftop across the street. Johansson pulled John in tighter to her chest. Kris shot to her feet. Thunderclap stood on the edge of the rooftop. He shivered, and bits of snow and ice clung to his coat and face, but he wore a scowl.

And, clasped in Thunderclap's arms, struggling against the iron grip clamped around his neck, was Calvin.

Kris' eyes widened. "Zero! Thunderclap, let him go!"

"I don't think so."

Calvin struggled, grappling at Thunderclap's hands, ice creeping from his arms in a swirl.

"Cut it out," Thunderclap snapped, in accompaniment to the burst of electricity that jumped from his wrist cannons and into Calvin's body.

Calvin grunted, and then slumped to hang limply in the big man's arms.

Kris' voice rose. "Put him down!"

"Let's make a deal," said Thunderclap. "We can't have you blabbing to everyone about the Boss's plan."

"Why because I'm not dead? Maybe you shouldn't have told me what the plan was, you big idiot!"

Thunderclap's lip curled. "Careful." He held Calvin out over the building's edge, three stories up. "Now, the Boss wants to talk to you. So, come and have a little chat. And keep your trap shut, you better not have told that cop anything."

Johansson glanced quickly at her, then drew John in tighter to her chest. "She's told me nothing. All she's done is beat up my partner. I should've shot her on sight."

Thunderclap laughed. "Don't worry, she'll be out of your hair pretty soon. Come and talk to the Boss, Pink Punch. I'll keep your little buddy... on ice... until then." He stepped back and disappeared into the darkness.

"Zero!" Kris shouted. No response. Not from Zero K, and not from Thunderclap.

"Not too bright, that one," Johansson muttered. "Pink, go, help your friend. I can't arrest you after this."

"And we sure as hell won't be touching those suits," John said.

He looked up at her, swallowed, and then forced out: "Thanks. I don't know who you are, but we're good. For now."

Kris nodded, then turned her back on her father. He'd be okay. She'd done what she had to, to help him. Now, she had to rescue Calvin, before Thunderclap hurt him too.

Stan materialised beside Johansson's police vehicle in a swirl of pink, and Kris climbed inside.

"Stan, we've got an appointment with TechCorp."

26

The gunmetal grey building reared up into the night sky. Save for the blue glow of the TechCorp sign that adorned its topmost reaches, and faint security lighting, it was dark. Kris gazed up at the behemoth and swallowed. Right in the center of Northberg, the biggest threat to the city stood in all its corporate glory.

"Kris," said Stan, as he idled behind her at the curb. "Are you sure you know what you're doing?"

"They've got Calvin."

"I know. But you haven't been doing this very long. You'll be walking right into the belly of the beast. If anything happens to you, your mother will sell me for scrap."

"She can't. Mum doesn't remember you. Or being Pink Punch. And that's because of the Boss. And after what she tried to do to Dad and the cops, what I had to do to stop him... Now she's going to hurt Calvin. What if she doesn't stop there? She could hurt my family, my friends, or this city again." Kris' hands were balled into fists at her sides, shaking. "I have to stop her."

"You're still hesitating," said Stan.

"Or course I am. Thunderclap is up there." If Thunderclap had decided to take her down himself, after he'd activated his device, it would have only taken a few hits. The only reason he hadn't was because he'd wanted to make it look like a cop had killed Pink

Punch. Kris squeezed her eyes shut and shook her head sharply. It shook the thought to the back of her mind but did not stop the pounding of her heart in her chest. "But that doesn't matter. I may be the only person who can stop this, and I need to do it now, before I chicken out."

"I was going to say being afraid is good," said Stan. "You realise this is dangerous. Just be careful, sweetheart. Your mother might not remember me well enough to hold me responsible, but that doesn't mean I won't."

Kris smiled faintly. "Thanks, Stan. I'll be fine. I mean, I have to be. With Mum's memory gone, someone has to petrol you up."

Stan grumbled. "I can petrol myself, but thanks. I obviously have to stay down here. But I'll be watching your progress, and I'll be there to talk to the whole way."

Kris approached the TechCorp building and pressed a hand against the big glass door. It didn't respond and all she could see inside was security lighting that dimly illuminated the entrance foyer. Pink Punch could break in easily, but that would probably set off an alarm.

The doors beeped faintly and then opened of their own accord. Kris gulped. She made her way across the foyer, her boots stomping heavily on the floor. The soft swish of the lift doors opening was amplified in the otherwise silent building. The lift took her skyward, numbers climbing to the highest on the buttons.

The lift doors opened on a massive office which took up the entirety of the top floor. Kris kept the thought of a shield at the back of her mind as she cautiously stepped out.

A battleship sized desk, made of the shiniest black wood Kris had ever seen, was at the far end of the room, with wall to ceiling glass windows behind it. Behind the desk, a woman rose to her feet. "Pink Punch. So glad you could make it. I'd love to be a little less formal, but I'm afraid I only knew your predecessor. It seems I have no idea who you actually are." A faint smirk touched the corner of the Boss' lips.

Kris balled up her fists and two gauntlets built themselves in a shimmer of pink. "My predecessor? You mean Rachael Mahrone? She's a good friend of mine. And first of all, you get her fired, just because she was worried about her husband. And then you get your stupid ham headed minion to put her in a coma..."

"Now, hold it there," the Boss said, holding up a hand. "Rachael Mahrone quit. She also stole our technology, the suit you're wearing right now. That belongs to me."

"I don't see your name written on it anywhere," Kris shot back. "And judging from what I've seen of your other stuff, you make that a pretty high priority."

The Boss' eyes narrowed. "I don't care what's written on it. I own it. I own the technology, I own all the information Rachael stole, I own every little bit of information inside her head."

Kris shrugged theatrically. "Yeah, well, she can't remember any of that, so I guess it belongs to no one now."

"Lucky for her. I hope you're a little more careful with your identity than she was."

"And I guess that means you won't know what hit you." Kris began to stomp toward the woman. "Because I can't think of any reason why I shouldn't just pick you up right now and cart you down to the police station."

"What about your little friend?" The familiar voice came from Kris' left.

There was a plush set of black furniture, couches and a long black glass table set up to the side of the office. Big enough that they had hidden Thunderclap sitting there. Now he stood to his full height and stepped around them.

Calvin struggled in the man's grip. His arms were held in thick handcuffs; a full sleeve of metal that completely covered the tattoos on his arms. The metal had flecks of white on it, tinged with cold and ice, but beyond that Calvin appeared unable to use his powers.

"Zero K, are you all right?"

Calvin's jaw was tense, and he looked a little pale, but he jerked against Thunderclap's bulk as he tried to break free. Not that he had much chance of that while clamped in Thunderclap's thick-set arms. "I'm fine, Pink. As soon as this big dumb brute lets go of me."

Thunderclap scowled. "Ham headed, you said? Big dumb brute? I should snap your buddy right here." He pushed in on Calvin's shoulders, his big hands crushing the boy's upper body.

Calvin winced, his shoulders shuddering, and then he let out a stifled grunt.

Kris fought the urge to rush over. "Leave him alone."

"All right, that's enough, Greg," said the Boss.

Thunderclap kept up the pressure on Calvin's shoulders.

"I said that's enough!"

Thunderclap let up and Calvin drew in a sharp breath. "I thought you wanted me to..."

"I'll tell you what I want. Don't forget who took you in. And don't forget I own those wrist cannons; I can take them back anytime I want."

Thunderclap looked down at his arms, his forehead scrunching up. "You took half my arms to give me these. If you take them..."

"Exactly. So, do what you're told. I don't like it when my equipment malfunctions." She turned back to Pink Punch. "So, let's talk. Is that something you're capable of? Of do you only know how to throw punches like Greg here?"

"All right, I'll talk. But tell Thunderclap to let Zero K go. He can't cause any harm in those shackles."

The Boss nodded to Thunderclap. The big man all but threw Calvin back down onto the sofa. Calvin glared daggers. All spite for the man that had captured him, until Thunderclap turned away. Then he looked to Kris and gulped.

Of course he was scared. Now that he knew who Pink Punch was, a girl no older than he was who'd only been bumbling around in the high-tech body armour for a week, he had to doubt she would pull off his rescue.

The Boss looked the suit up and down with a possessive leer, then trailed a finger along Pink's arm. "It really is a work of art, isn't it? I've always admired technology that does not skimp on form, whilst still being functional. After Rachael left, we never were able to figure out how she got the suit to recognise thought patterns such that it could recreate stable weapons. A neat trick, for a super-hero. But it would take a company like TechCorp to utilise it to its full potential."

Kris yanked her arm away. "Just tell me what you want."

The Boss' grey eyed gaze flicked up to meet Kris'. "You want Zero K back safe and sound?"

"And what? You want me to give you this suit? You've already sent people to kill me to try to get it back."

"Perhaps I was a little hasty. It's true, at first reclaiming the suit was my top priority, and what happened to you mattered little. But destroying you is proving more difficult than I thought. And I've found there is little point doggedly pursuing a course of action that keeps failing. Instead, I prefer to see obstacles like this as an opportunity. It's obvious you wield the suit well. So, I want you to work for me. Under certain conditions, I'd be willing to let you keep that suit."

"You want me to do your dirty work? Sorry, but I saw what one of your suits did to that poor cop."

The Boss frowned. "The VCU detective? I understand why Rachael was concerned for him, but all the VCU does for vigilantes like yourself is hound you. The VCU is a tool this city uses to keep those with powers in line. It's a difficult situation, and yes it needs controlling, but all they do is pick fights with the more well-known supers and make the rest of the vigilante population feel like outcasts.

"I am not a bad guy, Pink. By the VCU's definitions, I am not even a vigilante - I was unaffected by the Fallout and have no super-powers. I simply own a massive corporation, and therefore have the power to make things right. All those suits were designed to do was to give me control of a set of tools that were not being used effectively."

"So, the cops are just tools? And Rachael? She was only a tool too, wasn't she?"

"She was my employee. She misused her position, and she stole from me."

"And then you could no longer control her!" Kris snapped, jabbing a finger into the Boss' chest.

Thunderclap tensed and electricity sparked around his metal bound wrists.

The Boss held up a hand. "Relax, she's not going to hurt me."

Kris wasn't sure of that herself, but sure enough, she had stopped in her tracks and gone no further. The Boss had no suit, if Pink grabbed her hard enough, she'd snap like a twig. "And now you want to control me."

"That's not true. Your suit does not have the same technology as the police suits; you would always have full control."

"But I would be your 'employee,' right? And that would mean you own me. Just like you thought you owned Rachael. And Thunderclap."

"I'm my own man."

"Greg, be quiet."

Kris raised an eyebrow. "Seriously? You going to put up with that, Thunderclap?"

Thunderclap scowled but said nothing.

"A cheap trick. That might work with some of my other employees, but not with Greg," said the Boss with a faint smile.

"It's true, though, you believe you own him. What happens if he leaves you? You take his tech? It even says 'property of TechCorp' right on his arm." Just like it had Dad's. No way she could let this woman have anything she wanted here tonight.

Thunderclap looked down at his arm and swallowed. "Aunt Victoria, I'm more than just a tool, aren't I?" *Aunt Victoria?* There was the faintest hint of desperation in his voice, and it suddenly made the bulky man look a lot younger.

"I'll tell you why it won't work," the Boss said, her voice taking on an edge. "Greg here would be dead if not for me. When his parents died, and he himself was close to death, I chose to replace his damaged heart, free of charge. I saved his life. I also gave him those wrist cannons. Without them he'd be a weak, average human. He would have no superpowers. I've made him stronger, and now he works for me. He didn't just steal the technology, unlike a certain engineer we both know."

Kris gestured at her chest. "Rachael designed this, didn't she?"

"Whilst in my employ, and that makes it mine."

Thunderclap looked at his fists as electricity crackled over them. "Yeah, and I like being strong and powerful. I'm only here because I want to be. No one takes advantage of me!"

Kris whirled to face the man. "Then you're even stupider than I first thought. And I thought you were pretty stupid to start with."

Thunderclap growled low, and electricity built around his fists.

"Greg, power down!" The Boss barked.

The man's steely glare wavered.

"Sit," said Kris, "there's a good boy."

Thunderclap bellowed and the electricity playing around his hands built into a massive ball. He flung it at Pink Punch.

The electricity slammed into Kris' chest and the power crackled across her suit. It knocked the air right out of her and for a brief second her vision blackened. Then it cleared to a splintering array of light, blinking around her like fractured glitter.

For a second, Kris wasn't sure what the shards of light were. Until the pull of gravity snatched at her gut. The blast had thrown her clean through the building's big glass windows. She plummeted toward the street below.

27

Kris reached for the window ledge as it accelerated away from her. There was no hope of grabbing it. Not without something like a grappling hook. The device appeared in her hand, and Kris shot the hook skyward. The hook cleared the windowsill, the cable jerked taut, and Kris' body slammed into the windows several stories down.

"Kris," said Stan. "Are you all right?"

Kris' heart hammered in her chest. "It's okay. I'm not dead."

"Good to hear. But if the Boss thinks you are, Zero K might be in danger."

Calvin. Kris swallowed. "All right. I can do this." She slowly retracted the cable and moved toward the shattered windows above.

It wasn't up to the Boss, or any corporation, to control the cops. Her father had taught Kris that much. To think of them like some tool, for her to use to her own ends, even if that was what she thought of as better protection for the city, was nuts. Especially since she had no qualms about controlling, and even killing cops, to gain that control. And now she wanted Pink Punch on her side too.

Kris pulled herself up the last few meters and peeped over the window ledge. Shards of glass littered the space behind the big desk. Thunderclap and the Boss stood in the center of the room. The

Boss held a finger in Thunderclap's face. "You follow my orders, you hear me. Otherwise, I have no further use for you."

"But Aunt... Boss. I thought you wanted her dead? And it's armour. Surely it would've protected her. She might be hurt, but she's probably still alive."

"I can use her; haven't you been listening? Besides, she might have damaged the suit!"

Calvin was on the floor. His shades had been knocked off; his hood now flung back. He had a faint trickle of blood at the corner of his lip and his chest heaved as he caught his breath. He shuddered and wiped at the corner of his eye.

Kris built a tiny ball between two fingers, and then flicked it at Calvin. It exploded on his chest with a puff of pink. Calvin grunted and slapped a hand over the spot, then looked up. "I'm okay," Kris mouthed.

Calvin broke into a wide grin, opened his mouth to say something, and then winced.

Thunderclap and the Boss were still arguing. Calvin held up his shackled arms and shrugged.

Kris hauled herself over the ledge and ducked down behind the Boss' desk.

"I guess that little ice brat isn't much use to you now, is he?"

"That's enough, Greg. You want to dispose of him? I don't think I should give you the satisfaction."

Calvin scooted over to the desk. "I was worried for a moment," he said, voice low.

"Great, we can be happy later. We've got to stop the Boss." Kris grabbed at Calvin's arms as she spoke and turned over the metal shackles. "I think I can get these off; might hurt though."

"I've iced them up as much as I can. That might make them more brittle."

Kris squeezed the shackles. Calvin winced, but the shackles broke, fracturing with an audible crack. He shook the fragments off.

"What was that?" said Thunderclap. "Hey, where did that little rat go?"

"Find him. He can't escape. And yes, you can have some fun. But don't kill him unless I give the order."

"Sure thing, Boss."

"We can take him…" Kris whispered, even though her chest tightened at the thought.

"Only if he doesn't mess up your suit again. Hang on, I have an idea."

"Calvin, wait!"

Calvin winked at her, then shot to his feet. "Hey, you killed my friend! I'm going to rip you to shreds."

Kris gritted her teeth and fought the reflex to jump to Calvin's side.

"There you are," said Thunderclap. "You're going to join her soon." The crackle of electricity filled the air.

Kris peeked out from under the desk. Thunderclap and Calvin faced each other across the room. Calvin shot a blast of ice at Thunderclap's wrist. The cannon iced up, fizzled, and sparked, and Thunderclap dropped his arm to one side, grunting at the increase in weight.

He shot a blast of lightning at Calvin from his other cannon, and Calvin had to drop back behind the desk. "He can't use that EMP if it's encased in ice, right?"

"Right." Kris grinned and leapt to her feet.

"I threw you out the window!" Thunderclap swung the cannon to her.

Zero popped back up, and Thunderclap swung the cannon back with uncertainty. Then scowled and put a hand on his wrist, but only touched ice.

"That's right," Calvin grinned, "you can't use your new toy. This will have to be a fair fight."

"He doesn't need it," said the Boss. "Thunderclap, you have more than enough upgrades already to take care of such a small task. Do what you want with Zero K, but I want Pink and her suit intact. Or at least repairable."

Thunderclap built a blast of electricity in his un-iced cannon and pointed his fist right at Kris. Kris tensed. If he threw that bolt, she'd dodge it, easy.

"You think I'm stupid, huh?" Thunderclap growled. "How's this for stupid?" He flung his fist wide, pointing it at Calvin. The electricity shot out in a super powered ball and hit Calvin's chest dead center. Calvin slammed into the wall behind him hard enough to crack the panel in a spider web pattern. He slumped to the ground, head lolling to the side, eyes closed.

"Zero!"

"Now this is a fair fight," said Thunderclap.

Kris slammed into Thunderclap, on top of him before either of them knew it. The big man stumbled across the room, and they crashed into the opposite wall. The ice on Thunderclap's wrist shattered on impact.

The crackle of electricity filled the air. A sharp whack hit Kris in the chest, and she rolled back across the floor. Thunderclap's fist came down. Kris rolled again. The fist cracked a hole in the tiles.

Kris pulled out a sword in a shimmer of pink. She slashed it across Thunderclap's arm. He blocked it once, twice, the metal ringing. And then grabbed the blade in both hands and snapped it. He drew back a fist and hit Pink Punch in the jaw.

Kris stumbled back. Thunderclap hit her again. The blow knocked her back next to Calvin. Thunderclap grabbed her by the throat and hoisted her up against the wall. Then he slammed his other fist, crackling with electricity, right up into her chest. Kris gasped as pain blossomed across her rib cage.

"This is what happens when someone who isn't strong enough gets a bit of TechCorp technology," Thunderclap growled in her ear. "You think I'm stupid? Well, I think you're weak. The Boss is going to take your suit, and she'll give it to someone who can handle it. This is going to be just as easy as taking down Rachael Mahrone."

Kris forced her eyes open. Mum. She glanced down at Calvin, where he lay motionless against the wall beside her. She wouldn't let Thunderclap hurt anyone else she cared about. She reached up a hand, grabbed at his wrist around her throat, and squeezed. At first, nothing happened. Then droplets of sweat began to slide down Thunderclap's cheek, his jaw tensed, his arm began to shake. The grip on Kris' throat weakened. She could breathe again.

Thunderclap reached with his free hand to activate the EMP. Kris clamped her other hand around the cannon, now squeezing his metal bound wrist with both hands, and effectively blocking off his access to activate the EMP.

"Oh, no, you're not. Not this time. Fair fight. Remember? So, how's this for weak?" Kris extended Pink's fingers into knives and spikes, like she had to disable her father's suit, and tore right through the cannon, severing it from Thunderclap's arm. At the same time, she brought her legs up and planted her boots dead center of Thunderclap's chest and kicked.

Thunderclap slammed into the far wall and the building shook. It took him a few seconds, but he hauled himself to shaky feet and shook his head. His eyes widened as he lifted his arm. It was severed just below the elbow. Instead of blood, it dripped oil and wires sparked.

"Stop panicking and do your job," the Boss snapped. She'd backed up against the lift doors, away from the fight. "I gave you electric

wrist cannons, and you've still got one. You don't need a toy to shu
down her suit!"

Thunderclap swallowed and nodded.

Kris powered up a pair of gauntlets. She could hear Pink's sui
struggle and whine to build them, and the build was slower than
normal. This was likely the last set of weapons it would be giving
her for a while.

Thunderclap flinched as Pink raised her fists. He raised hi
remaining wrist cannon and electricity sparked around it.

Kris went for him. He threw a bolt of electricity, but she ducked
right under it, came up, and smashed Pink's fist into the bottom o
Thunderclap's jaw, not holding back one bit.

Thunderclap slammed back into the wall and slumped down
The electricity crawling around his fist died. This time he stayed
down.

Kris drew in a deep breath, then winced and put a hand to her
side. Her ribs were on fire with each breath, but as her heart rate
slowed, the pain let up. Pink's suit was fizzling. There was still a
faint spider web crack in the armour on her side. But she didn't
need armour to take down the Boss.

The Boss stabbed at the lift button. The lift itself showed a
number only a half dozen below the top level, climbing. Kris
stepped past the Boss and slammed a fist into the center of the lift
doors. They bowed in. "Oh, no you don't."

The lift dinged as it hit the top floor. The doors vibrated but
didn't open. The motor shut itself down.

The Boss held up her hands and backed across her office. "Now
settle down, Pink. Let's talk about this. Obviously, you're stronger
than Greg was. I can use that."

"No." Kris glanced across at Calvin. Still no movement. Her heart
caught in her throat. "For all I know my friend is dead..."

"Thunderclap did that."

"What? The guy you own? You ordered him!"

"I don't need to own you. It'll be a mutual arrangement."

"Yeah, right. You put Rachael in hospital because she stood against you. You nearly killed a cop. And no, I don't care if you think of them as just some tool. I am stopping you. Right here, right now, before you hurt anyone else." Kris grabbed the Boss' collar in both hands and lifted the woman clean off her feet. She stepped around the desk and held the Boss out the broken window. The woman's feet swung over clear air.

The Boss met Pink's gaze, and there was no fear in her eyes. "See, this is why you need someone like me in charge. The vigilantes, the cops, all of you... you're like a bunch of children with a stick. You're just running around hitting each other. Some of you think you're doing the right thing, but you're only creating a great big mess. That's why you need guidance. I am not a villain, Pink. I'm only trying to help."

"Well, I disagree with you. So, give me one good reason I shouldn't drop you right now and put an end to this."

The Boss didn't seem to have a response, either that or she was thinking very hard of her next lie. But it was Kris' own words that drew her to a halt. Her mother was not a villain. Pink Punch was not. And neither was she.

"Kris," said Stan, "don't do this. Your mother would have never..."

"I know." Kris took a step back and placed the Boss on her feet.

The Boss straightened her collar, like her clothing was the only part of her that had been put out of sorts by the threat of plummeting to her death. "Having second thoughts about my proposal?"

Kris swallowed. "No. Just about dealing with you like this."

The Boss raised an eyebrow. "Then Greg was right. You are weak."

"Pink..." Calvin hauled himself to his feet. He held a hand to his chest and winced, but when he gained his feet, he was steady, if a bit stiff. "What happened?"

Calvin was okay. Kris blinked a couple times. "I was... I was just wrapping this up, you know, whilst you were napping."

Calvin rubbed at the back of his head and looked around the room. "You took care of Thunderclap. Whoa."

"I'm glad you're okay."

Calvin grinned at her.

The Boss glanced between the two of them, scowling. "You realise I'm not going to stop my plans just because you ask nicely. This will only be a minor setback."

"Yeah, well, we'll see about that," said Kris. "The cops aren't going to take too kindly to you putting one of their own in danger. I think I'll leave you for them to deal with."

The Boss raised an eyebrow. "The police? You can't be serious."

"You put one of them in a suit that tried to kill him, or at least force him to kill someone else. And you tried to trick them into letting you control them. I'm pretty certain that's illegal. He knows what you tried to do, so do we. You have nowhere to hide."

The Boss shrugged. "If that's what you have in mind, go on, do your worst."

"We can't have her or Thunderclap slipping away. I'd suggest you hold still." Calvin shot an icy stream at the Boss' feet. Shards of ice grew from the floor, stopping just below her knees. "Don't worry, they'll melt. But by then the cops should be here." He turned and shot another blast at Thunderclap. He wasn't as careful this time. The icy shards that grew up fully encased both the man's sprawled out legs. If he woke, he wouldn't be going anywhere fast.

"Thanks." Kris smiled at Calvin faintly, then nodded to the lift. "Let's get out of here." She put her fingers between the scrunched-up metal of the lift doors and wrenched them open.

"I look forward to doing this again, Pink Punch," said the Boss. "Believe it or not, this isn't over."

"Enjoy prison," Kris shot back over her shoulder. She and Calvin stepped into the lift. It was still working, and they rode it to the ground floor. As they stepped out, the flash of red and blue lights greeted them beyond the front doors.

Kris and Calvin exchanged glances.

"You think they'll listen?" Calvin asked.

"Dad got hurt. Of course they will. You'd better pull that up."

Calvin flipped his hood back up. He pulled the edge down as far as possible over his face in the absence of his glasses. "Better?"

"Yup." Kris squared her shoulders and they stepped out Tech-Corp's front door.

A half dozen cops, already focused on the building's entrance, raised their weapons.

Calvin raised his hands. "Hey! We're not here to fight."

"Stand down." Chief Thompson stepped from the safety of the blue and red lights. "My detectives told me you saved one of their lives."

"Yeah, Detective Mahrone, is he okay?"

"He's been taken to the hospital, but he'll be fine. What I want to know is who's responsible."

"The Boss," said Kris. "Or rather, Victoria Vaas. CEO of TechCorp."

The Chief swallowed hard, and looked skyward, up to the top of the building. "That was what I was afraid of."

"We've got her all tied up, or rather, iced up, for you," said Calvin.

"That's all you did to her?"

"I was thinking of throwing her out the window," said Kris with a shrug. "But then I figured it might actually be in our best interests to do things the right way. I know us vigilantes give you guys a hard time. Maybe it's time we tried to work together." It was a long shot, but Pink had just saved all of them from making a monumental mistake.

"Maybe it would've made my job easier if you'd just tossed her out the window."

"Huh?" Kris frowned. She knew her father would have wanted her to do this the right, the lawful way. Surely his boss should feel the same?

The Chief shook his head, like he was shaking his own words off. "Sorry. And thank you for looking out for my guys. I screwed up; I should never have let John use that suit. We'll not be using anything from TechCorp ever again, I can promise you that. As for... the Boss... I'll arrest her myself. Now, I suggest you both get out of here. We've got bigger fish to fry tonight, but I can't promise I won't arrest both of you next time I see you."

Stan materialised at the curb, only meters away from one of the cop cars. It was rather a shock to the nearby officers. Kris and Calvin climbed in, and Stan tore away with a screech of tyres.

"I really need to learn to drive you," said Kris.

"Not until you're sixteen."

Calvin pulled off his hood, sighed, and sunk back into the passenger seat. "I am glad you didn't drop her. I don't care what your dad says, there is a difference between heroes and villains. You did the right thing."

"Dad would still say Pink should've left the whole thing to the cops."

"Maybe. But maybe he'll change his tune after Pink Punch saved him. Because you did save him. And me. And stopped the Boss."

Kris smiled faintly. "You didn't do so badly yourself."

Calvin blushed. "Thanks."

28

K ris woke late the next morning. Never before had she been so grateful for the arrival of the weekend. At least with the Boss behind bars, Pink Punch could take a break, and she could catch up on sleep. Still, she always found it hard to stay in bed once she'd woken. So, she made her way downstairs in search of coffee. Dad didn't like her drinking too much of the stuff, but she was sure she could get away with it today.

John sat on the living room couch. He looked groggy, and his wrist was strapped up. He smiled at his daughter. "Hey, sweetie."

"Dad!" Kris hadn't expected him to be home yet. He'd been a wreck last night; she knew she'd hurt him to get that suit off. She rushed over and threw her arms around him. "You're okay, I mean, you're hurt, what happened?"

"Not so tight," John gasped.

Kris hadn't squeezed him that hard. She wasn't in any condition for tight hugs herself; her side still ached where Thunderclap had punched her. She sat on the couch beside him. "What happened? Are you hurt?"

"What happened was you, and your mum, you were both right. I never should have put on that suit. I did, and it nearly killed me. I don't know what you kids would've done if something had happened to me, after everything that happened to your mother." He looked away and cleared his throat. "But, of all people, Pink Punch rescued me. I'm only here because of her."

"But you got hurt."

John smiled faintly. "Well, unfortunately, beating the crap out of me was the only way Pink Punch could get that horrid suit off. This is far better than the alternative, and I have no one to blame but myself. I'll be fine."

Kris' shoulders slumped. Dad wasn't mad at Pink Punch. "So, you're definitely not wearing those suits anymore?"

"Hell no," John snorted, then winced. "None of us are. The Chief has made that very clear."

"And what about... whoever made you wear them... they can't do something like that again, can they? Did you arrest them?" Pink had left the Boss in the VCU's hands. After what the Boss had done to one of their own, they had to have made sure she got put away good and proper.

"Don't go spreading this around, but it was your mother's old boss, the CEO of TechCorp." John's lips twisted into a frown, and he fixed his gaze on an indeterminate spot across the room. "If I'd listened to Rachael when she still had her memory, we might have had the time to build a better case."

"Wow," said Kris. It was probably quite shocking that a CEO would be responsible for something so devious. "Right to the top..." She frowned as she caught her father's expression. "Wait, what do you mean, don't spread it around?"

"Pink Punch messed up that woman's plans pretty good, or so Dave told me, before he yelled at me to stop calling him and get some sleep. I seriously doubt Ms. Vaas is going to pull something like that on the police, or anyone else, for quite some time. The publicity has been pretty bad for TechCorp. But..."

Kris shot to her feet. "The publicity? The cops arrested her, didn't they? I mean, Pink Punch did everything to... I mean, she had to..." Kris trailed off and threw her arms wide in frustration.

"But," her father continued. "I'm afraid it's pretty hard to pin much of anything on someone as well connected and powerful as Ms. Vaas." He picked up the TV remote, flicked through a few channels, and finally settled on one of the news channels.

The Boss stood outside the police station, surrounded, not by cops with handcuffs, but a flurry of reporters with microphones shoved in her face. "Yes, I've just been released from assisting with police inquires."

"Ms. Vaas," said a reporter, "what about the rumours that you were behind the rampaging TechCorp suit last night? The Chief of Police has told us that the suit itself was responsible, that it was its programming that caused it to malfunction, not any actions of the VCU detective trapped inside. Was this a malfunction, or was the machine intended to act that way?"

The Boss straightened her jacket. "The override was built in for safety reasons, and only something the VCU was supposed to have access to. However, it has come to my attention that the man responsible for designing the suits, TechCorp's Chief Engineer, Steve Blakey, retained access to this program. It's likely he caused the incident last night. I promised this city, when I took ownership of Vaas Enterprises, now TechCorp, that I would never allow our technology to cause this city or its residents any harm. That promise still stands."

John snorted. Kris' jaw hung as she stared at the screen. The Boss was blaming Steve, the man who'd given them information, tried to warn them!

"Will your Chief Engineer be held responsible?" another reporter asked. "What was his intent in retaining control?"

"You'll have to speak with the police about that," said the Boss. "I don't know how it works if the main suspect isn't around to answer questions. They tell me my Chief Engineer was found dead this morning; apparently a heart attack caused by electric shock. Perhaps he was working on something else to harm the citizens of this city." She smiled faintly. "Ironic."

"Although, you are responsible for your employees. The Chief of Police has issued a statement that the VCU will no longer be using TechCorp equipment, and have switched solely to your competitor, Gadgetco. Also, TechCorp shares have fallen by 30%, and..."

"No further questions." The Boss pushed through the bundle of reporters to a black limo waiting at the curb.

"Typical." John's voice held a hard edge. It took him a moment to fiddle the remote in his one good hand and turn off the television. He dropped it on the coffee table with a clatter.

"But, Dad, I thought you said it was her fault? Why isn't she in jail?"

"Yeah, but she's got lawyers, doesn't she? Look, I know what she did, the Chief does too. But unless anyone can prove that beyond a shadow of a doubt..." John sunk back into the couch and closed his eyes.

"But it's not fair."

"She's not going to cause any trouble for a while, Kris. Sometimes that's the best you can hope for."

Kris got up and paced the living room floor, her cheeks flushed. "But Pink Punch had her right there, didn't she? Shouldn't she have..." She'd had her. Right above a multiple story drop. She could've ended it right there.

"Done what, Kris?"

Kris swallowed. "Pink should've stopped her. Properly."

John shifted his weight forward on the couch. "I hate to admit it, but Pink Punch actually did the right thing. You know, mostly. She handed Ms. Vaas over to the cops. It's not her fault we can't pin anything on her. She's too powerful."

"What's the point of letting the cops handle it if you can't stop someone like TechCorp? That suit could've killed you. And she's going to get away with it."

"It'll catch up with Ms. Vaas eventually."

"It should've caught up with her last night. You can't tell me that just 'doing the right thing' will eventually pay off."

"You're right, it doesn't always catch up with the people who deserve it. But if I was always working around the law to catch criminals, if Pink Punch had just killed the CEO of TechCorp when she had the chance, we'd be no better than them. I don't want to become the very thing I'm trying to fight. I doubt Pink Punch does either."

Kris couldn't find any words. She looked away.

"Kris, you're a kid. You don't need to worry about this stuff. Don't get me wrong, it is frustrating for us when people get away with things. Not only can we not get at TechCorp, but you know Rick and all his bloody vigilantes? We thought we had them, they had this great big metal door in their basement and everything. But it turned out it was just a broom closet. We can't hold them for that. I should be more upset about that. But right now, I'm just happy I'm not some killer Robocop. Or dead."

"The important thing is, I'm fine. Your mother, she's fine, and they may even let her out of hospital by the end of today. We're going to have to work through some things, but it will be okay, I promise. Ms. Vaas getting away doesn't change any of that."

Kris drew in a breath and tried to still the thudding of her heart. They'd been so close. The Boss could still cause trouble. But she surely wouldn't be stupid enough to do so after almost getting caught. If all Pink had accomplished was protecting her Mum and Dad, and maybe setting back the Boss' plans, then that would have to be good enough for the moment.

Kris sat back on the couch. "Mum's going to remember you eventually, Dad."

John grinned. "I saw her this morning. She said she remembers our wedding, and how she felt about me then. You know, maybe this'll be fun. We can work through our marriage again from the start, maybe not make the same mistakes. And she won't remember all the times I've messed up.

"And you just let me and the VCU worry about TechCorp, okay?" John ruffled a hand through Kris' hair. "And remember, I love you."

Kris shoved him off with a grin. "Dad!"

* * *

Stan pulled up with a rumble in front of the Richardson's mansion. It was surrounded by scaffolding and the buzz of machinery filled the air. Kris had managed to get out of the house, once her father had admitted it was probably safe enough in the middle of the day. Seeing as she was only going to the skate park. She'd picked up Calvin and X from Mum's warehouse. As the cops had released Rick and Nim, they could go home.

"Rick and Nim don't mess around with fixing things," Calvin said. "And you can bet Rick made sure he used a building company that employs supers, so he probably didn't have to wait too long."

"I was wondering why that piece of roofing was levitating."

Rick stepped out the front door to greet them. "Hey, thanks for taking care of the kids." He winked at Kris. "I hope they weren't too much trouble."

It took half a second for Kris to realise she was assumed to be the adult of the three. "Er, yeah, I mean, I did have to save Zero's butt, but apart from that."

Calvin groaned and rolled his eyes.

"But he helped me a lot too," Kris added, aiming a carefully controlled punch at Calvin's shoulder. "I couldn't have done it without him."

Calvin flushed and sidestepped the punch. "So, the cops let you and Nim out?"

"Yeah, but we've got Elspeth and Max to thank for that. Max extended and reinforced the entryway to the Broom Closet, blocked off the end, and threw a few extra brooms in there. And Elspeth did the rest - used her powers to solidify the illusion of a simple broom closet, and cover over the obvious cracks that are present in most of Max's work, especially when he only has a day or so to construct something. After the cops spent all that time getting the door open all they found was, well, more brooms. I'm sure they're still suspicious, but they had nothing to hold us on, so here we are. The cops aren't too happy about it."

"Yeah," Kris couldn't help a faint smirk. Somehow, despite the frustration she knew this caused her father, it felt like she shared in the victory of the trick. "I can bet."

"Oh, I meant to ask you, Zero," said Rick, "before... um..." he trailed off, blinked a few times and swallowed hard. "... Everything happened here. Ah, did you manage to find out anything about the cops from that friend of yours? They're going to be on our tail even more after they were so close and lost us. Especially that Detective Mahrone."

Kris stiffened. Something must have slipped through, something Rick's empath senses could identity, because the man's gaze shot to her, and he frowned.

"Yeah, about that," said Calvin. Rick's attention went to him again. Kris wasn't sure if Rick had registered whatever he had sensed from her. "I'm not so sure hanging out with Kris Mahrone to get information about her father is the right thing to do."

Rick's brows furrowed and he folded his arms. "Yeah? Why's that?"

"Because..." Calvin swallowed, then lifted his head so he met Rick's gaze. "Because I don't think it's right to manipulate her. She's my friend, and just because she doesn't have powers, that doesn't mean I should use her to get information. I don't want to do recon like that anymore. But..." he chewed his lip. "Please don't stop me going to her school. I like it there."

Rick smiled faintly. "Zero, I'm proud of you for standing up for yourself. And I'm not going to make you do anything you don't want to. It's fine. You can keep going to school. Her school, specifically, if that's what you want," he added with a cheeky grin.

Calvin flushed.

"I just hope if you do hear anything from her or her father that would put us supers in danger, you'll tell us. Now, you and X go down to the Broom Closet. And stick to the yellow tape, half the house is still unstable. I want to talk to Pink Punch before she goes."

Calvin grinned at Kris, and then followed X into the house. That left Kris completely alone with Rick. He could hardly hurt her, but Kris still felt her stomach plunge. What had the empath picked up? "Listen, Rick, I really should get back home before I'm missed."

"This won't take a minute. I just wanted to thank you."

Kris blinked. "Oh."

Rick shrugged. "Well, Nim and I were both in the cop shop. Nim could hardly do anything to stop the Boss from there. I imagine if the Boss had taken control of the cops, she'd have made a point of keeping us locked up, lawful or not. And you looked out for Zero K, and X, even though I know you weren't too happy about how helpful we've been. I'd say overall you've proved yourself a pretty decent hero."

Kris felt her cheeks grow warm under Pink's visor. "Rick, it's fine. I was just, you know, helping." She'd only been helping her mother. Everything else had simply flowed from that. Kris glanced down at her pink-clad hands and clenched them. And here she stood, Pink Punch.

"Well, you did a pretty good job. Especially considering you're not the original Pink Punch. I'm certain you haven't been doing this for more than a few weeks at most."

Kris' gaze shot up to meet Rick's as her jaw dropped. "I, I don't know what you're talking about."

Rick held up his hands. "Relax. I'm not going to kick you out. I was a little bit nervous when I figured it out. Your emotions were different. You're a little more volatile than the original. But, at the same time, you're more open, and you were certainly more willing to work with us."

Kris stared at him, processing. Rick stood and waited, like he had all the time in the world for her to work out what she was feeling. Perhaps he knew her feelings before she did. "I think I just sought out your help because I needed it, because I didn't know what I was doing," Kris finally admitted.

Rick smiled faintly. "Like I said, I was a bit nervous at first. I'd partially based my decision to let you into the Broom Closet on what I knew of the original Pink Punch's personality, and deeds. But you've proved yourself. So, I hope you'll consider staying on and helping us. There are still villains to fight. And..." Rick's jaw tensed. "Shift is still out there somewhere."

"Rick, I'm real sorry about Pyro."

Rick smiled sadly. "Yeah, me too. But we'll find Shift eventually; he's not going to get away with it. Neither will the Boss. It's obvious now that Shift and the others were acting on her orders."

"She wanted to control the police force." And she'd asked Pink Punch to work for her. Kris wasn't sure she should mention that. "That can't be good, and she might try it again."

"Well, that can't be her end goal, she has to want to control them for a reason. But, after what you pulled, I doubt we'll find out what that is anytime soon. Though it pays to be vigilant." Rick smirked. "Just not to be vigilantes. But it sounds like there's work for all of us to do. So, what do you say, Pink Punch? Do you still want to help us take down all these villains?" He reached out a hand.

Mum might never recover her memories of being Pink Punch. For the first time, that thought didn't fill Kris with apprehension, but with excitement. She grinned, and clasped Rick's hand firmly. "Yeah, Rick, I'm in."

Laura Kinch lives in North Queensland, Australia, where she works as a mechanical engineer in the sugar industry. When she isn't engineering, she uses her problem-solving abilities to construct fictional worlds and technology and haul her characters out of the messes she creates for them. She likes reading and video games, has an entire room full of Lego and watches too many Disney cartoons.

A Note from the Author

Thanks so much for reading my novel. I hope you had as much fun following the adventures of Pink Punch as I did writing them.

Can I ask you a favour? I'd love for you to leave me a review. This is a great way to support authors and help other readers decide what to read next. Please spare a couple of minutes of your time to write a brief review, either on Goodreads, or wherever you purchased this book.

If you'd like to find out more about my writing, head over to laurakinch.com. There you can sign up for my newsletter and follow me on my social media accounts and blog.

Until the next novel!